Other books by E. R. Wytrykus:
Novels:
> The King of Coins
> The Money Run

The Connections Trilogy:
> A Stone To Roll
> A Road of Your Own
> On My Way Home

> The Girls of His Dreams
> Family Ties
> Singularity

Short Stories:
> By The Short Hairs
> The 9th Inning and Other Stories
> The Adventures of Rex and Lexi

Screenplay:
> The Money Run

All books published by and available from:
Wheat Field Publications
109 Kiwi Court
Lincoln, Ca. 95648
Wheatfieldpub@aol.com

IN THE MIST

a novel by

E.R.WYTRYKUS

"In The Mist"

Wheat Field Publications
109 Kiwi Court.
Lincoln, CA. 95648
NDWY2@aol.com

ISBN: 978-0-9839338-7-8

Chapters:

1. RETIREMENT

Self-pity and booze make affable partners, like bacon and eggs, or beans and franks, the one enriching the taste of the other. The combination can go a long way towards assuaging a damaged ego. But eventually it becomes destructive, irritating, and worse, boring.

I'm not sure when I would have escaped from the funk I'd fallen into, except for a conjugation of events that included the discovery of a decades-old file cabinet, a foray into an even older, forgotten cemetery sleeping in the backwoods of central Indiana, and a manuscript about very old people. All of it was about as bizarre as the behavior of my wife, Erin, she herself on the far side of fifty.

I had ignored phone calls until I heard Janice's voice on the answering machine. I was standing at the screen door, looking into the back yard. It had been raining heavily for three days, but now the downpour had dwindled to a light drizzle. The air smelled clean and crisp, the grass was as green as a leprechaun's hat, and mini-puddles dotted the low areas of the yard. A robin tiptoed across the lawn, seeking a meal. In the eaves above where a sparrow had built a nest I heard the cheeps of new life. I felt old.

"So what does a history professor do when he retires," Janice Jeffries asked, by way of a greeting.

"Hello, Jan. How are things in the Pit?"

"I… we miss you. Nobody to share coffee and gossip with."

"I miss you guys, too. I'll make a point to come around some day."

"You should."

Then there was nothing and I knew she knew.

"You heard about Erin."

She cleared her throat. "Yeah, ah, Kenny mentioned it. I'm sorry, Morg, really."

"Thanks."

"Do you know where she is?"

"Last news I got she was in Italy. Who knows?"

"I can't imagine why she'd…"

Good old Janice. Jan has had a crush on me ever since her husband dumped her. There was no affair in our history, just a sloppy, impetuous episode, shortly after her divorce. She was vulnerable, I was weak. A mistake I regretted but which I'd learned to live with. It was partially witnessed, and broken up by, the serendipitous appearance of our mutual friend, Kenny. He never said anything to me or anyone else, as far as I know; I don't think he even told his wife Amy, because her attitude towards me never wavered from its usual warm tenor. And the kissing and groping episode was never repeated. It was years before I'd even give Janice a hug.

"So… how are things there? How's the project coming along?"

"Going well. We have almost everything loaded. There are a few bugs with the search application, but it should be up and running soon. You'll be able to download every article and paper, just about everything ever written by or about the university and its professors."

"Yeah, after I'm gone."

"Morg, about why I called..."

My heart skipped. The last thing I needed from her now was to...

"We found some papers. They were filed in a cabinet in the sub-basement."

"The pit of the Pit? I was down there once, looking for what I no longer remember. It was cold and damp. What'd you find?"

"It appears to be letters and articles written by someone who was associated with the university several decades ago."

"Who? Someone I'd know?"

"A long time ago. Colin Bisseau."

"Colin Bisseau! You sure?"

"Some of the material is definitely his. The cabinet was locked and nobody in maintenance could find a key, so I had them jimmy it. There are accordion folders filled with papers, and dozens of what appear to be journals, or ledgers, but I haven't looked at those closely. There are other folders with names I don't recognize. I scanned a few of the letters, and Bisseau's signature is clear. Some of them are only signed with his first name, personal ones, I figure. Others, more formal letters on university stationery, have his name typed in, Colin Bisseau."

"These journals, are they diaries?"

"No idea, Morg."

"People have been looking for Colin Bisseau's papers for years; it was always assumed they existed somewhere."

"Anybody's who worked here has heard all kinds of stories."

"Who have you told?"

"No one yet. One of the temporary staff came across the file cabinet, but she had no idea what was in it. I had maintenance move the entire cabinet to my office. This stuff could be valuable, Morg."

"You can't keep it to yourself, Janice."

"I know. But I've got a temporary cover."

"How so?"

"Do you remember the Cultural Development Committee? Have you ever heard of it?"

I shook my head before I answered. "Vaguely, I think. Refresh my memory. Hold on, Jan. I'm going to get a cup of coffee and sit down."

Having retrieved the coffee I sat down and took a sip.

"Okay, hit me."

"It's a rather obscure organization, pretty much unknown. There were three members. We never…"

"We?"

"Yes, I was, am, on the committee."

"Who else?"

"That's the rub. The other two were Professor Courtney and Professor Goldman."

"They retired several years ago."

"That's right. At the time I sent a memo to the Board pointing out that we either had to appoint two new members, or close the fund. I never heard anything and quite frankly, Morg, I forgot all about it."

"So where's this going, Jan?"

"Well…I thought maybe you were getting a little bored and might be looking for a hobby."

I laughed.

"That's funny?"

"No, Jan. And yes. And I appreciate it."

"It's not that I…" She stopped then and I knew it was because she knew about Erin leaving, and knew, from Kenny, that I was fumbling around, trying to figure out what to do with myself.

I spoke up to save us both from embarrassing pauses.

"Are you saying you can get me access to those papers?"

"That's why I called. The by-laws say that in the absence of all three members of the committee, the majority present can make any decisions regarding project assignments and use of available funds that come under their purview. I decided an examination of these papers fell within the authority of the committee. So I called a meeting and no one showed up except me. I even contacted Courtney and Goldman to make it official---they thought I was joking."

"The Board will still have to know," I said, after laughing.

"Not until the annual report is due. And obviously no one has asked for a report from the Cultural Development Committee in years."

"It could be trouble, though, just because of who it is, you know, Colin Bisseau. It'll be a big deal for the university to say it has his papers."

"I know those guys, Morg. The first thing the Board would do is make a major announcement and then hire a team to scavenge through the papers, looking for something exciting, but excising anything that didn't smell good."

"How long can you keep it a secret, Jan?"

"I'm sure I can until I'm required to report, which won't be for several months."

"What'll you tell people about me?"

"No one from the Board is likely to see you or care if they do. Retired professors are always knocking around, giving a lecture or doing research at the library, or, as often as not, taking a nap."

I snickered, imagining myself asleep in the library, slumped in a chair, unshaven, shaggy gray hair long due for a trim, wearing a food-stained shirt because I had no wife to do my laundry, my heading jerking and snot running out of my nose, my snoring irritating the students who were trying to study, but were unsure of the protocol for wakening a formerly distinguished Professor of American History Studies. Janice was speaking and I shook myself out of my reverie.

"… comes out that you are working on a special project no one would be surprised. You have cred here, Morg; are you listening?"

I smiled; "Ah, yes, that's nice to hear, Janice. You're not going to make me work in the damp sub-basement, are you?"

When she didn't reply at first I knew I'd screwed up. A legitimate project or not, Janice might reason that with Erin gone I was fair game.

Icily, she answered. "I'm not doing this for fun, Morgan Miller. If you don't want the opportunity I'm sure there are dozens of scholars who'd love to get their paws on these papers. And like you said, I have to be careful with them."

"Sure you do."

"I suppose," Janice said, as I also started to speak. "What?"

"Oh, no, you go."

"This is silly," Janice said. "You're right, of course. No one can work in the sub-basement for long. You'd catch pneumonia. You still have an office waiting for you to use if you want. Or, it being you, I suppose you can be trusted to take the papers off-site."

I'd been offered a small office to use to tend to research projects and handle correspondence, or for whatever, and in return, occasionally representing the university at various events. I'd deferred, suggesting I'd return after a year or two of travel and escapism.

More coyly, she added: "But being the only committee member, I'll need regular updates."

"Of course," I agreed, warily. "Coffee break updates." I could almost hear her smile.

"Good. Morg, we haven't talked expenses yet."

"Oh, I don't need..."

"Yes, we need to do this properly. There's about sixty thousand in the fund as of now. That should be enough for an acceptable stipend and your expenses for a year, don't you think?"

"More than enough. This is supposed to be a hobby, not a job. Besides, you said you'd have to file a report within a few months."

"True, but I suspect that by then you'll either have tired of the job, or have it organized so well that the Board will authorize you to continue."

"When can I start?"

"How about we meet for lunch tomorrow and discuss the terms of your employment?"

Jan had finally made her move. Trouble was, I was only interested in her offer of examining Colin Bisseau's papers, not in any other offer she was implying.

"See you tomorrow; noon?"

"Ciao."

Colin Bisseau; well, well.

As my days as Professor of American History Studies at Lyman Wilson University dwindled down I began to think on what I would do when I retired: Erin and I would travel, I'd read all the non-History books I'd been amassing, volunteer work, write the Great American Novel, and try my hand again at that most frustrating of endeavors, the game of golf.

My nebulous plans never got off the launch pad.

First thing off, Erin left. She said she needed to find herself, whatever that means. Fifty-seven years old and now she's going to find herself? Where? She read some stupid book; eat and pray and love your neighbor, or some such rot. She said she didn't want a divorce, just a smidgen of personal space.

I assumed there was someone else but she insisted, before I accused, that there wasn't. The children, Gerald in Portland and Connie in Phoenix, hazarded no explanation, only condolences. They were too busy with their own lives to visit me, and I didn't want to barge in on them and spend the time slobbering. No one enjoys group hugs with a person bent on pummeling himself.

At my retirement party Erin smiled and laughed and talked to people in her charming manner, but I sensed a sham; there was no lilt in her voice, no glee. The next day she told me of her extraordinary plans. Actually, she didn't tell me much, or if she did I wasn't listening carefully, my psyche having been jolted into a stage of disbelief. I didn't want to hear what she was saying.

My best friend Kenny was sympathetic but didn't have any gems of wisdom to impart. Ed and Ellen, from across the street, said it was a tragedy, and that they were here for me. Yes, Ed and Ellen, whose home I'd never entered, were somewhere for me. The next thing they'd tell me was that I needed closure.

What is a tragedy? No one had died, there hadn't been a killer typhoon. The newspaper today reported that in New York a man had shot his wife and daughter, and then turned the gun on himself. The two women died, he survived; arguably a double tragedy. Everything is hyped these days; words are used in exaggerated ways to show one's displeasure with someone else's opinion. Who knows, Erin might come home happy and giddy and in love with me all over again, and instead of a tragedy it'll be a rebirth of our relationship. Anyway, if it was a tragedy, it was mine, not Ed and Ellen's.

Erin texted me every day the first week of her adventure. She asked me not to respond, but I insisted she keep me informed of her well-being, if not her where-bouts. Then the texts stopped and she sent postcards, from New York, then London, and the Paris. She did not write, "Wish you were here."

She was moving fast. Then there was nothing for a week until I received a card from Rome. Her words were scrawled as if she was in a hurry and resented the few seconds it took to write a legible note. That was two weeks ago.

When I tried to read my mind would drift to wondering where Erin was and what she was doing at this moment. If she's in Europe she'd be sleeping when I was awake; when I went to bed, she'd be starting her day. Then I'd set the book down, look up at the ceiling and ponder what went wrong, where had I screwed up, why didn't I see the signs of her unhappiness, why didn't I find a way to stop her from going. I'd get sad, then mad, and then think about writing again. Trouble is, I realized I had nothing particularly poignant to pass on to the world, no stunning advice to give, no great insights. You'd think a Professor of History would write the definitive account of his favorite historical era. But I'd written countless articles and three textbooks, and that was enough.

Travel? The adventures Erin and I were going to share while young enough to manage? When we'd talked about those exotic places we were going to visit I didn't realize Erin meant to see them without me. Maybe at the time she didn't realize it either.

Actually I did read a lot, went to movies, and dusted off the golf clubs I hadn't swung in over ten years. I found I played about the same as I had then, hitting one or two good shots per hole and routinely missing three-foot putts. Kenny took joy in beating me, even as he kept telling me Erin would come home soon and things would return to normal. I didn't want normal again. I politely declined his invitations to dinner with he and Amy, because I knew the conversation would eventually get around to Erin, and it would both irritate and embarrass me.

I met Janice at an off-campus café, lest former colleagues pestered me wanting to know how I was enjoying the golden years. News about Erin's defection had not been widely disseminated yet.

Janice looked good. She always was a pretty woman, and now, in her mid-fifties, was still attractive. Hell, at my age every female from age eighteen on up looks good. She wore blue, her hair was a dark brown, almost black when the light hit it at a certain angle. It shone brighter than I remembered when I last saw her, which was on my final day as a Professor of American History. There was no gray; I wondered if she dyed?

"Good to see you Morg. I didn't think you were going to disappear when you retired."

We hugged.

"Good to see you, too Jan. It's odd not seeing you and the others every day or so."

"Coffee breaks aren't the same. And I've still got several years before I can afford to retire."

"You envy me?"

She started to speak, then shrugged.

"Yeah, I know, it's not the way I planned."

"How could she do it, Morg? Why not earlier, if at all?"

"She said most of her life had been boring; thank you, dear."

"I'm sure she didn't mean it was your fault."

It was my turn to shrug.

"I thought she liked her work."

"She did most of the time. Lately, the last few years, I noticed a change in her attitude. She said that each year the kids got sassier and the parents were even worse. Everyone's child was the perfect angel and the smartest kid in class."

"Aren't they all."

Janice was childless. Her husband had left after eight years of marriage, deciding he'd rather stay single. He remarried less than a year later. Janice had stayed an attractive, eligible divorcee. I'm sure there had been men in her life, but she never brought one around and never talked about anyone special.

"What are you grinning at?" Janice asked.

"Oh? Didn't know I was. Just thinking about the curves that life throws at us."

"At least you haven't lost your sense of humor."

"Yeah, you say." We ordered iced tea and sandwiches and sat in silence for a half-minute.

"I told her we could afford for her to quit. She did, but then…this other thing came up."

"You mean to travel solo?"

"It's more than that. I'll give her this, though. She's using her own money."

"How so?"

"You know Erin's mother died late last year? Erin got a nice chunk of money, which became available shortly before my retirement date. She said she'd been thinking about going away for a long time, but didn't think it fair to use our savings. So, she's using her mother's money. At least so far; I haven't seen any unfamiliar charges on the credit card bills."

"Did she say how long she'd be gone?"

"She said three or four months would do."

"And you're suppose to wait and worry?"

"I've thought of waiting until she got back, then say, 'it's my turn', and leave. I've also thought of selling the house and moving without leaving a forwarding address. And I've considered filing for divorce."

"You won't do any of those things, Morg."

My grin was not subtle and not meant to disagree with Janice's assessment.

Food came; a sandwich for me, salad for Janice. We ate, made small talk about the people we'd worked with, and about Janice's project, which led us to Colin Bisseau.

"Can you tell me more about what you found, or think you found?"

"You doubt me, Morg?"

"No, of course not. It's…"

"Okay, you'll have to see for yourself. You can do that without making any promises. Look, I'm trying to give you an advance peek."

"Are you sure you're not just feeling sorry for me? Because of Erin leaving?"

"Hey, take it any way you want, Morgan."

I'd gone a bit too far. When she uses my full name, Morgan, I know she's not happy with me. So what if she was feeling sorry for me? Isn't that what friends are for?

She put her fork down.

"As I said, there are letters, some personal, others university-related. Also what appear to be drafts of articles and possibly outlines of his books. Some of it could be from when he was an Ambassador. I didn't check all the dates but they go back decades. The latest I noticed was from 1980."

"The year he disappeared."

"Yes, along with his wife. Vanished."

"Are you sure the university has authority over the stuff?"

"Why not? Remember when he disappeared? There was a worldwide search for relatives. Neither he nor his wife had any family. They hadn't had any kids. In fact, both of them had been single until they met in their forties. They'd only been married a few years when they disappeared.

"Several so-called relatives crawled out, claiming they were the heirs, but none could prove anything. No will was located but on the day the Bisseaus were flown into Alaska a check for a million dollars, made out to the Wilson University's Scholarship Fund, was received by the university, from an organization called The Bisseau Fund. It came from a bank in the Bahamas."

"I remember," I said. "It caused quite a celebration. At the time the Bisseau's weren't considered to be missing, just on a camping trip. The Board was planning a gala thank you event when they returned from Alaska."

"Yes, but they never returned and the only other assets located were household goods and a small bank account."

"What about the house?"

"They lived in an apartment."

"You'd think he'd have left a decent estate. And someone as organized as Bisseau wouldn't have died without a will or a trust."

"You wouldn't think. It was much later, after the story had quieted down, it is was revealed that shortly before he and his wife left for Alaska, Bisseau had sold all his stock and bond holdings and turned them into cash."

"Really? And the cash went where?"

"Vanished, just like the Bisseaus."

"What about the bank in the Bahamas?"

"They never heard of him and the Bisseau Fund had closed its account."

I frowned. "So where were these papers then?"

"I called Professor Vasilek. He knew Colin Bisseau. I asked him if he remembered Bisseau saying anything about his papers."

"Charley Vasilek; didn't know he was still ticking."

"Professor Vasilek remembered asking Bisseau if he intended to donate his papers to the university and Bisseau's reply was that he doubted he had anything worth saving. Vasilek said Bisseau was reticent to discuss legacies, as the professor put it."

"I wonder how he would have done in the computer age, with e-mails and cell phone messages that are never completely deleted."

"Maybe that's why he quit public life; he saw it coming."

"Did Professor Vasilek remember anything else?"

"I asked him about the storage space in the sub-basement, where the filing cabinet was found."

"Did you tell…?"

"No, no. I didn't tell him I found anything. I made up a story that the question arose in our project to collect old theses so we could digitize them.

"He said that at one time the storage area was walled up, as it was too damp and cold for anyone to work there.

"Then, a few years ago, it was opened because there was a busted water line and the workers had to get in through the sub-basement. They didn't wall it up again but normally no one had any reason to go there."

"Was the file cabinet there all this time?"

"Probably. When it was found it was in a dark corner and I doubt the workers had noticed it."

"So what was your assistant doing down there?"

"She said she got lost. She seems innocent enough, and she never mentioned Bisseau's name. As I said, the drawers were locked. She said she came straight to me. I sent a man to cart the cabinet to my office and that's where it sits."

A busboy came by to clear the table.

"Coffee," I ordered and Janice nodded. "Two," I said. "So we can talk here longer."

"Remember the movie they made about Bisseau's World War Two heroics?"

Janice nodded.

"He grew up in an orphanage, never knew any family. Joined the Army at nineteen, won the Medal of Honor at twenty," she said.

"You do remember."

"I did some research on his life before I called you."

"Please go on."

"The Army records said he saved the lives of six soldiers in a forest near Bastogne, on December 20th, 1944; in the movie it was twenty-six, and it was Christmas Day. Army records said he killed nineteen Germans, the movie implied a hundred and more. In an interview Bisseau said the most accurate part of the movie was the bitter cold.

"After the movie it was hard for him to maintain a low profile."

"I suppose he went to school on the GI Bill."

"He was sort of an intellectual phenom. He became the youngest professor in the history of Lyman Wilson University. Master's in both American and World History, also in Geography, and a PhD in History, later another doctorate in Education."

"When did he first teach here? It was long before my time began."

"I don't recall what he did immediately after finishing his doctorate, but his first stretch at Wilson was in the late 50s. A year or so later he was coerced into running for State Senate, using his war fame to boost his candidacy. He won, but I heard he was never happy with the job."

"He also ran for governor."

"Yes, he got pushed into it."

"He lost."

Janice nodded. "Apparently he ran an uninspired campaign. As if he didn't want to win. Still, it must have been a shock to him, to lose at anything. He avoided the spotlight for a few years, writing and traveling. Then he came back here and taught again in the 60s. Two years later he was appointed Ambassador to Tanzania. He wrote a book about the ravages of poaching, one of the early efforts to broadcast the disastrous situation of African wildlife to the public domain, and then returned once more to the University.

"He wrote textbooks which are still in use for studies of American History up to the 60s. Wrote a treatise on the state of education in America, which made him both renowned and hated. He said the problems in our educational system start with lack of discipline from the parents."

"Gee, who would of thought?"

"Parents all over the country protested at book stores that were selling his book."

"He was serving as a special education advisor to the governor when I met him."

"Here at the university?"

"Yes, that was his third time around. By then he was solely an advisor in the PhD program; we weren't getting many people interested in higher degrees in History and Geography. He gave lectures but didn't hold any classes. I talked to him a few times."

"What was he like?"

To my surprise Bisseau's face leaped into my memory. I saw it as clearly as if he'd been sitting across from me.

"He was very young-looking. He did have some gray at the temples, but the rumor was that he dyed his hair to make himself look older. I couldn't believe he'd been old enough to fight in the Battle of the Bulge."

"Something else Professor Vasilek told me; he said Bisseau was being pressured to run for Governor again."

"You mean shortly before he disappeared?"

Janice nodded.

"So what? You think he hid away to avoid politics? It's kind of hard these days to disappear, especially if you are known at all, own anything, use credit cards..."

"Yes, but it might have been easier in 1980."

"He and his wife disappeared on a camping trip; if he wanted to bug out of civilization I don't believe he'd do it by going to a remote area of northern Alaska. What did your Google search tell you?"

"I printed most of what I found to give to you. In brief, they, he and his wife, Elizabeth, were flown to an area near the Gates of the Arctic National Park. The pilot said he knew the area and there was a pristine lake perfect for landing a floatplane. He was to meet the Bisseaus there again in two weeks. The Bisseaus said they planned to hike and fish and they seemed to be well prepared and supplied. Bisseau was known to enjoy camping and fishing, so this trip wasn't unusual for them.

"The pilot returned when scheduled and waited two days. He then radioed for help and began a search. Nothing was ever found, not a shred of a campsite or any evidence that a human being had been anywhere near the area. It was like the disappearance of Amelia Earhart."

"No evidence of foul play?"

"Nope. Even if a bear had killed them, or wolves, there should have been something. The search covered an area as large as the Bisseaus could possibly have traveled, and then some."

"There are places in Alaska that aren't easy to get to. And if a bear killed them and dragged them away, it might not have been possible to find any trace."

"Still, there should have been evidence of a campsite. When the pilot dropped them off, it was already late in the afternoon. They had already begun to unpack, the pilot said, before he left."

"There's a slew of unexplained missing persons cases."

"So what do you think?"

"Like I said before, when do I start?"

2. A PROJECT

I accepted the offer of the office at the University before someone else claimed it. Maintenance wheeled the file cabinet from Janice's office to my new digs. I could have had the cabinet shipped to my house but I decided it'd be prudent to do most of my work in academic surroundings.

For one thing, I'd concentrate better, rather than pacing at home waiting for the mail, wondering if today there'd be a card from Erin. And rather than be alone at home I could take coffee breaks with Janice and Kenny, and occasionally share lunch with them. It'd be like I never retired.

When Erin told me her plans it was like a stab in the gut. She insisted she still loved me but said she couldn't be a good wife if she didn't 'find herself'. I got so sick of hearing that phrase I told her to shut up and go if she was going. Hell, she'd been a good wife for over thirty years.

I should have noticed something wasn't right. She'd been losing weight, not that she needed to, and hadn't been sleeping. Now I see she was anxious over what she was planning to do.

For years vacations had been planned around conventions I attended and spoke at. Erin never complained and I believe she enjoyed the trips. If it wasn't a convention then I dragged her to a Civil War or Revolutionary War battle site. Serves me right for not taking her to Hawaii or the Caribbean for luaus and snorkeling.

Maybe I was the shallow half of our partnership, as I never felt the need to 'find myself'. I studied what interested me, and worked at what I enjoyed. And phfft, phfft, where did sixty-three years go?

After the initial shock I stopped wondering if Erin loved me, but rather, did I still love her. It was like her words had ripped a hole in my emotions and my feelings for her had spilled out. Gathering them up was like trying to pick Jell-O off the floor with one's bare hands. I'd wake up each morning aware that she was gone but not sure how I felt about it. Each day sleeping alone became more normal.

In response to her non-subtle inquiry, I told Janice that if Erin returned before I got deep into the Colin Bisseau Papers Project, I'd drop everything to spend time with her. Janice's eyes flashed disappointment before she looked away but I needed to make that clear. But the longer Erin stayed away, the more my resolve might change. I might 'find myself', and discover I was okay on my own.

I eyeballed my environs: they weren't flashy; functional but not stylish, which suited me. The one colorful item was the bouquet of yellow flowers in a vase that I was sure I'd last seen in Janice's office. I would have to remember to thank her.

Before I started on the contents of the file cabinet I reviewed the notes Janice had printed out about Colin Bisseau. In the University library I found a copy of a biography, *The Search for Colin Bisseau.* Apparently the title didn't only refer to the search for Bisseau after he and his wife disappeared in Alaska, but an attempt to gain insight into the total man, as so little was known about his personal life.

I also checked out Bisseau's book, *The Death of Beauty: Genocide On the Savannah.* I'd read it years ago, and doubted that I would again now, as it was a sad book. It was expertly researched and well written, but a disturbing commentary on the slaughter of animals for other than food purposes. The book not only covered such ghastly deeds as the killing of elephants and rhinos for their tusks, but the likely coming extinction of the Mountain Gorilla and the Siberian tiger.

True, since then the awareness of the horrors of arbitrary hunting of animals for ivory or what some people considered sport, or to make bone soup, has reduced the dangers to many rare animals. But in some cases it may already be too late. I'd recently seen a documentary that claimed there are less than one thousand surviving mountain gorillas.

Bisseau did not authorize the biography, and he declined to cooperate with the author. Though known as a friendly, obliging person, Bisseau and his wife kept to themselves as much as possible when not involved in official duties. For a man who'd served in politics and diplomacy Bisseau shunned the spotlight and was disinclined to talk about his past. When he was among people he was known to be gracious and an interesting conversationalist, exuding a subtle panache and conveying a broad knowledge of multiple topics, but he rarely revealed personal information. He had a knack of stirring the discussion away from himself and towards others, which generally made people feel good that this fine and famous man was interested in them.

I spent my first morning on the project scanning the biography. I called it a project in my mind to convince myself I was doing something worthwhile. Janice said she didn't expect me to work eight-hour days five days a week, just whatever I felt like. At our ten o'clock coffee break I told Janice I hadn't even looked at any of the material in the file cabinet yet because I first wanted to brush up on my knowledge of Bisseau's life.

The Search for Colin Bisseau reported that Bisseau was born in Lakeview Valley, a woodsy village south of Indianapolis. Bisseau had produced a birth certificate at times when it was required, and it showed he was born in the home of Martin and Wilma Bisseau, on October 31, 1924---Halloween.

Colin Bisseau's parents died in a home fire when Colin was still an infant. The baby was rescued by a neighbor and placed in a nearby orphanage.

When researching for the book the author noted that the town of Lakeview Valley had a population of only 38 at the time of the 1960 census, and by 1970 it had become a ghost town. As pictures in the book showed, the buildings were dilapidated and crumbling and nearly all the windows were broken, victims of rock-throwing youths, no doubt. Knee-high weeds cracked the sidewalks and streets. The orphanage Bisseau grew up in had been closed long ago and no records could be located. Bisseau said he had no documentation to show he actually lived there.

It was the same with school records. Bisseau claimed he went to school in Lakeview Valley, including high school. He had produced a transcript when he applied at Wilson University, but the author was not able to obtain a copy. Nor could the author find any evidence that a Lakeview Valley High School existed at the time Bisseau would have lived there. Whenever he was asked about his early life Bisseau would deflect the questions with a shrug and a wry smile. His standard comment was that he hadn't had a happy childhood and preferred to put his pre-college life out of his mind. Bisseau claimed he lived on his own from the time he finished high school, but could not, or would not, provide addresses. It wasn't until his war heroics and his entry into Lyman Wilson University, in the Indianapolis suburbs, that much of a trail developed. From then on his history was fairly well known and documented. The author could not find any pictures of Bisseau prior to his college graduation, other than official Army photos and those published in newspapers, always with Bisseau in uniform.

What was odd as I looked at the college-days pictures of Bisseau was that the man looked older than what he would have been then, about 25, but later pictures, obtained from public records, and my memory of him, was that he always appeared so much younger than everyone else his age.

I joined Janice and Kenny for lunch in the cafeteria. Kenny is a colleague and a friend (my best, now that Erin in gone), and sometimes golf buddy. He is also recently retired and is engaged in a research project in the University library for a series of articles he's been commissioned to write. It was going to be impossible to avoid Kenny so Janice and I agreed to share with him the subject matter of my project, as long as he kept it quiet.

After lunch I opened the file cabinet. My first impression was of neatness. The top drawer of the four-drawer cabinet contained accordion folders, secured with drawstrings, labeled and lined up like soldiers ready for inspection. Right up front was a divider labeled *Colin Bisseau*. Behind the divider were folders with such labels as 'Ambassador', 'Board Notes', 'Curriculum', 'Dailies', 'Magazine Articles', 'Personal Letters', and so forth, twenty-five or more, in alphabetical order, some thick, most containing only a few sheets of paper. Many of the individual sheets of paper inside the folders were also in document protectors.

There were letters written while Bisseau served as Ambassador, as the Governor's education aide, as a member of the Board of Regents of Wilson College, and so on. There was also a section labeled, 'Letters Received'.

I'd read them more thoroughly later, but in quick scans I didn't note anything of earth-shaking importance. Nevertheless, our library will love to have this stuff, and likely a scholar specializing in Colin Bisseau's life will find these minutiae fascinating. There were letters thanking fellow diplomats for their cooperation in dealing with diplomatic issues, souvenir menus from important formal dinners, lecture notes, outlines for classes he taught at Wilson for all three terms, going back to the 50s, drafts of articles, some of which were published, some not. I suppose it might be of interest to read what Bisseau wrote that he decided not to publish. There were letters on plain stationery that I assumed were personal letters to friends or colleagues, unrelated to any official duties of his, and these I would also return to.

The second drawer contained more accordion folders, each one carefully and clearly labeled, then a divider with the name *Colt S. Boston.* I had no idea who that person was. After more labeled accordion folders came a collection of journal books. They were bound in some sort of leather, like deer hide, discolored due to age and stained from normal handling, from natural skin oils, or spills, maybe a liquid as common as coffee, or as valuable as blood. Each book had a metal inset near the top, centered, on which was etched a date. The first one I picked out of the Colt Boston section was dated: "1859-1862," so these could not have belonged to Colin Bisseau. I opened it at random; there were entries similar to those in a personal diary, though from the dates it wasn't a record that was kept religiously. For example, one entry was dated, "Oct. 6, 1859," then there wasn't another until, "Jan. 1, 1860." I set the book back in place and closed the drawer.

When I got to the third drawer I came across another name: *Cade S. Bunyan.* A series of accordion folders filled half of the drawer. Some papers were loose in the folders, others, as in the Bisseau section, were in document protectors; someone had intended the contents to last. A quick scan of dates indicated that the Bunyan and Boston papers were much older than the Bisseau papers. I wondered if these were people Bisseau had been researching; maybe they were his ancestors.

There were more leather–bound journals, similar to the ones in the Boston section, as if the same person had prepared them. The earliest one was dated 1901. The bottom drawer was filled with the ledgers Janice had mentioned. They were similar to the ones in the other drawers, but newer and, to my assessment, of a higher quality leather binding. Each one was dated, some covering one year, others several years. The latest one was dated 1980, and I noted the initials, 'C.B.' at the end of each entry. There were also spiral bound journals, showing considerable wear, as if the author had not had the chance to make these entries in the fancier journal books.

I ambled over to the library—the walk was good exercise, and researched the names. There had never been anyone named Cade S. Bunyan nor Colt S. Boston ever associated with the University, not as a professor, not as a student, not as an employee. I sensed there were going to be more mysteries associated with this file cabinet than the basic question of how it got where it was found, and whether it held any papers that would prove to be valuable.

I walked back to my office at a leisurely pace, nodding to students scurrying to classes and noticing the scenery of the campus, surprised how much I enjoyed seeing the trees and the buildings and the people without rushing to a class or to give a lecture, my mind so filled with what I had to do that I seldom saw the beauty of the campus.

Back in my office I began a Google search. The names Cade S. Bunyan and Colt S. Boston were not unique, but I couldn't find anyone by either name that had been associated with any University in the country in the past few decades. So who were they, or had been, and what were their papers doing in with Bisseau's?

I decided to call it a day. I passed by Janice's office and told her I was taking the biography home to finish reading it. She smiled and reminded me I didn't have to hold to a fixed schedule. And I reminded her I wanted to have the job done before she needed to report to the University Board. To myself I wondered where I'd be in six months if Erin hadn't returned. Or for that matter, if she had. Thinking about it gave me a headache.

First thing I did the next day was hunt down a new file cabinet, one I could lock, and transferred everything from the old cabinet to this new one.

It was difficult to stifle my eagerness to begin reading the journals. It was like the first day of a new school term, when enthusiasm was at its peak. At least in college students who took history were there voluntarily; in high school it was a class for naps.

Though eager, I restrained myself from reading journal entries, stopped wondering who Cade Bunyan and

Colt Boston were, and began to take a general inventory of the file cabinet contents.

The Cade Bunyan section did not have as many folders as the Boston section, but they were neatly labeled. There was a faded birth certificate showing a boy born to Martha and Jonah Bunyan in 1881, in Kentucky.

There were several folders with nothing in them, and I wondered if documents had been removed. There was a folder labeled 'Farm' that contained a deed to a piece of property in Illinois in the name of Cade S. Bunyan, dated 1902. There were other papers pertaining to taxes, land surveys, purchases of equipment and supplies, and bills of sale for animals and crops.

Some folders contained loose-leaf papers, faded, stained, and wrinkled. The writing was in pencil and so light the words were nearly impossible to read. There were also several small notebooks, the kind a young person might have used in school.

I found nothing to indicate whether Cade Bunyan ever got married or had children. There were two newspaper clippings, obituaries, one for Jonah Bunyan, dated 1929 and another for Cade's mother, dated 1930.

There were a few letters from people whose names I could not discern because the writing was faded; some appeared to be personal letters while others were related to farming matters. I wondered how Cade Bunyan made out during the Depression. I guess he prospered because in another folder, not labeled, there was a deed, or at least a copy, to property in southern California. Then I wondered if he'd abandoned the farm in Illinois.

I quickly concluded no, because I came across a letter from someone, a name I could not decipher, written to Bunyan regarding the farm. What I could make out stated:

"We reached the Illinois property yesterday...words cannot express how truly grateful my wife and children and I are to have been given this opportunity, especially now, in this time of great trouble for so many people. You can be sure, Mr. Bunyan, that we will be the best possible caretakers you could have found..."

So Bunyan must have done well financially, even when the Depression hit, to be able to keep the land in Illinois, lease it, and buy more land in California.

In the Colt Boston section I found a folder tagged, 'Grant letter'. Curious, I pulled out a document protector, which contained a sheet of yellowish paper. It was difficult to read because the writing was in a flourishing style. The signature appeared to be an indecipherable scrawl at first, but I am a history scholar---it looked like 'U.S. Grant'. In fact, I was sure of it. Authentic letters with Grant's signature have been known to sell for over $25,000. This was getting odder.

It was difficult to read the letter encased in the document protector, so I carefully slipped it out.

Colonel:

It is with honor and relief that I acknowledge your gallant efforts concerning the incident at Bolton Depot in the early hours of May 17 last, which forestalled the advance of a Rebel unit, and rescued the men of my command who had been trapped there. On behalf of these men and myself personally, you have my thanks, and my respect and gratitude.

Very Truly Yours,
U.S. Grant

Yes, I'm an American history scholar, but I haven't memorized every little skirmish in every war. I did a Google search and even that took some time, but there it was, Bolton Depot, near Champion's Hill. Now that rang a bell. I searched further and found I was right: Champion's Hill was the site of a battle near Vicksburg during the May, 1863 campaign. Bolton Depot was, I suppose still is, a ridge at a point about midway between the Mississippi towns of Vicksburg and Jackson. While I was at it I searched for a Col. Colt Boston, but got no hits.

I strode over to the library and checked the indices of books on the Civil War, but there were no entries for

Col. Boston. I sat down to read about the Vicksburg campaign.

The battle at Champion's Hill was no minor skirmish, but a key episode in the Civil War. It occurred on May 16, 1863, and between the two armies nearly fifty thousand men participated, resulting in over 6,000 casualties. Poor John Pemberton; a Confederate general, first he had to deal with harassment by Benjamin Grierson, who'd been sent by Grant along with 1,700 men to probe deep into Mississippi and wreck havoc on Confederate railroads and supply lines (an event fictionalized in a John Wayne movie, I recalled.)

Then, attempting to link up with Joe Johnston's troops, General Pemberton could not get past Champion's Hill. Union forces sliced and diced his troops and he barely managed to effect a retreat, aided by Union indecision. But stopping his movement was vital to eventual Union victory.

A few weeks later Pemberton presided over the largest surrender of Confederate troops in the Civil War, nearly 30,000. Most were paroled, as Grant did not have the resources to deal with that many prisoners, and afterwards Pemberton resigned (he was re-activated later at a lower rank).

Pemberton's surrender came at the same time, farther east, Robert E. Lee was also retreating with his tail between his legs, his troops having been decimated at Gettysburg.

These two events occurring virtually simultaneously spelled the death knell for the Confederate effort, though neither side knew it yet. It would take nearly two years of bloody fighting and thousands of casualties to end the conflict.

In any war, and in any battle comprised of over fifty thousand combatants, there will be incidents of heroism and of cowardice, most of which are noted by few people and often go unmentioned in an historical account of the main elements of the battle.

Maybe a detailed unit account somewhere in the numerous tomes written about the Civil War would clarify the action cited in Grant's letter, but I wouldn't know where to start other than with every unit involved in the Vicksburg campaign, a chore I didn't care to take the time to tackle.

Apparently in the big picture it was an incident of no importance. But to the men who had been trapped and came close to death or capture, it would have been a life-changing event, one that Grant acknowledged to Colonel Boston, who must have performed some heroic deed to save the men.

Gingerly I returned the document to its plastic protector and to the folder, fearing I had already damaged it. I then took the folder with the letter and stuck it in my briefcase. I'd show it to Arthur Allenby, the noted dealer in historical documents, and see what he made of it.

Another folder contained dozens of individual pieces of paper, each one in a protective cover. They appeared to be personal letters. I'd save these to examine later.

I made an appointment with Allenby, who maintained an office on the west side of town. I hadn't seen Arthur in a couple of years so we made plans to meet late morning and then have lunch. I told Janice I wouldn't be in the next day but didn't explain why. She sounded irritated.

It was humbling to try to explain to Arthur about Erin. Arthur had lost his wife to cancer and now his whole life revolved around old letters and other mementoes of historical significance. I could tell he was confused by my attempts at explaining Erin's action, as if it was the doings of an irrational juvenile or a crazed person. I hemmed and hawed and tried to grin my way out of talking about it. He nodded sympathetically and asked me about the letter.

"We found some papers at the University that appear to be Colin Bisseau's." That got a start out of Arthur.

"You don't say! People have been looking for those for years. How'd this come about?"

"Pretty much by accident. A temp bumped into an old file cabinet that had been locked and undisturbed for years. I have no idea how the papers got there, or when."

I explained to Arthur that I had retired recently and taken on the task of sorting through the papers to see what was there and whether they were of any value.

"I suppose the University will keep them?"

"Likely, but Arthur, please promise me you won't talk about this yet. We're trying to keep it to ourselves until I've had time to catalog everything."

"Of course. But what does this Grant letter have to do with Colin Bisseau?"

"The crazy things is there are other documents in the file cabinet that apparently have nothing to do with Colin Bisseau; very old documents, and journal books, like diaries. I'm even more confused about their origin, and how they got into the University's basement, than I am about the Bisseau papers."

"Diaries, Morgan? Could be fascinating."

I opened my briefcase and pulled out the folder that contained the letter signed by U.S. Grant. I handed the letter, still in its document protector, to Arthur.

"This was in a section of the file cabinet that supposedly belonged to a man named Colt, middle initial S, Boston. I have no idea who he was. You ever hear of anyone by that name in connection with the Civil War?"

Arthur shook his head while he read the letter. I gave him time to inspect it and study the handwriting. After several minutes he handed it back to me and cleared his throat.

"It *looks* genuine. I'd need more time to examine it if you're willing to leave it with me."

"Is it worth anything?"

"Hard to say. If it's real, and is one not known to have existed, the curiosity value alone could be substantial."

"Have you any idea what this incident at Bolton Depot may refer to?"

"Not off hand. Champion's Hill was a massive engagement, Morgan. Lots of fighting, lots of casualties; plenty of heroes and plenty of cowards. I assume you've done your own inquiry."

I nodded. "A bit. I suppose there are unit records where we could find this Colt Boston?"

"Probably so, if someone wanted to invest the time."

The way he said it indicated such time would be expensive. But he was teasing. He grinned and rose from his chair and walked over to where his computer sat on a desk in the far corner of the room. I followed him.

Arthur punched a few buttons, we waited, and then up came a list of persons with the surname, 'Boston', known to have served in the Civil War.

"Over two hundred!" I exclaimed.

"Wait," Arthur said. He punched in more data.

"No hits," Arthur said, "for first name of Colt, middle initial S."

"How complete is this database?"

"I can't guarantee that it's one hundred per cent accurate. But if this Colt Boston served in a unit in the Vicksburg campaign, it's seems likely he'd be in here.

"Morgan, even if the name popped up it wouldn't tell us what the incident was or why the letter was filed in the basement of the University, would it?"

"Not likely. I'm thinking Colt Boston was a relative of Bisseau's."

Arthur put a hand on my shoulder. "I don't mean to be ungracious, Morgan. I'll study the letter, get another opinion; that much I'll do for old time's sake. Now, let's go have some lunch. The club do?"

Arthur meant the Historical Club, a popular gathering place for history buffs, teachers, and researchers. "Perfect. I haven't been there since I retired."

Two days into the project and already I was getting sidetracked. I needed to forget about Colt Boston and Cade Bunyan and concentrate on working up an orderly and professional inventory of the contents of the file cabinet. With that end in mind, I designed a worksheet on the computer and set to the task of entering a description of each item, a job that surely would take a week, longer if I couldn't resist reading items that tickled my curiosity.

I finished reading the unauthorized biography of Bisseau that evening at home. When I was done I fixed dinner and while eating was stunned to realize I hadn't brought in the mail, and hadn't thought about it at all today. I smirked and decided not to get it now. Tomorrow would be soon enough. If Erin isn't in a hurry to let me know where she is, why continue to stress myself?

In the morning on my way out I checked the mail. It was the usual stuff, mostly junk, and nothing from Erin. I had mixed feelings; glad, because I was afraid anything I heard from her would be bad news, and angry, just because.

For the next few days I entered a detailed listing of each item, as thoroughly as I could describe them, and tagged the ones that seemed to be particularly intriguing, such as personal letters, property deeds, an so forth. Though my main duty was to categorize the Bisseau papers, I sensed that the journals of the other people, the older ones, might provide insight into life in the 19th century that an historian like me would find fascinating. In fact, I suppose it had grabbed Bisseau's attention and he'd been working on a research project.

When I'd finished that task, working as diligently as a fresh college graduate trying to impress his boss on day one of a new job, I began to pore over the latest Colin Bisseau journal, the one dated 1980. Most of the pages were blank. Colin Bisseau and Elizabeth had gone to Alaska in late May, when winter had not yet released its grip on many areas of that giant state. The last entry was dated May 20; I chose not to read it yet as I wanted to work my way towards it. I was perplexed by the fact that Bisseau was keeping a journal up to nearly the day he disappeared, yet the journal itself had not been located in his apartment, but instead was found thirty-five years later locked away in a dark and dank basement of the university.

Where had it been, or had whoever been in charge of gathering up Bisseau's possessions found it, and the other journals, and decided to hide it? Another mystery; I'd have to find out who handled the Bisseau estate.

I poured a cup of coffee from the thermos I'd brought with me and began to read.

3. COLIN'S 1980 JOURNALS

January 1, 1980

Happy New Year! Yes, another one has come around already; they seem to come quicker every year. I write the same opening each New Year's Day; I need to get new material.

This year will call for another change. I experience angst at such times but it needs to be done. This has been a good life, interesting and educational if not always uplifting. Meeting Elizabeth has made the last few years especially wonderful, and with her being like me, she understands the need for change.

The way the world is evolving, for the better, in some ways, but not all, makes it more difficult for people like us. This will take more planning than usual so it may be months before we can move on, so I need to get to work.

He'd lost me by the second paragraph. It sounds like he and his wife were planning to make a major change in their lives, but did it backfire when they went to Alaska?

Usually by this time I am set to go, but Elizabeth and I have had it so good I've been reluctant. Past experience tells me we must, however, before it's too late.

It will take an exceptional amount of planning. Elizabeth is not happy about it but she knows I'm right. She's not used to the complexities of modern society and thinks we can just pick up and go. As usual there are few people who can help us.

What did he mean, about his wife being like him? Similar in personality, in likes and dislikes, in a desire to shrink away from public life? Like him enough so that she won't pick up after thirty-five years of marriage to find herself? His words implied that a major change in his life was normal and frequent. Colin Bisseau had become a mildly famous person, not only in academic and diplomatic circles, but in the public eye because of his World War Two heroics and the movie. Maybe that was it, he and his wife were going to totally bug out and become hermits.

A few entries later I read:

Elizabeth is upset; she feels I'm not taking her into my confidence regarding our plans. I suppose not...I've become used to doing most things myself when the time comes to move on. I know I can trust Elizabeth, but she is not as cautious as I am, and I find myself making most of the decisions without consulting her. Then I remind myself, this is for two this time, not just for one.

A day later, the entry read:

When we are ready, I'll give the papers I currently have in my possession, and a few other older papers I recently retrieved from one of my caches for review, to Jay for safekeeping until I'm ready for them. I probably should put them in a more secure cache I have near the university, but I don't have the time, and I don't want anyone, even Jay, to know where it is, though I have left him information that will serve in case I need him to access it. He says he has the perfect storage place and the material will be safe.

Jay? Who is, or was, Jay? If he was the one who stored the papers in the University sub-basement, he must have been a professor here, or at least someone who had access to the innards of the campus. It was time for more coffee so I went to Janice's office to see if she would join me.

"You remember anyone named Jay?"

"Jay, as in the letter, or in the bird?"

"Yes, like the bird, J-a-y."

"Not that I can think of. I knew a Jay who'd been a friend of David's, a long time ago."

Her ex, David, a name she rarely mentioned.

"In what context?"

"It's a name Bisseau mentions in one of his journal entries. He says he was going to give his papers to this person Jay, to hold until Bisseau sent for them."

"Tell me more."

I gave Janice a thumbnail sketch of what I'd read.

"Sounds odd, like he was planning on dropping out of society."

I nodded. "My impression as I read the notes was that he was planning on a long, complicated trip, one to where he wouldn't be known. And, he wasn't telling his wife the plans he was making."

"Where would they go? Even in Europe or Africa Colin Bisseau would eventually be recognized."

"I dunno. Grow a beard, wear dark glasses."

"Sounds silly, but at the same time, it sounds like fun, to get completely away from the familiar, the everyday mundane trappings…"

"Trappings? Do you feel trapped, Jan?"

The way she looked at me I felt she was weighing the odds of running off on her own, giving up on snatching me away from Erin, or ever having another intimate relationship with a man. It might be she envied Erin, doing what Janice, a single person, could more readily do without hurting anyone. It made me sad. I had never, not intentionally, since that one encounter, given Janice the sense I cared for her in any way other than as a friend and a colleague. She looked away, embarrassed, as if she knew I could read her face.

"It's a word, Morgan. It doesn't mean...yes, sometimes I do. It passes," She looked at me and smiled. Her eyes glistened.

"Let's go back to my office and search for this Jay bird."

We returned to her office and she brought up a computer file listing past and present professors, administrators, students, you name it, who had ever had any connection with Lyman Wilson University.

"Jay's not a common first name, but it could be a nickname," Janice said as she culled through the lists.

"Can you sort on first names?"

"Yes," she answered, "that's what I'm doing now."

There were dozens of James, Josephs, Johns, some Jacks and Jacobs, one Jed, a bunch of Jims, Jeffs, and Jeromes, a couple of Jaspers and even a Julius and a Jeremiah, a Jared and a Jackson.

"Okay, it must be a nickname."

"Or it's not anyone ever connected with the university," Janice suggested.

"I think it is, else how did the papers end up here?"

"Beats me."

"Hey, go down to the end."

"End of what?"

"Sort on the last name of all these people whose names began with 'J'," I said.

Janice deftly stabbed the keyboard.

"Now what?"

"Go to the end." She scrolled down.

I moved closer to the screen. I could smell her hair. A strand of it brushed my cheek. I edged back and reached with a finger to touch the screen.

"Scroll up a bit," I said.

"There, maybe."

"What? Who?"

"See this name, Jack A. Yadron. Who was he?"

"Oh, I see, his initials may have given him the nickname. Let's see."

Janice brought up the bio of Jack Yadron.

"Professor of Literature, years, ah…about the same time as Bisseau, so they probably knew each other. Oh my…"

"What is it?"

"Look there, Morg." Janice pointed to the last paragraph in Yadron's biography. I read it aloud.

"Yadron tragically died on June 3, 1980, in an automobile accident on his way to Wilson University. He was struck by a hit-and-run driver. The driver was later apprehended. Yadron is survived by…"

"June 3 is about the same time the search for the Bisseaus was going on," Janice said.

"Yeah, yeah. That would explain why the papers are still here."

"How so?"

"If Jay Yadron stored them for Bisseau, but didn't tell anyone, then he died, then Bisseau died, the papers would have just sat in the file cabinet, shuffled around a few times, until it ended up in the sub basement."

"Maybe that's where Yadron put them in the first place."

"It's possible," I agreed. "Yadron may not have known how long it would be before Bisseau asked for the papers, so he hid them where he figured no one would look."

"Why the secrecy in the first place?"

"It might not have been meant to be secretive. Could be Bisseau planned on doing some writing, wanted to get away to where he'd have privacy, then when he was settled in he would have Yadron send him the papers."

"Hmm, yeah, I suppose. Strange, isn't it?"

"What are you saying, Jan? You don't think it's more than a coincidence, do you?"

She seemed startled by my question.

"No, I never meant to suggest that. Just that it's a shame that two fine educators, both still young, died in accidents."

"We don't know how Bisseau died."

"Or when, for that matter," Janice added.

I backed away, far enough so the scent of her hair wasn't as alluring.

"I need to read the report of how Yadron died, and also the report of the Bisseau search party. It seems odd that they found absolutely no trace of two people and their supplies."

"I already gave you everything I found," Janice said.

"I'll go back to my office and read it again."

"Let me know what you find. The committee wants a report."

I smiled and nodded as I left Janice's office. I almost turned and asked her if the committee had any funds to buy dinner for its staff, but I was wary of our relationship turning towards anything other than business. I was too old for romantic games. Besides, I still had a wife, somewhere, unless she's already been to Reno and forgot to tell me.

It's amazing what you can find on the Internet these days, some of which is true. I read an article on the death of Jack Yadron, known to his friends as Jay, the story stated. There was nothing suspicious about his death. He was hit by an intoxicated driver who'd had two prior DUI convictions. A follow-up story a few days later, when the driver had been located and arrested, mentioned that Yadron had been a colleague of Colin Bisseau, a former ambassador and author of several books on a variety of topics. By then the Bisseaus were in the news as they had not yet been located, having gone camping in Alaska, and not seen since.

I then found a summary of the Bisseau search party report. It mentioned an article that gave the entire account, which I located in the library. Originally the pilot had said that the two people he dropped off, Colin and Elizabeth Bisseau, had been setting up their campsite when he flew off. Later, he said his earlier recollection was incorrect, and that his passengers were still rowing their way to shore the last he saw of them.

What didn't make sense was that if some disaster had struck them, such as an animal attack, surely there would have been camping paraphernalia laying around. And even a bear attack would have left evidence, if nothing other than bones. But there was no trace of humans having been anywhere near where the Bisseaus were last seen.

What also didn't make sense was the later news that before going to Alaska Bisseau had sold his stock holdings and converted them to cash, but there was no record of where the money had gone. Some accounts said Bisseau had held over ten million dollars in stocks and realty. Certainly he hadn't taken millions of dollars in cash with him to Alaska.

I returned to Bisseau's journal, but contrary to my original plans of chronological reading, I skipped ahead to the last few entries.

May 18th:

We are about as set as we can be. Elizabeth is not happy that I kept most of the details from her; I told her it was for the best until I had my plans in place. So today I explained everything to her, with the exception of certain names. And that's because people along the way who will be aiding us want it that way, not to reveal themselves any more than necessary, or any earlier than necessary. I don't blame them; I've acted the same way when I've been in a similar situation.

I'm not as sure about this as I have been the other times. The world has changed: it's become much more technical, open, inter-connected, than I've ever known. Credit cards, social security numbers,...it's become difficult for anyone to slip through the cracks and still be a part of normal society.

And Colin Bisseau became much better known than I intended. It seemed to get away from me, but I have no intention of being a lonely wanderer or a hermit for the rest of my life. I dare not even mention in these notes the exact nature of my current plans or where we will make our residence. When... if... I ever write the story...but should I?

Jay will clean out the apartment and take care of my papers. Being younger than me, he plans to stay at the university for several more years, and I've learned I can trust him, which is rare. But trust him I do, and when I contact him in a few months to forward the papers, I'll have them sent to a storage site that I can monitor before claiming them. I didn't make it this far by being careless.

As many times as I've had to do this, this time it seems more burdensome. If it wasn't for Elizabeth I'm not sure how I would handle it, or maybe I wouldn't.

Am I getting tired of the process? The thought sounds foolish when spoken aloud, yet I have heard rumors of those who literally walked off a cliff rather than face the process one more time. Even Marcus gets a bit grumpy at times; he insists that the world never really changes, it just finds more efficient ways to destroy.

What I do see is that life is going to become more complicated. It wasn't so long ago that a person could walk away from one life and not be concerned that he would be located if he had reasons why he wanted to start his life anew. That was before modern communication systems, before fingerprints, before the scientific method was developed and science itself was known as natural philosophy.

Time was a person could slide into the nebulous crannies of the world and vanish like a vapor. Every generation or so I pick up the Book again and see if there are insights that make more sense in light of social advances, or should I say, recent social adjustments. I noted that James writes, "For what is your life? It is a mist that appears for a little while, and then vanishes."

The question is, does the life vanish, or merely the material aspects? Some of us seem fated, favored or doomed I have not yet determined, to have the unlimited opportunity to study the question.

It has been a productive era and I take minor pride in my accomplishments of the last three decades. It is time, though, for contemplation and a total review of where we go from here. There is no hurry.

Reading this give me a queasy feeling in my gut, as if I'd snuck into my older sister's bedroom and read her diary. What was this about 'every generation or so?'

It seemed clear that Bisseau was gearing up to abandon the rat race when he and his wife suddenly disappeared. Even if they intended to vanish from public view could they have done it so well they were never heard from again? Or did some tragedy truly strike them in Alaska?

Bisseau's manner of writing had a mystical, even spiritual tone to it. It rang as if written by an older, slightly cynical person, one who's been around the block a few times. It reminded me that in his book on the crisis facing African wildlife he tended to wax lyrical about the simpler ways of life before civilization rolled across the globe.

His final entries were:

May 19th

Marcus has the outline of our plans. He needs to know the details in case anything goes wrong. If Elizabeth and I get separated, I have instructed Marcus to forget me and make sure she is taken care of. Nothing is fail-safe. Assuming our transfer to PB goes smoothly, I'll give Elizabeth the rest of the plan so she then will be able to implement it if anything goes awry. I think my plans are solid and I am beginning to feel confident of success.

I will have a surprise for Elizabeth. I hope it will smooth her agitation that I haven't been as open with her as she would like. With a bit of luck I've located one of her old friends, one she had lost contact with. We will stay a few days with her and her husband and I think Elizabeth will enjoy linking up with them after all the years they've been separated.

There's nothing left to do. We will take a shuttle to the airport in the morning. I wanted to give the car to Jay but we both agreed it might be awkward to explain if someone recognized the car as having belonged to me. So I sold it and insisted on giving Jay the money to compensate him for all he's done and will still do to help the transition. I hope when the time comes for him I can be of help.

May 20th: Herein I copy the note I left for Jay:

Jay, thanks for everything…I'm sure you'll continue to have a fine career at Wilson, or wherever you chose to go. I count on you to find a secure place for these papers until I can send for them, which will be in a few months. I hope we can get together some day…I have a soft spot for the University and would like to stay informed of its progress. Be well, old friend.

Colin

P.S. sorry I can't make it to The Rendezvous this year…timing is everything…Have fun and say Hi for me.

The rest of the pages in this journal book were blank.

I sat back and mulled over what I'd read. Bisseau obviously had plans beyond Alaska, but what was the real reason he and his wife went to Alaska in the first place?

4. WAR HERO

Confused and a bit disturbed I turned to the earlier journals of Colin Bisseau. The earliest one was dated 1944-45. Before the dated entries was a prologue.

Most of the time while in the Army I had to write notes on small pocket-sized booklets or on whatever scrap of paper I could lay my hands on. Sometimes there was nothing to write on. So these entries have been either re-written from whatever notes I made, or are based on my best memory of events. But because it was difficult to maintain a regular log there are fewer entries for this period of time than in other years.

January, 1944

I've finished basic training and am now off for advanced infantry training. I wish I could convince them I know all this. I must admit the weapons are newer than what I've been used to, and the tactics employed are different. It's a new kind of warfare.

I didn't get this at all. Colin Bisseau in 1944 would have been twenty years old based on available records. What weapons could he have been used to other than hunting rifles? I scanned several entries, most of which were mundane recollections of training and Bisseau's wishes for combat duty. For example:

We keep hearing rumors than an invasion of Europe is imminent. Sure wish I could get in on the action. Haven't been to Europe in a spell. Of course, charging in as an invader isn't exactly the same as visiting as a tourist.

I'd come across nothing to suggest that Bisseau had been to Europe prior to the war. When would he have had the opportunity? I continue to quickly eyeball entries until the following:

June 7, 1944

It's happened: the invasion of Europe. Eisenhower's troops landed yesterday on the beaches, the beautiful beaches of Normandy. I suppose they are not so beautiful today, red with blood and littered with bodies and equipment. From the rumors it was carnage, but the Allies managed to get ashore and are holding on. I'm still stuck here in Georgia waiting and training.

In October Bisseau wrote:

Finally, I am going to the war! Why am I so eager? I guess because I have known people to do bad things but

I've never had to confront pure evil head on. And Hitler
sounds like the epitome of evil.

Again, his writing had the sound of a person experienced beyond his years. Maybe he intended to write his life story in novel form, or the 'Great American Novel' about World War Two. Like most ambitious writers he never got it done. (Though his non-fiction is impressive.) I skipped ahead; I wanted to read what Bisseau had to say about the event that made him a famous war hero.

I came across an entry wherein Bisseau reported that he was with the 90th Division, in General Patton's Third Army, that it was fiercely cold, and that the hopes of the war ending before Christmas were no longer accepted as a possibility. The Germans weren't yet defeated, but they were on the run and the soldiers talked about playing it safe, having made it this far. No one wanted to be the last soldier killed on the last day of the war.

Dec. 22, 1944: (copied from scraps of notes I made after the described event)
Two days ago was a day like few in my life. The Germans have counter-attacked in great force. We are reeling. My platoon has been cut off from the main body and in trying to re-join them we became separated into two groups and got ourselves lost. It is bitterly cold, colder than I can remember experiencing. Breathing hurts. There is no

sun to provide the slightest hint of warmth. The sky is overcast and gray, and the light that does manage to drip through the trees to ground level is barely enough to read by, had one anything to read.

The bare branches of the trees are dark and menacing. At night, in the light of the moon, they resemble disfigured ogres out of a horror story.

Snow falls steadily. It is almost miraculous to see it fall, accumulating soundlessly, unstoppable. It is bright and the white blanket is beautiful but it makes it difficult to keep oneself dry. We shiver to keep warm, but shivering makes it a challenge to shoot straight.

We were attacked from three sides and several of the men were hit. Two died immediately. Everyone else, six men, except me, were wounded. Why I've been spared I don't know. I may live a charmed life but my flesh can be mutilated by bullets as easily as anyone else's. With what I've been through it is remarkable I've never had a serious injury. Is there a built-in immunity along with everything else?

His writing at times sounded spiritual, at other times fanciful.

I tended to the wounded as best I could, interrupting my nursing to fire a few rounds from different locations, to keep the Germans guessing as to how many of us were alive. As the sky turned to a deep-gray, mid-afternoon, the firing from the Germans lessened. By nightfall the attacks on us ceased altogether. I think the enemy thought we were dead but didn't care to prowl around in the dark to ascertain.

Around 4 a.m. I told Cpl. Lansing, the least severely wounded, that I was going to try to break through and get to our lines, and bring help and medical assistance. I gave him my remaining ammunition. The way he looked at me I think he suspected I was lighting out, abandoning the men.

I wasn't more than a hundred yards away when I heard rifle fire. I hesitated, but without ammunition there was nothing I could do. I moved as fast as I could, plodding through the snow. A few bullets winged past me but I think they were wild shots from Germans shooting at any movement in the forest.

My instincts were true: I found headquarters and staggered into camp after first being halted by guards. I collapsed as I tried to explain who I was and what I needed.

Long story short, it was going to be an hour or so before they could spare anyone. I rested ten minutes, ammoed up, and began my return. Someone tried to stop me, told me they were bringing a tank up and I could ride on it. By then it might be over, I said; they need ammunition now. I tried to lug the machine gun ammunition but it was too heavy to carry in the snow and would slow my return.

It was quiet as I neared our encampment and I feared the men were dead. As I spied the site of our tawdry foxholes, barely inches deep, as most of the men were too weak to combat the frozen ground, the first whisper of daylight revealed gray uniforms barely ten yards away. I opened fire. No one joined me as my comrades were completely out of ammo, not to mention weak from loss of blood.

Bullets zipped by my head and I heard them crack against the trees and the ground in front of and around me. I don't know why I wasn't hit. One by one the Germans fell. I loaded a fresh magazine. A bullet tore through the sleeve of my jacket. I raised my gun and fired wildly, spraying back and forth, up and down. I heard screams. Four Germans rose from the ground and turned and ran. I shot them dead.

Why did I do this, I have asked myself. Why did I return? No one would have blamed me if I stayed at headquarters. Why do I take such risks when I have so much to lose? Isn't my life worth more than theirs? Why do I keep doing stupid things?

An interesting question to ask oneself: isn't my life worth more than others'?

Christmas Day, 1944:

Help came to us an hour or so later and all the wounded men survived. Later I visited them in the hospital and they acted like I was some kind of hero. Actually I felt foolish. I don't like to be noticed. I don't like to take chances. But what's done is done, and had I not gone back for help, we would have all died, so I guess I have to live with being a small time hero. Hopefully, amidst the chaos and noise I will be soon forgotten. To that end I've asked for a transfer. My excuse is that my unit was so badly shot up they'll be out of action for weeks, whereas I'm rarin' to go. I was told to take a few days off and catch my breath. Later today we heard that the General had reached Bastogne to relieve the men surrounded there.

New Year's Day, 1945

Happy New Year! It's difficult to feel happiness with the war still going. The Germans showed they weren't done fighting with their latest series of attacks. Why don't they surrender? But I'm sure this will be the last year of the war; at least in Europe.

We are exhausted. We had to retreat several miles in the face of the German attacks, but the word is that we have stopped them and as soon as the skies clear and our planes can fly we should be able to push the enemy back across the Rhine River.

It is sad for me to see lovely villages and farms blown away, the people's lives shattered, the putrid bodies along the sides of the roads; people, horses, cows. This used to be such a beautiful land. Maybe I shouldn't have been so eager to return.

Once again Bisseau referred to having been to Europe before. I 'm wondering if he was writing these notes to provide a basis for a novel. He may write that he doesn't want to be remembered as a hero, yet I get the impression he intended to exploit his actions in the war. Maybe he wasn't quite so humble as his persona implied.

March 26, 1945

It's all over but the shouting. We have crossed the Rhine and what's left of the German Army is in tatters and in retreat. Sadly, men are still dying and it looks like Hitler is determined to take his country down in flames. I can't understand why his generals don't overthrow him.

I've managed to hook up again with the Third, though with a new company. We keep moving forward and the men are eager for this to be over, but also reluctant to take chances.

I thought by transferring I could escape the fame, or notoriety, of the 'event in the woods', but yesterday the General himself (Patton) pinned a Silver Star on me. He smiled and said I had done a wonderful job of 'killing those bastard Krauts.' I smiled and saluted.

From my readings I recalled that Bisseau's award was later upgraded to the Congressional Medal of Honor. Harry Truman, as one of his first presidential duties, presented the medal to Colin Bisseau.

I leafed through the rest of Bisseau's diary for the remaining weeks of the war in Europe. He apparently saw no action after receiving his medal. It took him a few days to realize why.

April 1, 1945:

April Fool's Day, and I'm the fool! I've being shipped home to promote war bonds to help finance the war against Japan. I'm to be paraded as a hero who saved over a hundred men from sure butchery by the SS! I'm so much in the spotlight now that even if I did manage to disappear, and in a shattered Europe I could with no problem, I'd probably be discovered, because I don't think our Army will be leaving Europe any time soon, end of war or not. I didn't have time to think through my options, and my resources would not be easy to access in these chaotic conditions. In fact, I can't be sure they are safe. So I'm on my way home, like it or not.

His resources? Bisseau was either writing fiction or he was confused due to the trauma he experienced fighting in Europe. Or he's had a past totally unknown to anyone, and he obviously wasn't going to reveal it easily.

Would he if I read all his diaries religiously? Is there some big secret that would be eye-popping to know about this man, or nothing more than the confused ramblings of a soldier who's seen and felt the horrors of war? He would not have been the first soldier to lose track of reality during times of shock. He'd seen many ugly things, seen the horror people can inflict on one another. It is not unusual for people in those situations to block out the outrageous events they have been a part of, and blend in memories of things that never happened, but which could block out the memories their minds couldn't deal with. Most of these people, once returned to home and safety, lead normal lives, with only an occasional sweat-inducing dream to remind them there are things hidden inside, waiting for a weak moment to wreak fear. Bisseau certainly led an active and seemingly ordinary life after the war, without any evidence on the outside of any mental trauma. Who knows what goes on inside a man's head? Or inside the mind of a man's wife's head?

I was surprised that there were few entries for the next several months, and those were short. I'd say Bisseau was not happy with his time as a poster boy for the United

States Army. His last entry of the war was in August, shortly after Japan surrendered.

So what will we, the world, do now? Will this be the end of wars, or the beginning of even worse conflicts? What will I do next? I need to find a new vocation.

I quickly scanned through his notations until I came to 1946.

I'm starting college—again. Well, there's always something new to learn. I suppose I'm cheating a little this time as I'm going to study history; hell, I could teach the course. But it will allow me time to brush up on events of the past few years and to sort out my resources.

The war has played havoc with economies of the world and I will need to realign some affairs. During the Spring I'll make a trip to London and see how issues are there. Lawson (as he likes to be called now) contacted me and said most everything is safe, though there were some losses. He wasn't specific.

Again Bisseau indicated he'd been to Europe, even before the war, and writes about his 'resources'. And who was Lawson?

He didn't write much the next few weeks, mostly notes relating to school. I skipped ahead to April 1946.

April 16, 1946: Edinburgh.

Lawson hadn't told me he'd moved my accounts here from London during the worst of it, back in 1940. He said he wasn't sure if his communications were secure and didn't want to alarm me. Lawson is trustworthy so I have no problem with his actions. He may have saved me a considerable amount of effort and fortune.

I will make some re-allocations so I can access anything I need from the States. I have to handle this quickly while Lawson can help, because he will be leaving his position soon. As we have come to learn over the years, best of friends or not, it is always safer to withhold some information until one is safely re-settled. So it may be three or four months before I hear from him again.

The next two entries confused me because they were written in French, at least, what I identified as French. I don't read or speak French so I'd have to get these translated. Where and when did Bisseau learn French? There were no more entries until ten days later, and then it didn't say anything I understood.

April 26, 1946

The re-allocation is complete. Lawson will be leaving in a few days. We had a going-away party, just the two of us, with the best wine we could find in torn-up

London. It is truly a shame what happened to this beautiful city, but there are numerous cities in Europe in even worse shape. At times like this I feel guilty for being alive when so many have died. The uneasiness flows through me and eventually I have to shrug and get back to living, sort of like standing under a shower and crying over a lost love, letting the hot water wash away the malaise.

Without Lawson to help me until he is re-settled, I won't have anyone I can trust to handle my resources, but I can do some things anonymously. Now I need to get back to the university.

Again he refers to 'resources'; does he mean assets as in money? There was no indication what he did for funds at this time in his life so maybe that's what he was referring to.

The rest of the 1946 journal consisted mostly of notes regarding his studies and other aspects of university life. I read quickly and found no further mention of 'resources' or other oddly phrased commentary. His notes made no reference to any close friends (other than the earlier mention of Lawson). He occasionally described women he dated but none of the names were mentioned more than once or twice.

Yet, the unauthorized biography reported that Colin Bisseau was popular and wasn't short of friends, male and female, during his school years. Handsome, popular, a war hero, it's amazing some pretty girl wasn't able to latch onto him, until the woman named Elizabeth, many years later, which was another mystery: there was virtually nothing in the biography about the woman Colin married, other than that they met in 1972 and were married shortly thereafter. This was when Bisseau was working as an education advisor to the governor. Again my interest jumped, this time to Bisseau's wife. I wondered if there was anything about her in these journals, so I searched for a journal that covered the 1970s.

Sure enough there were several, almost one for each year of the 1970s. There was sure to be interesting reading regarding his time as ambassador, and I'd be curious to read what he had to say about returning to Lyman Wilson, if only because there might be entries covering the time I was starting my career there.

It took a while, because I kept stopping to read entries that caught my eye, like this one from 1976:

We finally had the time to go on a photographic safari. Elizabeth has been badgering me ever since we came to Africa, but my duties made it difficult. Now that my time here is almost concluded, I figured we needed to do this soon, as I was as eager as she. The times we had the opportunity to visit parks or even venture into the wild brush it was always in the line of duty.

What was surprising to me, almost as fascinating as seeing wild animals romping over the grasslands (several variety of antelope, zebras and giraffes), or laying lazily under a shade tree, untroubled by our caravan of jeeps, smug in their authority (the lions), as if they knew we wouldn't dare come close enough to aggravate them, and the enormous size and strength and magnificence of the elephant, with intelligence in their eyes that was piercing, as if saying to us, I know my place, and you need to keep yours, was Elizabeth's daring-do in getting as close as possible to take pictures. More than once our guide had to caution her and escort her with his weapon at the ready. I reminded Elizabeth it would be quite embarrassing if the wife of the author of a book castigating the gratuitous hunting of wild life should be the cause of the death of one of these creatures.

I realized I'd gone too far so I flipped back to 1972:

I have seen her! We met and spent the night together, mostly, believe it or not, talking about what we've been doing these dozens of years since we lost each other. I dare not write more lest I find myself heart-broken again.

I went entry by entry the rest of 1972 but found no mention of 'her' until this terse comment in October:

We were married today.

And that was all he said about the day or the event.

I walked over to see Janice. It was time for an after noon coffee break. I must admit it is always a pleasure to see her. She seems to get prettier every day; how can that be at her age? It must mean I'm turning into a lonely old man. Anticipating such thoughts, last night I sent a text message to Erin. I had resisted contacting her because she had asked me not to. When I had not heard from her for weeks I still resisted because I was playing the game of 'if you don't miss me, I don't miss you.'

I was genuinely concerned about Erin, but at the same time I was intrigued by my new work. I wondered if I should be doing something aggressive to get Erin back home, and if by not doing so I was indicating I didn't miss her, didn't love her. I wanted to know where Erin was and that she was safe, but right now, between working on this project and my feelings for Erin being garbled in my mind, I didn't want her home yet, because when, if she did return, I wanted us to understand what we expected from each other. I don't want to be surprised by a sudden return, and not knowing if it meant she was staying, or she was packing for good. Later I would admit to myself I was being plain, damn stubborn.

My text to Erin was steely: "Where are you Are you OK? I am fine. Please answer."

"Hi, Morg. I was wondering if you'd come by. I've got a fresh pot unless you want to walk over to the cafeteria."

"Let's walk, I need the exercise."

As we walked I filled Janice in on my latest readings in the Bisseau journals.

"Jan, can I get access to Colin Bisseau's transcripts from when he was enrolled here?"

"Normally you wouldn't, why?"

I told her about the entries in French.

"So he could write French, so what? He was educated and widely-traveled; why does that surprise you?"

"Because these entries were written in 1946, in his first semester here. When did he learn French?"

"High school?"

"When he was in high school, if you took a language it was typically Latin or Spanish. And I doubt if that podunk school he went to in the woods of southern Indiana taught him French. I'd like to get those entries translated. You know anyone?"

"You're lookin' at her, Morg. Didn't you know I could speak and read French? Spent a year in France, though I may be a bit rusty."

"No, I didn't know. Would you give it a shot?"

Janice said she would and we made small talk while we drank our coffee. She didn't ask about Erin and I didn't tell her I'd texted her. I don't know why I didn't.

On our walk back from the cafeteria I again broached the subject of Colin Bisseau's transcripts.

"I'd still like to know if he studied French here."

"And what if he didn't?"

"Then I might be curious to know where he did learn French."

"Self-taught?"

"Maybe."

"Okay, I'll look."

A short while later Janice called and said that Bisseau's transcripts did not show him studying French, but rather, he studied Chinese.

"The writing in the journal was definitely not Chinese," I said.

"Bring me a copy and I'll see if I can translate it."

"How soon can you do it?"

Janice hesitated and I got the feeling she was thinking of making a bargain. I'm positive I heard a sigh.

"I'll try to do it tonight; I have nothing else going."

I ignored the hint. "I'll bring a copy over now."

After I dropped off the copy of the entries I wanted translated, I told Janice I was leaving for the day. She looked disappointed, or was it my imagination? I got the impression that each day she hoped this was the one where I asked her to come home with me. It made me sad, then I'd feel bad because I should be thinking about Erin's feelings, not Janice's.

When I got home I noticed a message on the landline voice mail. It was Erin; her voice was tired, or stern, certainly not very friendly, far away in both body and spirit.

"Hi, Morgan. I thought I should call to let you know I am fine. I suppose it's just as well I didn't find you in. Or maybe you are in and are listening to me speak. I can't blame you if you don't want to talk to me. But I appreciate your message. This I something I think is best…I'm sorry I can't be more specific. I'll try to call you when I know better what I'm doing. Be safe, Morgan, and be happy. And, oh, yes I am fine, so don't worry."

No "I love you," no "I miss you," but somehow I should be happy. Like hell! If she loved me and missed me she wouldn't be away. She didn't even say if she was still in Europe or back in the States. Who'd she meet, some Italian gigolo? Then again, maybe if I truly loved her I'd be chasing her to the ends of the earth.

I came in late the next day, missing morning coffee break. I ate leftovers at my desk for lunch. Shortly after noon Janice showed up with the written translation I'd asked for.

"You all right, Morg?"

"Yeah, I was up late last night watching an old movie. I slept in."

"Oh, hey, you're not on a time clock, it's just that you're usually here early."

I pointed at the paper she held in her hand.

"Did you translate it?" I asked.

"Yes, the best I could, but it doesn't make sense to me. I don't have the context of what else he wrote."

I read the translation to myself. Then I opened Bisseau's journal to the place he'd first written the entry. I read the April 16, 1946 entry out loud to Janice. Then I read the translation aloud.

"I've known Lawson a long time. We were fortunate to find each other, and to find out that we are alike. Both of us have found that it can be dangerous to reveal oneself too soon, as usually it leads to problems. There is no one I trust more than him, which really doesn't say much since he's the only other one I have any connection with these days; these years.

Still, as cautious as he is, he can get careless. He practically told me where he would be, either because he feels he can be more open with me, or because he wants me to know, in case of trouble. I should warn him that he should trust no one with his changeover information."

"I told you it made no sense," Janice said.

"Let me read the next entry."

"Much of the European investments are gone. Fortunes made, fortunes lost. Fortunately (a lousy pun), the commodities survive. I can move them back to London now, and will have to find a way next summer to move them with me. Wilson University will, I believe, make a comfortable and safe haven for the coming years."

"What does he mean, 'haven'? It sounds like the university was a safety zone or something. And those other words, 'changeover' and 'commodities', what do they mean?"

I shook my head slowly.

"You sure he wrote this in 1946? He was only twenty-one or twenty-two years old then."

"It's in the journal that covers his years in World War Two. Unless it's meant to be fiction."

"You mean even his heroism?"

"No, no, that's substantiated by other people. I was wondering if at one time he meant these notes as a source for a novel. Maybe even science-fiction."

"Science fiction? I don't know what this sounds like, but it doesn't sound like science fiction," Janice said.

"I'm thinking out loud, and probably way off base. I find it odd that this young man who grew up in an orphanage and went to school in a town too small to show up on maps became a war hero, was familiar with Europe, knew French, and writes as if he was...much older than he was at the time."

"Some people called him a genius, Morgan. A child prodigy, super-intelligent, learned quickly, maybe had a photographic memory."

"I've never known anyone with all those talents."

"Don't be jealous," she said with a smile.

"I'm not, Jan, but I'm curious about Colin Bisseau in a way I never anticipated. I wish he'd left journals of his younger years, before the war."

"What are you thinking, Morg, that there's some big mystery, or some horrible facet to his life that you'll discover?"

"I'm not thinking horrible, but mysterious, yes."

"Not everybody advertises their life all over the Internet, Morgan, or writes on Facebook about every little thing that happens to them. Some like to keep their privacy."

"Yes, and a few decades ago it was easier to keep one's privacy. Yet, Bisseau kept notes and journals, and asked this fellow Jay to keep them for him, then both Jay and Bisseau disappear, at virtually the same time."

"And the papers remained buried under the university for the next thirty odd years, Morgan. What does that mean to you?"

"Actually, that part of the mystery makes it more of a coincidence. I can't believe Bisseau wrote in his journal that Jay was to take care of the papers, if he hadn't expected him to do so. And while Bisseau's disappearance is mysterious, Jay's death is not."

"What else do you find mysterious?"

"The papers of these other people, Colt Boston and Cade Bunyan. Who were they and what was their relationship to Bisseau, that's what."

"He could have been on an academic research project, Morg. Bisseau was a historian first, before he was a politician, diplomat, or writer."

"That's possible, but if so, what was so fascinating about those two guys to make Bisseau spend his time researching and writing about them? That alone might be interesting to learn."

"Well," Janice said with a heavy sigh, "I gave you the job, so you do it the way you want. Just have something interesting that I can present to the Board." She turned to leave, then stopped. She didn't face me as she spoke.

"I, ah, wondered if you'd like to run over to the Historical Club and have a drink after we finish today."

I felt a knot in my throat. "Ah, no, not today, Jan. I have some errands to run after work."

"Could I run them with you?"

"No, thanks, it'd bore you. I'll see you tomorrow."
She dashed off as if the tea kettle was whistling.

When I was twenty-one I would never imagine turning down a sweet looker like Janice.

Timing is everything.

5. MORE JOURNALS-1

The next day I picked up with Bisseau's journals of his days as a student at Lyman Wilson University. I didn't come across anything spectacular or confusing, at first. The entries were not regular, often nothing for a week or more. Most were commonplace, about classes and various campus activities. Often he noted that the classes were easy and he felt he was experiencing de ja vu. I did come across this mystifying entry:

Out with Sandra again last night. She is loads of fun but I think she's taking our relationship too seriously. Getting married again is not in my plans. Lawson agreed when we spoke of the problems it can cause. He said he'll never tie the knot again unless he finds someone just like him. I think he's right on.

Now when could Bisseau possibly have been married? If he'd been married, he must have been a teenager, and it couldn't have lasted for long. Maybe he and some gal from high school eloped and got hitched by a backwoods preacher, and later the girl's parents had it annulled. Maybe that's why he was so secretive about his life before his time in the Army. And what does Bisseau mean that his friend wants someone just like him?

His 1947 journals contained some intriguing entries:

March 2, 1947:

It's been over a year but I finally heard from Lawson. He called from New York and will be here Wednesday. We have lots to discuss.

No date

Met with Lawson…(who is using the name 'Marcus' now)—he told me where he'd been and it was as I suspected. I suggested he was becoming predictable. He disagreed but I didn't pursue the subject.

Marcus was a name Bisseau mentioned in his last entries in 1980. So he and this fellow, called Lawson and then Marcus, remained friends for a long time. Someone else I may need to investigate.

May 23, 1947

Lawson, I mean Marcus, and I spent hours discussing plans for the coming years. We agree that the United States will be the world's power for the near future, and for a long time, though we both know how fleeting fame and power can be.

As usual he suggests that land, especially in the West, would be a great investment. Feeling guilty that I hadn't confided in him sooner, I told him I already own considerable property in California. He frowned, then laughed and said, "We all have our secrets, don't we? So do I."

As usual he's seriously into high finance so he'll be spending most of his time in New York. He's quite willing to share with me his suggestions for investments in exchange for my so-called expert opinion on world politics, and my willingness to travel when business requires it.

And, big news, he's made arrangements to bring some of the gold and other commodities to the States. He said it's expensive so I shouldn't be shocked at the surcharges, as he mockingly called the up-front price he had to pay. He'd left about half in London. I told him that for his usual fee I'd let him handle my investments in the stock market. He suggested the oil and steel industries, and I agreed. I also told him I wanted a significant position in the company known as International Business Machines. I anticipate that technology will develop exponentially in the coming decades; I don't necessarily look forward to it in and of itself, but I believe it is coming and I want to make investments when possible in companies I expect to grow. We noted, somewhat ironically, that as the world evolves we have more opportunities, yet at the same time more risks. It is amazing how much easier and faster it is to get from one place in the world to another, yet more difficult to keep one's movements confidential.

*It'll get worse, I maintain. Technology is developing
that will track everybody, everywhere, all the time. It'll
make communications and travel faster and cheaper, but
it'll make secrecy difficult. Marcus slipped into a
melancholy mood, as he is wont to do, so I ordered
another beer and we talked of less gloomy matters, like,
had either of us gotten laid lately.*

How had this young man acquired a horde of gold
that he was having smuggled into the country, with more
stashed in London? And if Colin Bisseau bought stock in
IBM back in 1947, he became an extremely wealthy man
by the time he disappeared.

What concerns me are the implications in Bisseau's
journals of secret and possible criminal activities. If this
feted Medal of Honor winner had been involved in illegal
international financial dealings, that would be a story worth
telling. But who would do the telling? Besides, I had no
proof of anything. And I could not get a handle on how this
young man, raised in the woods of rural Indiana, could be
world-wise, traveled, and a budding Goldfinger.

It spent a half-hour on the Internet before I found a
story in an Indianapolis newspaper from 1980 that claimed
Bisseau had sold his IBM, and other stock holdings, in May
of that year, a few days before he disappeared. The story
reported that Bisseau was thought to have owned in the
neighborhood of one hundred thousand shares of IBM

stock. At that time, the story continued, IBM stock was selling in the range of $54.

What would have enticed this shrewd investor to cash in over five million dollars worth of IBM stock, and possibly more in other stocks, and what happened to the proceeds?

I returned to Bisseau's journal, began to read, and realized I'd missed the regular coffee break time. Janice probably thought I had done it purposely because I had rebuffed her yesterday, and was now avoiding her. I sighed and contemplated the fact that since I didn't understand the mind of Erin, a woman I'd been married to for over thirty years, I certainly wasn't going to understand Janice.

Finally I came across a posting by Bisseau that would make headlines if revealed.

May, 1947

There was a Communist coup d'état in Czechoslovakia recently. Our former allies, our so-called World War Two allies, the Russians, or the Soviet Union, are certainly not our allies any more. As tired as the allies were of war and death, it is incomprehensible to me that we allowed the Russians to take over Eastern Europe. Now they are our enemies (I realize that during the war they were allies of convenience, not dear and trusted friends).

When the war ended we should have thanked Stalin for helping us defeat the Germans and told him to pull his army back across their borders. To let them in effect annex Poland, Hungary and other countries I do not understand. Yes, it would have resulted in more fighting had they resisted, but we had the army, we had the weapons, and soon we had the atomic bomb.

It's not like Stalin was a paean of respectability. He was a demon like Hitler. Yes, I can understand they wanted a piece of Germany as reciprocity for their war losses, but they had no right to take over other nations.

Had it been me in charge, I would have made Germany, at least the western half, into an American state; the Brits and French didn't like it, I would have reminded them that it was us who pulled their asses out of the fire— twice in the last twenty years. We would have defeated the Germans without them. It wasn't as if the atrocities started with Hitler. Remember mustard gas in the trench warfare of the First World War? And German U-boats firing on passenger liners?

Now, and I suspect for a long time, we will live in the tension of what some are already calling a 'cold war' with Russia.

(Needed to get that out of my system; saying it out loud sounds foolish; writing it gives me a release.)

Now here was something; had this diatribe become public I doubt Bisseau would have ever been elected to anything higher than dogcatcher, or been selected as an ambassador. Surely even Roosevelt and Churchill, actually it would have been Truman, not Roosevelt, by the time the Germans surrendered, could not have convinced their public to carry on against the Russians. I doubt anyone expected that the Soviet Union's domination of Eastern Europe would turn so cruel.

Bisseau's comment were likely the musings of a young person who, two years after the war had ended in Europe, was second guessing. Still, this was an interesting find.

There wasn't much more of note as I scanned the journals for the rest of Bisseau's time as a student at Wilson. He broke up with Sandra, traumatic for her, he claimed, and occasionally mentioned that Marcus had invested wisely for both himself and Bisseau. There was no mention of gold. He noted that Marcus frequently asked, "Have you found her yet?" And that Bisseau would answer back, "I'll know her when I find her." Marcus then would reply, "Make sure she has a sister as pretty as she."

Bisseau graduated in three years, began teaching history at a local high school; (he wrote that the text was boring and badly written and he needed to write a history textbook some day). He also went to graduate school.

There was one journal book for the years 1950 through 1954, and his entries were sparse and rather boring. One entry did catch my eye.

February 13, 1954

I've received an offer of a small fortune for the property I've been leasing to the Johnson family. Not sure what to do. They have been good tenants, never a problem. Still, the offer is fantastic. I will have to give this some thought. Will contact Marcus for advice.

I found a follow up in an entry a few weeks later:

Marcus said to "take the money and run", but it's not like I need the money, and I hate to throw the Johnsons out. I called Allan and told him not to assume they would pass on the farm to their children, that once they were retired I would sell the land. But I told them I could sell them a couple acres nearby at a price the family could afford.

These entries reminded me of the note I saw in the Cade Bunyan section of the file cabinet. I scoured through the Bunyan papers and found the letter related to property in California. When I looked at the signature again, a scrawl, it looked like it could be "A. Johnson."

Bunyan must have been a relative of Bisseau's, but why did Bisseau write, "I've been leasing"? Did Bisseau inherit the land from Bunyan, whoever he was?

Despite the label, '1950-1954', there were no entries in this journal dated between late 1950 and early 1952. In 1950 Bisseau finished graduate school, and according to the unauthorized biography, he worked on his doctorates in 1954 through 1956, after which he came to Lyman Wilson. There was a gap in both the biography and in Bisseau's journals. I recalled that there was a similar gap in the 1960s, after Bisseau lost the election for governor. There were similar gaps, sometimes years, in both the Boston and Bunyan collections. Of course, some journals could have been lost, or the men lost interest at times in keeping a regular accounting of their activities. Numerous times I have begun to keep a diary, but never got far with it for lack of exciting events to record.

I was pondering what to do next when my phone beeped; it was Arthur Allenby.

"Morgan, the letter appears to be genuine. At least, that's my opinion and also Jameson's; you know him?"

"No, but I've heard of him. Had he ever heard of the incident mentioned in the letter?"

"Heard of it, yes, but not the specific action Grant referred to. But that's not unusual. No one could ever catalog every minor engagement."

"Is it worth anything?"

"Yes, but how much is difficult to say. Jameson and I agree it's genuine but any potential buyer might want another opinion. Would you be interested in getting some feelers?"

"Oh, no, Arthur, I can't do that. I don't have the authority. But send me a bill for your time to make this official."

"If you insist. Please let me know first if it goes on the market. Or if you find any more like it."

We chatted a few more minutes, me eager to get back to the Boston section of the file cabinet, now that Arthur's call had diverted my attention from Bisseau. I reopened the folder I'd glanced at the day I came across the Grant letter. I thumbed through loose sheets of paper, faded and thin, with writing in pencil that was nearly the same shade as the paper. They'd probably been that way before they were placed within the protective sheets, which didn't exist at the time Boston, or whomever, wrote the letters.

Of the papers I could decipher, there appeared to be letters discussing business matters: potential land acquisitions, farming matters, and investment opportunities. Seemingly odd items for a young man of the wilderness to write about. And to whom was he writing? If Boston wrote the letters, how did he get the originals back, and how did Bisseau acquire them? As I noticed that the handwriting varied in the letters, as did the paper itself, I examined the signatures and realized that some of these were letters written by Boston, others written to him. Most everything referred to business deals.

For its time, the 1860s, the writing I could decipher was remarkably free of spelling errors. Though the penmanship was superb, reading the letters was difficult because of the age of the papers and numerous stains.

One letter that was in better shape than the others I was able to read easily. As I browsed through it my eye caught a familiar word: Depot, as in Bolton Depot. I read the complete letter. It was here that Boston told the story of what happened, and what he'd done that resulted in General Grant's appreciation.

...the fierce fighting ceased late in the afternoon when Pemberton began to withdraw. There were thousands of casualties and I lost several fine fellows. Sherman's Corps bivouacked at Bolton Depot, while McClernand and McPherson settled in a bit farther west and south. It appeared that the bulk of Pemberton's forces were high-tailing it to Vicksburg, though he placed himself and about 5,000 men (as I learned later) east of the river.

It was only due to my inability to sleep, still tense from the day's activities, that I overheard a sentry mention that two scouts had not returned. I inquired and set out with Sgt. Owen and two privates whose names I did not know at the time but as I now know were Pvt. O'Leary and Pvt. Doniphon.

We crept as close as we could to the Rebel lines and from the light of a fading fire spotted our scouts huddled along the banks of a ditch, a tiny rivulet, apparently an offshoot of the Big Black River, a minor one not featured on our maps.

Between their position and us we spied five or six of the Rebels moving to surround my scouts. I feared for my soldier's lives and also realized that if the Rebel's captured or killed them they could use this ditch to sneak troops along our right flank.

I ordered one of the privates to return to camp and tell Cpt. Rivers to send troops to shore up our flank and to find the outlet for this ditch. Unfortunately as he departed he stepped on a twig, which snapped and gave away our position.

The Rebels spun in our direction and fired a volley at us without bothering to aim. One round struck the Sergeant, incapacitating him, and another struck one of the privates who I feared was killed but was only knocked unconscious. Our two scouts in the ditch began to fire on the Rebels but in an instant more enemy soldiers appeared, from the other side of the ditch, and they began to discharge a stream of deadly bullets.

I do not know what compelled me to rise up and attack, there being a half-dozen of the Southerners holding ground between myself and the two scouts in the ditch. I charged the Rebel soldiers, bayonet fixed, and emptied my rifle as I ran. I struck one of the enemy and he fell. Two of them shot at me and I felt the wind of a projectile pass my ear.

I pierced one of them with my bayonet, then swung my rifle like a club. Another Rebel attempted to shoot me down but his rifle jammed. I stabbed him. The others swirled around and made for the ditch.

The enemy from the other direction also let loose with a barrage, and both of the scouts in the ditch were wounded, but again I felt lucky and blessed by a grace I certainly do not deserve, to have not been struck dead.

I re-loaded and aimed in the direction of the Rebels just as they reached the ditch. I discharged my weapon and one of them toppled over and, I suppose inspired by my actions, the two scouts, gladly not seriously injured, also fired. The Rebels reversed course and scampered away as if lightning-struck, the situation having swung against them, probably terrified that there was an entire platoon of us on the move.

I helped the scouts to their feet and led them through the darkness back to camp. By then Cpt. Rivers had situated Company B on the right flank at the spot where the ditch merged with our lines. Because of the thick brush this ditch had not been noticed and it would have allowed the enemy to sneak snipers to the edge of our *headquarters. We were firmly entrenched, but they could have raised some havoc.*

With mighty thanks I learned that our soldiers survived their wounds. Back in camp, settling my nerves with hot coffee, I found damage to my uniform from bullets in three places, and marveled that the bullets had merely scorched my uniform and not struck my flesh.

Again I was surprised by the style of writing and the lack of spelling errors typical of the average person of those days. I marveled at the courage of the man, similar to when I read Bisseau's account in World War Two. I am not a courageous man and doubt I could have done what they had. Still, one never knows what one is capable of until the situation arises.

Boston concludes with this remark:

Why do I take such risks when I have so much to lose? Isn't my life worth more than theirs? Why do I keep doing stupid things?

I was stunned. I knew those words. I'd read them recently. I retrieved the Bisseau journal for 1944 and re-read his entry that ended his description of his actions that earned him the Medal of Honor. The words were exact.

Had Bisseau copied them from Boston's journal? Had he read Boston's journal and the words stuck in his mind, and without meaning to, wrote the same thing? Such a coincidence was near impossible. Besides, how would Bisseau have had Boston's journals?

Of course, eventually Bisseau did acquire Boston's journals, since I now knew he'd given his papers to Jay, and they ended up in the same file cabinet as the Boston papers. I felt queasy; butterflies fluttered in my stomach. If it came out that Bisseau had purposely copied another man's thoughts, even for something as simplistic as a personal journal, it would bring into question not only Bisseau's published works, but even his account of his actions during the Battle of the Bulge.

Boston had one more comment related to the incident, after he had received Grant's letter:

While I am pleased to be recognized by the General, and the accolades of the men are appreciated, I feel they strew words of honor too hastily. What is heroism, after all? Is it simply doing what needs to be done, kismet having put one in position of having to perform the deed? If one is a favored child of the gods is it heroism to throw one's body into the fire, knowing that soft, cool rains will keep one safe?

The man wrote of stabbing and shooting people in one moment and waxes philosophically in the next.

If there was a kinship between Boston and Bisseau, possibly Colin inherited property. Bisseau was born in 1921; this man Boston, writing in 1872, must have been at least in his early thirties. He would have been old when Bisseau was born, but it's possible he could have still been alive. However, Bisseau's early history shows a lack of relatives, or any friends that he was close to.

I continued to scan the journals. I hoped to get an indication of Boston's age. But for all he wrote about financial matters and every day life, it was as if he took care not to impart facts too personal in nature. A man by the name of Kittredge was mentioned often, but only as it related to business matters.

There were letters from Boston to someone named Clare, endearing letters, though I did not find an indication that Boston married the woman. There were letters to fellow soldiers; these might be of interest to Allenby. I made a mental note to tell him about them.

For an account of daily life in the late 19th century I'm sure these journals will be of interest to other historians besides me. I might consider taking on the task of having them edited and published myself, on behalf of the university.

For a long time the entries were rather mundane, referring to common daily events, such as:

Marched 10 miles today; weather fair, no sign of Rebels.

Rained last night and today; stayed in tents except for necessities.

Another boring day; some drills, then it rained again. Salt pork & hardtack for dinner---again, no vegetables, none since last week.

No enemy nearby...we played ball, washed clothes; Hurrah!--four ounces of beef for everybody plus fresh peas, corncakes and molasses.

And this one gave me a laugh:

Won 12 dollars at cards, then loaned it back to the losers, so they could buy tobacco from those they had lost it to in an earlier game. Some people shouldn't gamble.

There was surprisingly little mention of actual fighting. I jumped ahead to April 1865 to see what he might have written.

It is over a last; the war is done. And Lincoln is killed. Some fool ambushed him in a theatre, as we hear the story, and shot the president in the head, in the presence of his horrified wife. The murderer escaped but rumor is that since then he has been tracked down and shot to death. What did he think, that he could reverse the results of the war, even after Lee's army had been defeated? What a shame, after we fought this long and bitter war, to have our dear leader shot down at the end; a great shame for the country.

There were no entries for the rest of 1865 and I found no papers dated for the next several years, though it's possible they are here and I'll find them later. These files are neatly arranged and stored, so I suspect if any had existed for the years immediately after 1865 they'd been lost.

Then I came across sketch booklets, similar to those in the Cade Bunyan section, like the ones used by students of the 19th century. These were in fair condition and were easier to read than the faded letters on loose pages.

I couldn't determine where Boston's home was, but apparently he settled in the New York after the Civil War ended. He mentions involvement in the shipping and the import and export business.

The narrative picked up again in 1872.

Sept. 29, 1872:

Met with Kittredge (Jonathan Riker when I first met him). He does a fine job handling the financial end of the businesses. Most everything he invests in does well so I don't mind paying the fee he imposes; it is fair. Generally he recommends buying real estate so he and I (each under 2 or 3 pseudonyms) are becoming large landowners. Who would have thought, all those years ago tanning hides under bleak, gray skies thousands of miles away, that I'd be a landowner? Who would have thought I'd even be alive today?

I came across a few comments Boston made related to historical events of this time that he would have heard of or read about. For example, in July of 1876 he writes of the spectacular news of a massacre at the Battle of the Little Big Horn. Boston wrote:

I met Gen. Custer once, in early 1864, when I was in Washington on Army business. It was at a party where we shared a few words about the status of the war, and how much longer the South could hold out. It was difficult to garner much of his time because he was so in demand; very popular after his exploits at Gettysburg, Brandy Station, and other places. I still have a copy of the Harper's Weekly *of March 1864, featuring the dandy Custer leading a cavalry charge in the raid near Charlottesville.*
I never served with him but the stories of his deeds and fearlessness have become legend. They say he has (had, sadly) an enormous ego, but I have known a few competent military leaders, and most have a gigantic admiration for their abilities.

I had hoped to get a glimpse of Mr. Lincoln, maybe even meet him, but no such opportunity arose.

An unexpected pleasure was to share a few minutes in the company of General Custer's lovely bride, commonly called Libbie. As gracious and beguiling a lady as I have met since...

The entry came to an abrupt end and there were no more of particular interest for the rest of the year 1876.

After a gap in time the next batch of notations was in a bound tablet dated 1879, and indicated that Boston had settled in Chicago. In reading through I found the answer to the missing dates.

It has become a burden to maintain and store my journals in my home. I worry about theft or fire. I also believe I have included too much information regarding my financial activities since the end of the war. So I have moved the papers I've accumulated since the end of the CW...

(I assume he means the Civil War.)

to a safer location (one of my usual ones).

I grow weary of keeping a journal. At one time I thought the journals would be useful for some future purpose, or for historians, or as family records. Sometimes I think I should keep better accounts, so people will know about…what I know…and other times I think I should burn everything. Why bother with these journals if I'm worried that some day someone will learn the truth? What is the truth about the others and me?

I shuddered when I read those words. My skin tingled and goose bumps rose, and I'm not sure why, but I have this sense that I do know why, but can't accept it.

So whatever journals he maintained for over a decade are probably lost for good. In another folder I did find a notebook dated 1880.

It is time to move. Kittredge and I agree we need a presence in the West. It was there we first met, but we were sidetracked, which is in itself a long story. (And long before I met him I'd had a few years there and built up some resources. I recounted both those episodes in the journals that were lost, sadly enough, and I don't think I care to take the time to re-write them.)

He will stay in New York and I will seek out properties that may suit our desires. It should be much easier traveling west with the train and the Indian situation a bit calmer.

Kittredge said he has met someone, the daughter of one of the brokers he frequently works with. He says he thinks she may be his "one". I worry about that because it can be tricky and if he's wrong, it could ruin his business and drive him out of the city. He promised he will be prudent and all I can do is wish him luck.

We have cashed out of 'B&K Imports' and the profits will keep us both in good stead, and provide me with seed money for real estate in the West. As I was leaving Kitt wished me "good luck", and I looked him hard in the eyes and told him to "be careful." It has become our standard way of seeing each other off when embarking on a new venture. I fully understand how difficult it is to not have a woman at one's side on a regular basis, and my own reasons I may put down again some day, but long ago as it was, the tragedies of Catherine and Clare and the children still haunt me.

As I'd noted before, at times Boston wrote long entries, full of information on daily life but short of personal specifics. His writing reminded me of Colin Bisseau's style: he was enigmatic, rather purposefully or as a style I couldn't say. If they were related, or had worked together, that might explain it. But the time line didn't fit for them to have known each other as adults.

And like Bisseau he refers to events that don't fit with the age of the writer—the *long ago tragedy of Catherine… and the children.* Added to the mystery was the mention that earlier journals were lost.

Boston's reports of his transcontinental crossing were filled with descriptions of the landscape and commentary—almost gossipy—on the manners, dress, and conversation of the people he met on the train. There was much talk as to whether the passengers would see wild savages or herds of buffalo, the former by now mostly confined to reservations, the latter, while the remnants of the once-gigantic herds still ranged on the prairies of the West, were fast nearing extinction. Boston commented:

It is horrific what we do to the lower forms of life. We are not good caretakers.

The entry reminded me of Colin Bisseau's writings regarding the disregard shown by humans towards other species, driving them so near to eradication. Then there was this fascinating entry:

June 2, 1881--
...the train began to slow down and finally it came to a complete stop. Someone opened a window to look out to see what was the cause of the delay. The air from the outside carried a stench that caused most everyone to gasp.
The terrain we were passing through was flat and it was possible to see a long way, both to the South and the North. I held a handkerchief to my nose and stuck my head out the window. On the plain were numerous objects, some whitish, others more yellow or brown. Then I heard

two noises. One was the grunting of some animal, the other sounded like rifle shots.

I exited the train to see better what was occurring. Crossing the track, what had delayed our train, was a small herd of buffalo. There were only a few dozen animals, not a massive herd of a few years ago that could block a train for hours.

As the beasts crossed someone was firing at them. I saw one go down, then another collapsed to its knees. As the animals fell a few of the passengers who had gone outside cheered and applauded. It was then I realized what the objects were dotting the plains hundreds of yards away. They were the rotting bodies of buffalo that had been shot for their hides. Or shot just so the Indians couldn't use them. Or for the "sport" of it.

I walked toward the front of the train and saw two men who were taking turns firing at the buffalo.

"Cease that at once!" I commanded.

One of the men glared at me and swore an oath.

He turned from me and aimed his gun at a buffalo that had crossed the tracks and stood meekly not twenty yards from us. I grabbed the man by the collar and yanked him around to face me.

"You needn't be so impolite, sir," I said. At the same time I ripped the rifle out of his hand.

The scoundrel came at me but I sidestepped him and stretched out a foot, which tripped him and he fell face *down onto the ground. As he lay there, grimacing and swearing all the more violently, I smashed his rifle against the side of the engine, cracking the barrel.*

The other man had stopped shooting and he also swore at me, words I do not care to write down, and swung his arm to hit me. I dodged his attempted blow (my experiences in hand to hand fighting an asset now), and I hit him in the stomach. He groaned and bent half over. I wrenched his rifle from him and destroyed his weapon in the same manner as I had his associate's.

I then reached into my wallet and threw two fifty dollar bills on the ground and told the men that was compensation for the damage I'd done to their rifles. I strode away quickly, lest my fury cause me to inflict more harm to these miscreants.

I was fascinated and read the entry a second time. This was real life history. I felt the skin on my arms prick and I yearned to read everything I could about Colt Boston. I wanted nothing more than to find the journals he said had been lost. I also wish he had said whether there was any additional trouble between he and the buffalo shooters, but his entry ended with no further comment.

Within a few more postings in the journal, Colt Boston had reached San Francisco. His entries then reflected his search for properties to buy and business relationships he engendered; the man was constantly on alert for investment opportunities.

Early October, 1881

    Have returned from a trip to the south of Arizona, in the neighborhood of Bisbee and Tombstone. The silver mining industry is booming and I am considering investing. However, there is a tension in the place that makes me circumspect. I spoke to Behan, the sheriff, and also a man named John Clum, who publishes a newspaper. Their moods were optimistic but I sensed their enthusiastic comments were based more on hope than realistic expectations.

    Shortly after that entry Boston noted:

    Heard rumors of a ferocious gunfight in Tombstone. Law and order is taking its sweet time in coming to some of the more rural parts of the country. Come it must, and I plan to be ready for it, though I think it will squash much of the excitement and passion that has permeated this country since the Rebellion. The days of the likes of the mountain man John Johnson, Daniel Boone, Wyatt Earp and others will soon be relegated to the history books, if anyone remembers to write down their stories.

Other entries indicated Boston purchased a variety of properties, but because he thought it not important to enter specific descriptions in his journal, or not safe, it was impossible to know exactly what investments he had made. He then stated that he was going to the southern part of the state.

Some fine folks from Germany mentioned that a few of their associates had moved to near the Santa Ana River in the southern part of the state, to a community they call Anaheim. I recognized the use of the German place name, 'heim', or home, from the old days, and it gave me a few moments of warm reflection. I was told Anaheim was a growing community of carpenters and other craftsmen, but was also developing a thriving agricultural industry. Think I'll go there and do a bit of snooping.

The entry implied Boston had a German background, but if so, he, or his father had changed the surname as 'Boston' did not sound Germanic.

Months later, after succinct entries related to business dealings, which included purchases of several hundred acres of land, which brought a smile to my face and made me wonder if the man had been prescient, Boston wrote:

I took Mary S. to see Helena Modjeska perform. I had read about her, the famous Polish actress who specialized in Shakespearean roles. It turned out that Mary's father is a patron of the arts and we had the opportunity to speak to the members of the cast. I was tempted to ask Helena about her life in Poland, but resisted bringing up the subject.

Whoever inherited Boston's estate must have become very wealthy. Yet, with a world of information available at the click of a mouse, I could not find anything about a person named Colt S. Boston that fit with the person who wrote these journals.

There were no papers or any notes of any kind for the years 1885 through 1890. Boston's entries ended so curtly I felt cheated. Nothing for years...

March 2, 1891,

Have contracted with Wells Fargo to handle our holdings in California. They are a fairly new firm but have competent people. Our assets are being held in other than the names Boston and Kittredge, but for obvious security reasons, as per my habit, it's best to keep that information in one of the usual secure locations.

And that was it, another entry that smacked of secretive, if not illegal activities, and then nothing. There were no more booklets in the Boston section of the file cabinet. There was one manila folder I hadn't looked at yet. In it, in a sheet protector was a clipping from the *San Francisco Chronicle*, dated July 11, 1901. The article read, in part:

Police and fire officials are still baffled by what caused a fire that destroyed a small building near the wharf. The building had apparently been used as an office by a man named Colt S. Boston. Mr. Boston was known to own a fishing business with a fleet of over a dozen boats. The fleet was operated by a Mr. Kittredge, who said that Mr. Boston rarely came by, and let Kittredge manage the company. However, Mr. Kittredge, who said he lived nearby and was alarmed by the smell of fire, having run to the site but too late to gain entry to the building, claimed Mr. Boston had contacted him earlier in the day and said he would be at the office in the evening, but that Kittredge needn't bother to come by.

A fire alarm was called in a few minutes before 11 p.m. on July 6th. After officials were able to enter the building, once the fires had been extinguished, though not before the structure had burned nearly to the ground, a body burned beyond any possible identification was found inside. On the floor, underneath a pane of glass, which enabled it to survive the flames, was a wallet with an identification card for one Cade S. Boston.

The address given for Mr. Boston was a New York City address, but at this time officials in New York maintain that no such address exists in the city. Mr. Kittredge said he had no idea where Mr. Boston resided when he was in the San Francisco area. Further efforts to locate Mr. Kittredge have been futile and no one in the neighborhood knew of anyone by that name residing nearby.

I was jolted both by the story and by Janice's voice. I jumped.

"A little touchy today, are we?"

"I was concentrating, too hard I guess. You surprised me."

"I guess so. Have you eaten today?"

I looked at my watch: 2:30. "No, I was so engrossed, but now that you mention it, I am hungry."

"Let's go to the café. I need a cup of Joe and you might be able to find a snack. You can tell me what kept you so spellbound you missed lunch."

I summarized for Janice what I had read in Colt Boston's journals.

"You seem to be spending more time with those than with the Bisseau papers."

I nodded. "There's some connection, Jan. I'm not sure how but something syncs Bisseau and Boston."

"A common relative?"

"Maybe. Boston gives no indication of having married or having had children, and he died in 1901. Bisseau wasn't born until twenty years later. But there could be someone in between."

"Did Boston have any siblings?"

"I have no idea. But he must have been a wealthy man, and someone inherited his estate."

"Unless he died without a will."

"No way. His writing is fragmentary in places, but I can tell he was meticulous about business matters."

"Maybe he left everything to charity," Janice suggested.

"Lots of maybes. The way he writes, it's like he's tempting the reader. In some places he gives great detail, down to the dialogue, and at other times he draws the reader in, then stops, and doesn't tell the rest of the story; then there are gaps. Frustrating, but titillating."

"You're hooked, aren't you?"

"I'll admit it. But I do think that if I can find the connection it'll tell us something about Colin Bisseau."

"Something we need to know, or something we'd be better off not knowing?"

I grinned. "Good question, Jan.

6. MORE JOURNALS-2

Janice's mood was brighter than when she walked out of my office yesterday, and I was tempted to see if a rain check came with the previous day's invitation. But at the moment I was more interested in the journals and letters I'd been reading than in taking a step that might lead us both into a chasm. So I said I was going to lug work home and I'd see her tomorrow.

My eyes were tired from reading. I rounded up the faded papers I had looked at earlier to take with me. I would go back to them this evening to see if I could learn anything about Colt Boston prior to the Civil War, reading backward into this man's life.

At home a cup of soup and a small sandwich perked me up. I poured a glass of a Merlot and sat down to leaf through the Boston journals. Again the task seemed arduous. I began with the earliest dated book, "1859-1862." The words were faint, probably written with insufficient light and the stub of a pencil. The pages were stained and smeared from dirt and grease and the ashes of a fire. Not all were dated. The first entry was either Mar, for March, or May, 1859. I strained to read, even got out a magnifying glass. The first page bore the title, *"New Journal."*

After I read this entry I sat back and closed my eyes. I had stepped back in time to a period I had often read about, studied, and taught, but never knew as intimately as I felt I did at this moment.

It has been over a week since what I crudely refer to as "The Disaster". Clare and the child are gone. It is my punishment for being so rash as to take on a family when I had for so long kept my promise not to do so.

Until now I have not yet been able to bring myself to begin a new journal. I say begin a new one because the others have been lost.

It was a year ago January that I found myself in love again, a notion that is considered quaint on the frontier. One does not marry for love, but for someone to share the burdens of life, and to build a home and raise a family.

Ever since Catherine I've been strict about this. Still, a man alone is not as good as a man with a woman to love and care for and vice versa. No one can raise a family in the wilderness alone and expect to survive for long. But I digress.

We were near the North Platte, which is normally a shallow river and easy to cross. There are dangers in this country but not nearly as common as written about in the sensational reports that appear in the Eastern newspapers. Still, one needs to take care.

One danger that is far more likely than being attacked by the wild natives of the Plains is that of the weather. A storm that blows wildly and drops more rain in a few minutes than the gentle spring rains of the Ohio Valley do in a day can be more deadly than a band of crazed Kiowas.

We encountered both. Clare drove the wagon while I scooped the child from her and carried him as I urged my horse on. But the band kept gaining on us. I signaled Clare to stop. She looked at me with fear, not understanding. When she slowed I handed the baby back to her, and told her to move out as fast as the horses could handle, and that I would catch up. She screamed "No!" but I slapped the nearest horse and they galloped away.

I dismounted and pulled my horse down with me. The poor animal, ignorant of its coming fate, gave me cover from the arrows and bullets aimed at me but sure to pellet him. The band of hostiles was near enough now and I took steady aim. Two of them spread away to go after Clare and the wagon. I whirled my rifle around, took two shots and watched both of the riders tumble to the ground, their bodies kicking up whirlwinds of dust. I turned my attention to the main band and fired again. Another attacker screamed and pitched backward off his horse. I then quickly shot down two horses and they and their riders tumbled to the ground.

The Indian's losses were already too high for the possible gain of one man and one woman and a wagon full of goods the Indians likely couldn't use. The remaining Kiowa gathered their dead and wounded and fled. As they galloped off lightning crashed and the rain poured from the sky as if Niagara Falls itself had been loosened from the black clouds above. Thunder broke from the sky, booming like cannon fire, rolling from one end of the sky to the other.

Fortunately the Indians had not hit my horse except for one small nick on his haunch. I remounted and urged the steed on to catch up with Clare and the wagon. I reached the Platte and saw that it was already a raging, uncontrollable torrent, flowing far over its banks. The wagon was not in sight. Fear struck me as sharply as if I'd been hit by one of the Indian's arrows

I knew I could not cross here, and Clare could not have either. I began to search along the bank, or what was left of it, first one direction then the other. It was dark and everything, the sky, the ground, the water, was shimmering shades of ebony. Then, in the light from a flash, I saw the white canvas of the wagon, stuck in the brush, nearly a hundred yards from me. Water crashed against the wagon and I saw it torn out of the brush as I exhorted my mount.

In the few seconds it took me to reach the spot where I'd seen the wagon, its remains were already far beyond my grasp, careening down the river like a pinwheel. The canvas was ripped apart as I stared in horror, the slats and wheels of the wagon thrown about as easily as I might toss a twig into a pond.

I chased along the bank of the river but had to constantly alter my route as the water continued to rise. As it did it sucked the dirt and foliage into its maw and spat it out like a child spitting out bitter medicine, branches and clods of dirt becoming deadly projectiles.

Trembling with fear, the horse reared up as if challenging the bolts of lightning being slammed down at us by Zeus. I fell backwards, saved from injury by the thick layer of mud. The horse sped off and I crawled until I was exhausted, finally far enough away from the river's scope to rest and catch my breath.

I found the horse the next day, unhurt but shivering. I searched for three days along both sides of the river but found no trace of the wagon, of Clare, or of the baby. It is not nature's fault, nor the Kiowa, but mine alone.

I guess if one lives long enough history can repeat itself.

The papers and the journals are gone. Usually I store the journals of the others in a safe place. Unfortunately, this time I had decided to move them with me. So now they are gone, those of Carson Baker, Coleman Baxter, and Cyrus Bisseau. The older ones are still stored where they have been since long before I immigrated. Best I leave them where they are.

Cyrus Bisseau, I noted. So there was the connection between Colt Boston and Colin Bisseau. I would bet a month's pension that Cyrus Bisseau was a common relative. I also had the feeling that I wouldn't find anything on the Internet about a person by that name.

Boston's entry ended with this plea:

Colt Boston is now twenty-one years old, though with his beard and shaggy hair looks a few years older. Surely he has been around long enough to know how to protect his family.

It is times like this that I am confused by the gamut of human existence. Why am I still alive when they are gone? Clare, much younger than I, the baby, dear God, hadn't ever the chance to run in the tall grasses of the prairie, to feel soft rain on his face, but only the cold, unforgiving waters of a rampaging river. How does it make sense, how does it fit some master plan? How is Colt Boston to know what to do?

For a moment I thought someone else was writing, but then I realized that Boston was switching back and forth from the first to the third person. Maybe it was confusion due to the grief he was experiencing. Certainly he was being hard on himself, a man of twenty-one years, young even in frontier days. If this was being written in 1859, then he was born in 1838. He died, according to the obituary I'd found yesterday, in 1901, age 63. Not exceptionally old, but fairly long-lived for the times.

By skipping around instead of reading the papers in chronological order I was getting myself confused. The Catherine he referred to must have been a sister, as Boston was too young to have lost a wife and children in some similar, earlier incident, as he implied in one of the later journals. And who were the other people he mentioned, and why would Boston have their journals?

My project was spreading out like an octopus prowling the muddy sea floor on the hunt for food. I was confusing myself as to how and where I should concentrate my efforts. Go back to Bisseau's papers exclusively, read everything and catalog them for possible future publication? Or make the job more intriguing by reading all the Boston writings and then tackling the ones of Cade Bunyan? The project was getting unwieldy and I hated to admit to Janice that I was swinging madly in several directions, not progressing as the organized and objective historian I was trained to be. But how could I be dispassionate about what I'd been reading? And now I had what I thought was a definite relationship between Colt Boston and Colin Bisseau, and I was sure any study of Colin Bisseau would be far more revealing if I could clarify what the connection meant.

Not so to the average person who gets his news from the Daily Show or the latest Twitter blog to go viral, but Bisseau 's disappearance still ranked up there close to Amelia Earhart's in historical interest. And the so-called "Greatest Generation" still savored their war heroes.

7. ETTA

Colt Boston apparently didn't maintain a journal for a long time after the disaster that took his family, as I found nothing until early in the Civil War, which brought me back to the time of the Grant letter.

Glum is not a fancy word but it describes how I felt. I leaned back in my chair, closed my eyes and thought of Erin. I was shocked to find that it took a while before I could picture her face. What had happened? Like the young Colt Boston I wondered why I hadn't done a better job of protecting my family.

Not from bandits or raging floods, but from the uncertainty and chaos of modern life; from the anxiety of worrying about children or money, of being alone when one got older and needed care and company. Evidently Erin didn't need my care and company, and I wished at this moment that I could walk into the pages of Colt Boston's diary and disappear from this life.

For what I had accomplished, as I look backwards from the threshold of the Medicare Years? I had taught classes, I wrote some books, I gave some lectures. Who remembers them? Who cares who they had for a history professor? Who cares about history? Certainly our leaders don't, else they wouldn't make the same mistakes over and over. Or would they; are humans simply prone, generation after generation, to have to learn again what was already learned?

Nothing I had done seemed important. Nothing except, I hoped, raising two kids, who, though not particularly close to me, seem to have turned out okay, with good jobs, nice families, and no major troubles that I'm aware of. In a few years I will die and the memory of me, of anything I did, will become dust as sure as my mortal remains will.

And now I, who buried his life in history books, in the pages of the past, in battles of yore and people who actually accomplished something, have nothing. No companion, no one to talk to, no one to *not* talk to. And now I am doing it again, submerging myself in other's lives, dead people, but people who did things.

And what did Colin Bisseau do that was so wonderful? Teacher, like me. Small-time politician, big deal; he hated it. A writer, like me, albeit his books actually sold; diplomat, okay, that's something, but did he do anything the next guy in line couldn't have done? Do any of us make a difference?

Of course some do; just read those history books. Still, most of us, by far, don't make a difference. We are born, we grow up, we go to work, get married, have a family or not, read some books or write a book, fix cars or leaky faucets, pack groceries or build houses, but generally nothing that the next person coming down the road couldn't do just as well. Are we merely filling space for a time, and when our allotted time passes another body replaces ours? Bisseau had found a quotation, about life being like a mist, that is, here today, gone tomorrow.

What matters? Is it being happy, or making someone else happy? Can you *make* someone happy? Obviously I hadn't made Erin happy, but was it my fault? Had she made me happy or was I merely happy with her? I thought we were happy with each other; or did we just get used to being around each other? Maybe, like me, Erin is seeing the hands of time moving quicker, as the years seem to fly by faster as one ages, hands that cannot be stopped by any worldly power, and she wants to find what else is out there in the winter of her life. But weren't we supposed to spend the winter together, keeping each other warm and comfortable as the years and days dwindled?

The next thing I knew the clock was chiming. I heard four chimes but when I glanced at the clock it showed five o'clock. I shuffled to the bedroom and crashed onto the bed without taking my clothes off. I slept until eight and woke up angry.

I reached for my cell and typed out a message to Erin:

"Come home or meet me in Reno."

I had no intentions of going to Reno; the word was symbolic, but I figured Erin would get my idea. I hit 'Send', and immediately had seller's remorse.

Once I hit the Send button the proverbial die had been cast; we could never go back to the way we where. But then, hadn't that been the case since the moment Erin left? Maybe our relationship shouldn't return to what it had been, but evolve into something better. I sent a second message:

"Ignore previous message. I was mad. Please come home and let's talk."

I undressed, showered and dressed again, pulling on a clean pair of jeans and a blue Polo shirt. I stopped at Leon's for coffee, a pastry, and the USA Today, and shuffled into the Wilson parking lot a bit after ten.

I ignored the note on my desk from Janice asking if I'd come across anything of "scholarly interest" in the Bisseau papers and went back to the Cade Bunyan section.

I realized I was bouncing around like a beach ball in the grandstands, having totally lost the methodical approach I had intended. The Bunyan papers were neater and cleaner than those of Colt Boston's. They were, of course, not as old. When I'd last left Bunyan he had gone to California, shortly after the turn of the 20th century. A few later letters indicated he had returned to New York City having "re-organized the Western holdings", as one of his notes reported. The next I knew it was 1907.

Aug. 2, 1907:

At Rutledge's request I went to see Winslow Oates, of 'Oates, Carswell and Simpson', who, I was told, would provide me with instructions regarding a possible investment opportunity in properties a few miles outside the city. Instead, Winslow gave me a message from Rutledge asking me to meet him in Chicago as soon as possible as he was, as he put it, "onto something big", regarding a land deal "too good to be true."

I chuckled because, as shrewd as Rutledge was, he frequently came across opportunities "too good to be true", and as I had often pointed out to him, they usually were exactly that. However, I must admit, his acumen has made me a man who can afford dinner in the finest restaurants anywhere in the country.

I thanked Winslow and as he was accompanying me out of the building I caught a flurry of color off to my left. Amidst the black and gray of business suits and high hats the bright blue dress of a lady walking quickly in my direction was like a lightning strike in the midnight sky. She had apparently just come out of Mr. Carswell's office and was scurrying along the aisle at a pace definitely not ladylike. She caught the attention of all the gentlemen, including myself. In her haste the lass bumped a chair and dropped her purse and her handkerchief, the latter fluttering down onto my shoe like a sparrow's feather searching for a resting place.

"Oh, my goodness," she gasped. I studied her in that brief moment. She had light brown hair, shoulder length under a hat that, like most ladies' hats, does more to distract from a woman's good features than adds to them, was fairly tall, slim and sported a tantalizing figure. She was striking.

"Madam, allow me." I reached down to pick up both the handkerchief and the white handbag. Both articles were embossed with the initials, 'E.P.'

"Ethel?" I suggested. *"Esther? Emily?"*

"Oh, Etta, Etta Place, I mean, no, I'm not, I mean…"

"You've forgotten your name?"

I've never been one to cause women to get flustered around me. I do treat women well, and I've had a number of satisfying relationships, but I'm an average looking man. This beautiful woman, maybe in my imagination, seemed flustered by my manner, or by me, or was embarrassed by her clumsiness.

"No, you see my cousin, Etta, we have the same initials. I'm Emily Parker, she made these things for me, we are close in mind and spirit and she thought it would be fun if we had similar articles with our initials, you see."

She was lying, of course, but who am I to criticize someone for using a pseudonym?

"Cade Bunyan, at your service, Etta, I mean, Emily Parker."

I hoped I wasn't coming across as an oaf, as by now every man in the room was staring at us, the business of the financial world sabotaged by a lovely young lady stumbling into a chair.

"May I see you out?" I pointed the way as I handed the handbag and handkerchief to her.

"Thank you, sir." She gained a modicum of composure. I nodded to Winslow, then to the others gawking at us, and guided Emily by the elbow towards the exit.

Outside, I said, "Perhaps a cup of tea? The Continental Room *is just around the corner.*"

"I'll think on it as we walk, thank you," she replied.

A moment later, as we reached The Continental, she said, "I think I would like tea, Mr. Bunyan." She smiled, and I knew Rutledge's big deal would have to wait.

It has been a long time, far longer than I can remember, since I have been as fascinated, as struck, by a woman. I studied her face and listened to her voice and tried to analyze what it was that so attracted me. It was impossible not to sink into her blue-gray eyes, which gleamed with excitement and enthusiasm, but also hinted at a soupçon of sadness, maybe some recent unhappy news. I scrutinized her bone structure, the shape of her lips and nose and chin, burning her face into my memory so I could never forget it, no matter how long before I'd see her again. And I knew I would see her again.

We sat and sipped tea and talked for over an hour. I cannot recall exactly what we talked about, but we spoke as if we'd known each other forever. She was obviously intelligent, and far more versed in the ways of finance and economics than the average woman of the day. When I asked her why she had been in such a rush she blushed and said it was something Mr. Carswell had said.

With a flitter of her eyes Emily—I will use the name she prefers—suggested we were overstaying our welcome and she was surely being forward in occupying so much of the time of a stranger.

As we reached the sidewalk outside the hotel I asked, "May I see you again, soon? Dinner tonight?"

Emily put two fingers near her mouth and created a whistle any twelve-year-old boy would have been proud of. A carriage sashayed over immediately, the horses clomping in satisfying rhythm.

"I shall be occupied tonight," Emily said. She climbed into the carriage. As it began to pull away she stuck her head out and called to me.

"Perhaps tomorrow. I am at the Dakota."

Assuming someone wasn't running a massive scam on me, and I was beginning to consider that possibility, I'd run across another bit of fascinating history.

The legend of Butch Cassidy, the Sundance Kid, and Etta Place is more famous for the Hollywood version than as important American history. The movie made the characters an engaging historical footnote helped by clever casting of attractive actors who made the outlaws the quintessential loveable losers.

Butch, Sundance and Etta, (she possibly The Kid's wife), to elude the Pinkertons, expanded their bank and train robbery careers to South American. There, likely in 1908, Butch and Sundance died from an extreme case of "lead poisoning." The conspiracy-lovers don't believe it; they insist the outlaws escaped and mended their ways to live quietly for many decades, along with Jesse James. These same folk also believe that Jack Kennedy survived the assassins' bullets and lived another thirty years, albeit in a vegetative state. All fantasy, but the fate of Etta Place is a real mystery and one that Western scholars have long tussled over.

She is thought to have been living alone in San Francisco in 1907, having left Butch and Sundance in Bolivia, and never saw the men again. I find it interesting that in Bunyan's journal the woman uses the name 'Parker', which was Cassidy's name, that is, Robert Leroy Parker.

A quick search told me that the Pinkerton Detective Agency described Etta Place as having "classic good looks" and that she was born in 1878 or thereabouts. So she would have been 29 years old when Bunyan met her. Harry Longabaugh, the Sundance Kid, and his pal Butch would still have been alive in South America. If Etta was dealing in high finance I have to wonder if the trio had been successful in their escapades and she had returned to New York to invest the spoils.

Certainly if she could afford to reside at The Dakota she was financially in good shape. The Dakota is one of Manhattan's most expensive and prestigious residential buildings. It was built in the 1880s and its name, supposedly, came from the fact that at the time it was considered so far out in relation to the inhabited area of Manhattan that it was as remote as the Dakota territories.

In modern times it became infamous as the site of John Lennon's murder. It has also housed a number of famous actors, actresses, and artists. I returned to Bunyan's next entry, which was dated several weeks later.

Sept. 3

The last few weeks have been glorious. Suffice it to say I have spent nearly every hour, night and day, with Emily. I am seldom so careless with whom I keep company, without knowing everything I can about them, but the woman enthralls me.

Each morning we linger in bed until she is ready to rise, which is just before the maid arises, lest we be found still snuggled together. The maid, a gray-haired, frumpy but pleasant lady of sixty years old or so, also prepares breakfast, simple but tasty fare. Emily and I enjoy it in a

139

nook of the six-room apartment, lingering over a superb view of the park. Our evening meals are generally at restaurants in the city.

(I assume he means a view of Central Park, which was near to where The Dakota was built.)

The furnishings, obviously expensive and made from the finest wood, and the artwork (at least one of which I recognized as an original Cezanne, the famed French artist who died last year) belong to the apartment's owner, from whom Emily is renting, though she will not divulge the name of the owner. I am endeavoring to find out, as it may help me learn more about this fascinating and mysterious person. I mean, she may be married to a wealthy financier now traveling in Europe, who will one day return, find me in bed with his wife, and shoot me dead while I sleep.

Each week I send Rutledge a telegram telling him I am involved in a "major opportunity in New York", and his Chicago plans must be put on hold. Eventually he caught on and replied, "Does she have a friend for me?"

The days are filled with walks in the park, visits to the finest cafes and art galleries, shows, and parties where the men gaze at Emily and then stare at me trying to compute how I fit in. Who am I to be dominating this beautiful woman's time? I am not a major player in business, that they know of, nor a politician, artist, or a member of European royalty. They are envious and I strut while knowing I am being foolish but I don't care.

Sept. 21

Rutledge has wearied of my delinquency and cabled me that the least I could do was meet with a man he is sending to Mr. Oates with a slew of legal papers that need my attention. Mr. Oates will have the details. All right, I agreed, despite the meeting being scheduled on a Saturday, and it meant forgoing the early day delights I had so quickly become accustomed to, as I was expected at Mr. Oates' office at nine in the morning.

I gave Emily my regrets but promised I'd be back by mid-afternoon. I could not avoid a long meeting, including lunch, discussing financial affairs I normally take pleasure in. But today I was eager to return to Emily. One would think I could give up a few hours with her but if anyone is aware of the evanescent bubble that a love affair can be, it is I. When I could finally get free I promised the carriage driver double his fare if he would urge his steed to its utmost performance.

I dashed up to the apartment as eager as a bride gliding down the aisle of a church, her face aglow as she sees her beloved waiting for her at the altar. When I entered the apartment I sensed something amiss. The furniture was the same, the pictures on the walls were the same, but the air was different. It was as if it had been sucked out of the apartment and replaced by something stale; it hinted of decay.

"Emily!" I called. I ran from room to room calling her name. I looked out the windows thinking I'd see her walking outside, impatiently waiting for me to return.

In the bedroom I sensed her aura; I could smell her, almost taste her, but my senses were responding to my desperation, not to reality. The closet was barren of her clothes. The drawers were empty except the ones where I kept my things. My heart thumped, my throat felt dry and as if a hard-boiled egg was stuck in it. I ran back into the drawing room and there I saw the letter. I felt I had swallowed the egg.

"Dearest Cade," it began. "I am so sorry. I should not have let this go on as long as it did, but you gave me such joy I could not stop. I don't know why this was so, something between us I cannot identify. But I must leave and you must not follow. The apartment is paid through the end of the month, use it if you wish.

My love, always, E."

E, she wrote, only E. Was that for Emily or Etta, or something else? I am shattered.

Sept. 24

I spent two days searching the cafes and galleries Emily and I had frequented. I sought out people we knew or had encountered; no one had seen her. I returned to the apartment each evening and slept in her bed—our bed, fantasizing that I'd awaken to see her sitting on the edge smiling at me, her eyes vibrant with desire. I don't remember taking meals though I suppose I did else I would not have had the energy to walk the streets of the city for as long as I did.

It wasn't until the third day that something occurred to me and revived the hollow feeling I'd first experienced when I found the closets void of Emily's clothes.

Back on the 13th of the month Emily and I had joined thousands on the bank of the River Hudson to delight in the arrival of the Lusitania, the new Cunard Line steamship, which was completing its maiden voyage from Liverpool. A few days later we were among those who were able to take a guided tour of the ship. It is a magnificent ship, more massive than anything I've ever seen, but as I write this I am not prone to spending the time describing it any further. Suffice it to say I remember how avid Emily had been to see the ship and learn all she could about it.

I soon confirmed that the Lusitania had departed at 3 PM on the 21st on her return journey to Liverpool. At the time I was hieing back to The Dakota to spend what was left of the day with Emily she, I feared, was watching the city fade away as the ship slipped out of port.

I shook myself from the web of distress I was manufacturing in my mind and hastened to Sandy Hook, in

Lower New York Bay. It only took a few minutes of glib conversation and a few dollars to obtain access to the passenger manifest. There was no Emily Parker, nor Etta Place listed. There was however, an Ethel Place, and I was surprised she would make it so easy for me to discover her movements---or maybe she never considered I might follow her. However, she now had a three-day head start on me and would land in Liverpool on the 27th. By the time I could get across the Atlantic she could be anywhere. Or was she trying to draw me to her and I merely had to follow the clues?

Sept. 25

I am still wrought over what to do, but have decided I should first go to Chicago, meet Rutledge and assist him in his work there. He has informed me that the opportunity to purchase a valuable piece of prime realty will evaporate soon if I do not get personally involved. She will wait, he said, not realizing how much it hurt me to read those words. Once business is complete I will follow Emily.

Post script: something I thought odd was that all of Emily's jewelry was gone except for a cameo locket she often wore around her neck. It was lying on the table next to her side of the bed. I'd never examined it before. I did now and found that it opened to reveal a photograph of Emily, a slightly younger Emily. The locket was the sole item I took from the apartment.

I couldn't help but feel anguish for this man I never knew and who had long ago expired. Right now I think I do not want anyone else to ever read this. Yet historians would salivate over this journal entry and more than one would cross the ocean to see if they could find Etta Place's trail and solve the mystery of the Sundance Kid's woman. Did Bunyan follow? The next entry in the journal was dated months later, in April of 1908.

I have wasted enough time. No, I shouldn't say wasted, as I have visited cities I had not been to in years, plus new ones, and met new people, and that is never a waste of time. But I have found scant trace of Emily.

I tried bribery, pleading, and threats, but no one in Liverpool remembered anyone answering the description of Emily. Certainly a beauty such as her would have caught the eye of the average male.

I tracked down a few passengers on the Lusitania's *voyage, and while some did remember an extremely attractive young woman, traveling alone, no one remembered her name as Emily, or Etta, or Ethel. One man said it had been Rita, another said Eva.*

I went to Queenstown, the stop before Liverpool, and questioned the Cunard agent there. He said a woman wearing a bright blue dress had gotten off the ship, but she had her hat pulled low over her face.

I spent two days trying to track her from Queenstown but found no one who recalled seeing a young, pretty woman, blue dress or otherwise. I thought none but myself could disappear into thin air as if they'd never existed. It makes me wonder.

Bunyan made no further entries for months. It was as if the spark had been sucked out of him, the joy of life dashed beyond repair. When he did return to his journal the entries were a series of comments regarding business affairs, mundane except for one that referred to a suggestion by his friend Rutledge to invest in bonds being sold to finance the construction of an aqueduct in California.

Quoting his friend, Bunyan wrote:

The project sounds impossible, but I have met the man in charge and he literally oozes immense confidence and ability. As you have been impossible to contact lately, brooding still, I suppose, I have made a substantial investment for us.

Based on the date of this entry I assume it referred to Mulholland's massive, ambitious Owens Valley water project to bring water from northern California to the burgeoning city of Los Angeles.

I think Bunyan immersed himself in work after Emily's departure. If I had been sad last night, now I felt I could have joined the Blue Man Group, and would not need makeup. I sat back and tried to imagine Cade Bunyan striding into the apartment and finding Etta is gone; much like me coming home to my cold, empty house.

"You look like you've lost your best friend," a voice said. Then, "Oh, sorry, Morg, I guess that wasn't in good taste."

I shrugged and stifled a sigh.

I picked up the note Janice had left and waved it.

"A few articles that I don't think were ever published..."

"On?"

"Mostly on the woes of the American educational system. Much more seething than his book, it rips politicians and parents. Probably no publisher wanted to rankle the public. There's an article on the ravages of the buffalo hunters in the late nineteenth century. More of a short story, actually, told in the first person, as if he was living it.

"Some letters to fellow profs, bemoaning the fact that new students don't always know the two sides in the Civil War."

"Which Civil War?"

"You see?'"

"I was teasing, Morg. Lunch?"

"Yes, but let's go off campus for a change. I'm tired of the cafeteria."

"Who's buying?"

"The Fund? We'll talk business."

"Whoopee."

Maybe I should tell her about Bisseau's rantings regarding our allowing the Russians to take over Eastern Europe.

"Let me put this away." I'd had some of the Colin Bisseau journals on my desk. I opened the bottom drawer and as I shuffled files to make room I notice a light-blue colored file folder lying on the bottom of the drawer. "This must have slipped down," I said.

I scooped it up and opened it. There was one sheet of paper, with one line of type data. The line, typed in bold italics, read:

LV, row 4, 103124

"What is it?"

I stared at the paper for two seconds. What was amazing is that the memo made sense to me.

"Doesn't look like anything." I put the file back in the drawer, in front so I'd find it easily when I returned.

8. ALASKA, MAY 1980

Gates of the Arctic National Park is larger then the states of Massachusetts and Rhode Island combined. The entire park lies north of the Arctic Circle. There are no tourist amenities, no established campsites, no roads, no ranger stations. No one visits because they happened to be passing by.

The floatplane slipped out of the clouds and glided gently down onto the sparking waters of Nutuvukti Lake, as if placed there by a giant hand. A person not wearing sunglasses would be blinded by the glare of the sun ricocheting off the water.

The pilot expertly settled the plane on the water and brought it to a stop after a few gentle bounces. A door opened and a yellow object flew out, which instantly inflated into a diagonally shaped kayak. A man stepped into the kayak, and then turned to receive several backpacks from someone inside the plane. Then a second person, a woman, also stepped into the kayak. The two people waved to the pilot, sat down, and began to row away from the plane towards shore.

When the kayak was safely away the propeller whirled and the plane began to skip across the water until it shot up, sending a spray that nearly splattered the kayak and its passengers. The two people watched the plane, and then waved again as it circled around. The pilot waved to the people below with both his hand and the wings of the plane. The plane climbed higher into the cobalt sky and turned southeast to return to its home somewhere near Fairbanks.

The couple in the kayak rowed to shore, stepped out, and unloaded their gear. Then the man deflated the boat and repacked it to the size of a small suitcase. He finished just as a thumping sound from the west caught his attention.

The helicopter alit a hundred yards away on a flat, sandy area, about fifty yards inland from the shore of the lake.

"Do you know him well enough?" the woman said.

"I've told you, he's one of us," the man answered.

"How long have you known him? Is he another one you've kept secret from me?"

"Since…a very long time."

"I resent being left out of the planning."

"He insisted I keep him out of it until the last moment. Besides, you had your end to take care of." The man looked at the woman and placed a hand on the back of her head.

"I'm sorry, I've become so wary over the years. Haven't you?"

The woman hesitated before she spoke, sighing first. "More so, like you, as time goes on. It does get more difficult. Still, I don't think you need to be so secretive with me."

"You're right, and I apologize. Come on, let's lug this stuff over there."

Soon they had loaded their gear onto the helicopter. The pilot kept the rotor spinning, making it too noisy for conversation. Not a word was spoken as the man from the kayak handed the gear up and the pilot accepted it and tossed it in the back of the cabin. The pilot, his face covered by heavy goggles, mumbled, "Ma'am" when the woman climbed in and took a seat in the back, but she couldn't hear him.

When the gear was aboard the pilot glanced over at his passengers, the man now seated at his right, the woman behind, and nodded. The man from the kayak nodded back.

The woman's mouth opened as if to speak, then she reached a hand and tapped the pilot on the shoulder.

"Marcus?" she called out, trying to raise her voice above the noise.

The pilot turned, smiled, and lifted his goggles.

"Hello, Liz," he shouted.

The woman smiled broadly, then laughed as she touched the man lightly on the cheek. Then she cupped her hands around her mouth and moved her head forwards, yelling into the man's ear.

"Marcus! What a nice surprise! I didn't know you could fly a helicopter." She punched her husband in the arm and said, "You could have told me it was Marcus!"

"I'm not just a pretty face, Liz," the pilot said.

The man in the passenger seat said, "Let's do it."

The pilot nodded; "Colin," he said as the helicopter began to rise.

When they were high enough so that the lake below looked like no more than a country pond, the pilot steered the helicopter towards a north-easterly course.

"North?" The woman said in surprise. She tapped her companion on the shoulder.

He turned to her and said, "Prudhoe Bay; a bit east of there, actually."

The woman nodded.

The rest of the flight, a little over 350 miles, was made without conversation, until they began to circle over an offshore oil derrick. The man the pilot had addressed as Colin pointed to it and turned to the woman in back.

"An old one, abandoned. Everything we need should be there," he said, nearly shouting. Colin nodded to at the pilot, who returned the nod and began the landing procedure.

Colin and Liz exited the helicopter and with the help of the pilot unloaded their belongings. The two men spoke for a minute. The woman watched their lips moving but the words were snuffed by the noise of the rotors. Then the men grasped each other by the shoulders, smiled and hugged. The pilot returned to his craft and the other man retreated to where the woman waited. They watched as the helicopter rose and until it had shrunk to the size of a tiny bird.

"Who is he, really?" the woman asked.

"You've known Marcus for years, Liz. He was with me when we found each other in Chicago."

"Yes, but like you, he's so secretive. I don't even know if he's married."

"Not now he isn't. He's helped me, and others, many times. Does a great job. He'd be hard to replace."

"What else does he do?"

"Been around long enough to learn a few things. He's older than I am."

"That doesn't exactly answer my question."

"You should come to the Rendezvous some time; get to know a few of the others. They'd like you."

"I went to one a long time ago. I was bored; everyone acting so smug, talking a lot but not saying anything."

"Like someone I know?"

"Smart ass! So now what?"

"You can't see it from here but there's a powerboat waiting for us, loaded with more supplies."

"You hope."

"It'll be there. Marcus has never let me down."

"I thought you always said never trust anyone."

"I'm getting mellow in my old age."

The man and the woman took turns helping each other strap on backpacks. Then they each picked up another pack to carry.

The splintered wooden planks of the old derrick creaked as they crossed to the opposite end. There, a stairway led to the sea level. Tied to a post, bobbing like an apple in a bucket of water, was the powerboat.

"Like you said."

"I'll take these packs down, then I'll come back. Then you follow with the last one."

"I see why you insisted on small bags."

"Mainly what we'll need for the first few days. We'll get everything else later."

The man lowered himself carefully down the rungs of the ladder, holding on with one hand while he held onto the backpacks with the other hand. When he was a few feet from the bottom of the ladder he dropped the packs into the boat, unloaded the one from off his back, and then climbed back up.

Once they had loaded the luggage into the boat, the woman spoke.

"Do I dare ask where we go from here, or is that another secret?"

"We'll hug the coast until we reach the McKenzie River, then south to the Great Bear Lake where a plane will be waiting for us. Then we keep hopping south until we get to Thunder Bay. Someone will meet us there and fly us to Cuba."

"Cuba? Is it safe?"

"Safe, yes, and quiet. From there we'll make our way to a few smaller islands, then to the Canaries, to Casablanca, to…"

"You have tickets for all this?"

"Ha, ha, yes, dear one, I have better than tickets."

"It seems awfully complicated."

"Yes, it is complicated. Not as easy as it was in the old days."

"I'm used to picking up and moving without much planning."

"Once you could do that. Move from one coast to the other, or London to Paris, Paris to Rome. Change your name and no one would know you for who you once were. Now, it's not that simple."

"And you think it will be this time, with you being as eminent as you have become?"

The man frowned and nodded slowly. "I will have to change my appearance; a beard, dye my hair, colored contacs. Even so, we need to lay low for a spell. I know a score or more wonderful coastal towns and islands that will be comfortable homes until we have been forgotten. And once I'm sure we're safe, I have a special place in mind where we can hunker down for as long as we care to."

"How long?"

The man shook his head slowly, gazed at the sky as if examining paint samples. "Nice shade, weather looks good, at least we lucked out on that."

Then, returning to the woman's question, "Years, quite a few years I think. I need a long rest."

"I haven't been to London or Paris since..."

"Not the big cities, not yet."

"Coastal towns and islands? Do they have running water?"

"You'll enjoy it." He looked the woman stern in the eyes and put his hands around her shoulders.

"Elizabeth, listen carefully. All the plans I've made, including contact information, are sewn into the lining of the smallest bag, the one you brought down the ladder. If anything goes wrong, if we get separated..."

"Colin, no, you said everything would be..."

"It will be alright, trust me. But on rare occasions unforeseen forces screw up the best-made plans. I've known it to happen to others even when they had thought of everything. Marcus will be available if you need help."

"What if something happens to him?"

Colin ignored the question and kissed Elizabeth on the cheek, patted her shoulders, and smiled. "I honestly don't think there'll be any problems, I just want you to have options. I mean, what if I suddenly drop dead!"

"That isn't funny!"

"Okay, let's get moving. There's a campsite waiting for us I want to reach before dark."

9. CEMETERY

Janice was in a cheery mood, and she looked and smelled good, sweet and crisp, like an unpredicted April rain shower.

Still, it was hard to keep my mind on her or on lunch. I was thinking about the blue sheet of paper with the enigmatic notation, **LV, row 4, 103124**.

I set those thoughts aside, storing them in a box inside my head that I would retrieve later, and told Janice about some of the journal entries I had read: Bunyan's pining for Etta Place, a name Janice said she'd never heard, Bisseau's opinion on the Allies allowing Russia to move into eastern Europe after the end of World War Two, and Colt Boston's confrontation with the buffalo hunters, among others.

"How are you cataloguing the papers, Morg?"

I was embarrassed; me, trained to perform tasks logically and in a disciplined manner, was floundering.

"My intentions were first rate, Jan," I said. "And I will get back to a more organized process. I must admit that I've gotten caught up in the writings of these people and I've kind of forgotten this is supposed to be about Colin Bisseau, not the diaries of other people."

"Maybe you should take the other ones out all together, put them out of sight so you aren't tempted to spend time reading them."

I nodded and tried to look as if the suggestion was a good one, but I knew it was now impossible for me to forget about Cade Bunyan and Colt Boston. I forced the conversation away from work and to other, run-of-the-mill topics.

Janice surprised me by asking if I'd heard from Erin.

For a second or more I debated how to answer. "No, not since…I texted her, but haven't heard back. I'm a bit worried."

"Should you call the authorities?"

"What authorities? I don't even know what continent she's on!"

Janice pulled back, startled.

"Sorry, didn't mean to yell."

"And I didn't mean to upset you. But I can see I did." Cheery mood gone.

I wasn't sad to get back to my office, lunch completed with little further conversation.

I sat holding my head with one hand, as if it might fall off if I didn't keep a grip on it. The best thing about this project, and especially the journals, was that it kept my mind off Erin for long stretches of time. When I tried to do the mundane work of cataloging the contents of the file cabinet my mind wandered to thoughts of Erin: was she safe, was she ill, was she cheating on me, was she even alive. Damn, I wondered, what if she's dead, beaten and raped in a dark alley in Rome, maybe all her identification stolen so that she lies in cold storage, a Jane Doe, waiting for someone to claim her.

What would it be like if she were dead: would it be any different than it is now? Or would I be relieved of having to wonder about her any more? Would I feel remorse?

I sent another text:

"Please respond, Erin…you're beginning to worry me. Love, M."

Still unsure about the status of my emotions, but feeling a bit smug that I'd done all I could for now, I picked up *The Search for Colin Bisseau.* I flipped through the pages looking for a photograph I'd seen when I first read the book. I found it and read the caption:

"Lakeview Valley Cemetery, grave of Colin Bisseau's parents."

The picture showed a close-up of a tombstone that was engraved:

Martin Bisseau   *Wilma Bisseau*

1899-1926   *1900-1926*

A plain tombstone, nothing to note that two young people had died in an infernal, which besides killing them had left orphaned a two-year old boy named Colin.

In the background of the picture were rows of other above-the-ground tombstones, an old-fashioned graveyard not as common today. Even in this picture, taken over half a century ago, the forest is threatening to absorb the grave markers and blanket any evidence that a village existed here in the woods, not ninety miles south of a major crossroads city.

I suspected the grave of the Bisseaus was located in the fourth row, based on the message in the blue folder. By now, decades after this photo was taken, trees may have marched completely over the cemetery, slowly but resolutely conquering the land, making it impossible to locate a particular tombstone.

I debated telling Janice. If I told her I was going to the former site of Colin Bisseau's hometown she might want to come with me. And I'm sure she wouldn't approve of what I intended to do.

The next morning I loaded a few things in the trunk of my car and left the house as the sun was poking its head over the horizon. I stopped to pick up a cup of coffee and a pastry and continued driving. Around seven o'clock I called on my cell and left Janice a voice mail saying I would not come in today.

The drive to where Lakeview Valley used to exist took a tad over two hours, far into the countryside and nowhere near any cities large enough to have a high school football team. The map I had did not show a

Lakeview Valley, nor did the index to my atlas include the name.

Based on the information in *The Search for Colin Bisseau,* Lakeview Valley had been located midway between the towns of Solsbury Hill and Freedom Farms, two towns that exist on one of those thin gray lines on the map, the kind that are described as "Other roads—conditions vary, local inquiries suggested."

The sign as I entered the village limits of Solsbury Hill revealed that the population was 184. I drove slowly through the town, seeing no one outside, other than a dog. A café appeared to be doing business, there was a gas station, a hardware and feed store, and a 'Karen's Grocery.' The tallest building was a two-story wooden structure with a flagpole in front of it, a United States flag hanging limp, with signs in the windows informing any and all that inside was a realty office, the Solsbury Hill City Hall, Business and License Department, and the Post Office.

A kid on a bicycle crossed the street in front of me, staring at me as he'd never seen an automobile before. I debated stopping at the café for another cup of coffee but decided I didn't want anyone to get a good look at this stranger, so I continued on until I was again cruising amongst walls of thick, dark forest.

In a few minutes I came to a sign for Freedom Farms, population 167. So I must have missed a road that would take me to where Lakeview Valley had existed. I turned around and drove back in the direction of Solsbury Hill, driving slowly and looking for any turnoffs, or anything that looked like it might have been a road at one time.

After a few minutes I saw it, a narrow, pebble-covered lane, scraggly weeds populating the edges, off to my right. I turned and ushered the car along at no more than 20 MPH. The tires rolling over the pebbles made a crunching noise and through the rear view mirror I could see gray dust blossoming upwards. I wasn't sure what I was looking for but if there were any people in the vicinity the dust would announce my presence.

After a few minutes the road narrowed and became more weed-strewn, tall as a white-tailed deer's eye, and I stopped the car. In back of me the dust was settling and soon there would be no sign that a car had come this way. I was leery of straying far from the car, as I wasn't sure I'd find my way back, the trees and shrubbery on either side of the rustic road so thick Daniel Boone might have gotten lost.

Well, I had the entire day, I reasoned, time to get lost and find my way back. I decided I'd go no farther than one hundred steps in any one direction, then backtrack, and go in another direction. I started out, using the sun as a guide, opposite it, to the west.

Nothing but trees did I see in that direction. The buzz of thousands of insects greeted me, but the forest went quiet once I entered. As I walked the only sound was the noise I made whenever I stepped on a twig. If I stopped walking the faint buzz of insects would recommence. I felt like I was the only life form around, but in actuality the forest teemed with life, flora and fauna. After one hundred steps I halted, examined my surroundings three-sixty, then turned and walked back to the car.

East would take me back the way I drove in, so I tried north. As I reached one hundred steps I saw what looked like a building farther ahead, barely visible through the branches of the trees.

Using twigs, I made an arrow on the ground pointing the direction to the car. Then I continued towards the building, wondering as the grass became taller whether there were any snakes hiding in wait.

I broke a branch off a tree, hoping I wasn't violating some conservation law, and used it to swish at the grass ahead of me. The sun was high in the sky now and though its beams had to struggle to break through the ceiling of foliage, I began to feel its warmth.

As I neared the building, which looked like nothing more than the skeleton of an old barn, leaning like the Tower of Pisa, still standing thanks to the thick foliage that had grown up along its sides, I stepped on something hard.

Whatever it was, it was covered with dirt. I knelt and brushed the dirt off until I uncovered what felt like concrete. I brushed more and found a broken slab, with letters and numbers. It was a portion of a tombstone. I had found the Lakeview Valley Cemetery.

I whacked at the grass ahead of me and soon I was hitting more tombstones, many standing, some fallen over, and all nearly hidden by the grasses and weeds. How to find row 4?

First, I carefully counted my steps back to where I'd made the arrow. Then I returned to the car. From the trunk I took a shovel, two large garbage bags, a hunting knife I'd received as a gift and which I'd never used, a pair of garden shears, and a liter bottle of water. I also took out a small suitcase, and put the garbage bags, bottled water, and shears in it. The knife I clasped to my belt. I then lugged my gear to where I'd found the tombstones.

For the next two hours I swung away with my stick trying to locate tombstones and snipped at the grass with the shears; I should have brought a scythe. When I located a tombstone I cut around it until I could read the name and dates, which on the first several were not later than the early thirties. If Colin Bisseau lived here long enough to go to high school you'd think there would be some dates later than the thirties.

Soon I was wishing I'd brought more water as I began to sweat and feel the heat of the noonday sun. I was also getting hungry.

I was pondering driving back to one of the villages to get food when I bumped into a tombstone I hadn't yet seen. I pulled the weeds away and saw the names:

Martin Bisseau   Wilma Bisseau
1899-1926   1900-1926

I stared at the tombstone, and then I looked around in all directions, feeling guilty over what I was doing, and what I was planning to do next. I was about to become a grave robber.

It sounds grotesque, but I shut my mind to what someone else would think, especially Janice, convinced I was on to something I couldn't define.

Whereas a minute before I was ready to go to one of the nearby cafes, now I didn't want anyone to see me, to wonder what this stranger was up to. I struck the dirt with the shovel.

After digging a hole about two feet deep and four feet around, I hit something that clanged. It was either a big rock or the object in the grave wasn't buried very deep. I suspected the latter. I dug around the object and soon I knew I was right: it wasn't buried deep, and it was not a casket, it was a safe.

The safe was buried on its back, with the door facing up. It was much too large for me to get my hands around, and probably too heavy, and I'd have to dig a much bigger hole to attempt to pull it out of the ground. So I made my next intuitive stab.

I turned the knob around until I'd passed zero three times, then stopped at 10. I turned the opposite direction, passed zero, and stopped at 31. Went the other way and stopped at 24. The numbers in the blue file, Halloween, Colin Bisseau's birthday.

I turned the handle and heard a creak. For a split second I wondered if poison gas would gush out of the safe, or an explosion scatter me among the detritus of the forest.

Nothing so dramatic happened so I pulled on the handle until the door opened. I heard a beep, like the sound on my cell when a call is coming in. Inside were four metal canisters, about 12" x 12", I estimated, and 2 inches thick. They were locked.

And on the door side I noticed a pulsating green light, which was also the source of the beeping sound. I had activated an alarm. But to where, local police? I doubted that. If it was, I was a dead duck. More likely, it's to someone a distance away, and maybe meant to scare off an intruder as much as provide an alert.

"You wanted adventure in your retirement, Morgan, so now you've got it."

I pulled one of the canisters out, grunting, as it was heavier than I anticipated. I was not going to be able to move all the canisters in one trip. I heard a noise behind me and instinctively reached for the knife. I imagined the headline:

"Noted history professor arrested on grave-robbing charge."

Two deer looked at me, more startled, I think, by my presence than I was at theirs. Likely they rarely saw human beings this deep into the woods. They slowly walked away as I breathed again and let my shoulders sag. I then slugged down the last drops from the bottle of water.

I carried two of the canisters to my car, then returned for the other two. I shoveled dirt back over the safe. I figured it wouldn't take long for the forest to repair the damage I'd done. Unless someone shows up soon to check on the beeping green light.

I was a mess. I was sweaty, my clothes were dirty, my hands were filthy, and I was tired, hungry and thirsty. By the time I'd managed to turn the car around and get back to the main road, my mouth was as dry as the dusty road I'd exited and begging for water. Yet, I didn't want to stop at any place nearby.

I tortured myself by driving for a half-hour until I was in an area resembling modern society. The car needed gas by now, so I stopped to fill the tank and also bought two bottles of water and a pre-made sandwich from the shop attached to the gas station. I ate the turkey sandwich and drank one bottle of water before I'd gone three miles. I noticed a helicopter overhead and for ten minutes I could swear it was keeping pace with me. I was relieved when it finally it veered up and away and for a moment I wondered if I should drop my contraband in a ditch and forget I'd ever seen it.

As I drove home I thought about how to proceed. First, I have to open the metal canisters I'd stolen. Then I'd have to decide what to do with the contents. Do I tell Janice? Do I explain how I found these or make up a story even more far-fetched? I found myself grinning as I drove, realizing I'd done a really crazy thing, and feeling good about it. Until I remembered the alarm. Who had been notified, and could they track me? The helicopter still bugged me.

I knew I hadn't anything at home interesting for dinner, so I stopped at a grocery store a few miles from home (I was still looking pretty ragged and didn't want anyone who knew me to ask what I'd been doing--robbing graves, Morgan?), and bought a steak and a handful of green beans, and, to celebrate today's triumph, a pint of butter pecan ice cream.

Between the time I'd entered the store and when I exited the sky had turned from light gray to deep purple. It began to rain, a spattering at first, but soon heavier drops fell, making a rather solid, pleasing sound as they splattered the windows of the car. Then the rain fell faster, slapping the windows like a whip. The wipers whipped back and forth as fast they could, but they couldn't keep up with the deluge and I couldn't see and I became frightened, thinking that I had suddenly become a frail old man, unable to cope with a few drops of rain.

Just as suddenly the deluge fizzled to a sprinkle and I was in familiar territory and I felt foolish that I had been near panic. The sky lightened and water gurgled alongside the curbs as I turned onto my street. I slowed as I neared the house because something didn't look right. The lights were on. Were the police waiting for me?

I got out of the car quietly, shut the door without slamming it, and approached the front door of my house. My cell was in my left hand, thumb posed over the numeral '9'. I stood at the door, listening, heard nothing, and inserted the key. I turned the knob and entered.

A lamp in the front room was lit, and light came from a room off the hallway. I heard the shuffle of feet, and as I looked down the hallway a person emerged and moved towards me. Shadow covered the face of the person but I knew her.

"Hello, Morgan."

"Erin. You came back."

"Yes, for awhile."

"A while? Why then at all?"

She moved towards me and I gasped. Her face was shallow, as if she'd been starving herself. Her eyes were dull, and the dimples on her cheeks were more prominent than ever. She stopped inches from me.

"I came home to die, Morg."

10. ERIN

Erin was an attractive woman, something I'd taken for granted for too long. Even now, in her late 50s, looking like she hadn't eaten in a month, her features were pleasant to gaze upon. She had never been heavy, always watched her diet and eschewed desserts. Why had she said she needed to lose weight, a stupid notion to pass through my mind at this moment?

Long forgotten memories were resurrected as I remembered when I first saw Erin. It was at somebody's party, and she wore a white, angora sweater, tight, and it emphasized her breasts, and I stared at them, then up and down at them and her face, an appealing face, and she caught me, and I looked away, but she smiled and turned a bit, as if to examine a painting on the wall, but really to give me a side view, as if she were auditioning, and I was half-inclined to walked over to her and gently surround her breasts with my hands and squeeze them, and she would look at me and say, "Thank you", but I didn't, not then.

"What?" My first split-second thought was fear that she wasn't joking or exaggerating.

I gripped her shoulders with my hands, to steady myself as much as to look her straight in the eyes, eyes that used to sparkle but now were empty of joy and stared at me with sadness. Was it sadness for me, for herself, or for us, the once and former us, the partnership that once was?

"What are you talking about? Are you ill? Talk to me."

"I will, give me a moment. You're wet." She moved out of my hands and her mouth gaped and her eyes widened as she examined my clothes.

I ran my hand through my hair, damp and sticky from the rain that had mixed with dust during my foray in the woods.

"What have you been doing? Your shirt is filthy, your knees…you've ruined those pants."

"Oh, yeah," I followed her gaze, and then wiped my hands on my shirt, too late to clean them, having already soiled her blouse when I grabbed her shoulders.

"Kind of a long story. I've got a job."

"What, digging ditches?" She smiled and laughed, and the smile emphasized the creases on her face, put there by lack of food or illness, and the possibility that she was ill instantly ripped from my mind any negative thoughts I'd developed towards her since her sudden departure.

"Let's get a drink, and we'll talk. Have you eaten?"

She nodded but I wasn't sure I believed her.

I poured two glasses of wine, my hand shaking from fear of what she would tell me, while she waited for me to speak first. I did, glad to avoid having to hear what she would say, that she was only back to pack her clothes, or that she had truly come home to die.

"It's at the university. A research project."

"Oh? With Kenny?"

"No, not with him; he's working on something of his own. We, uh, a student assistant, came across some papers of a man who used to teach there. Remember Colin Bisseau, many years ago he and his wife disappeared? No trace of them was ever found."

Erin nodded, not convincingly. "I think so, yes, I remember. Did you know him?"

I shook my head, at the same time remembering when I had met him.

"I can't say I knew him, but I did meet him and speak to him on two or three occasions. He left shortly after I began to teach there."

"Is Janice working on it?"

A simple enough question but it was loaded with innuendo, curiosity, and accusation. How long had Erin wondered if there was anything going on there? My eyes darted to hers involuntarily, and as quickly I looked away.

"I'm working on my own. Technically, she's my boss, but it's my project, cataloging and reading old papers to see what's there, whether there's anything useful for the library, and so on."

"And is there? Anything useful?"

"I believe there is. It'll take some time to sort it out."

"How does that explain your dirty clothes?"

I snickered at the image of me sneaking through the woods and desecrating a grave. Who would believe it?

"Field work. But enough, Erin, let's get serious; what's going on?"

She sighed, took a sip of wine, put the glass down, then sat back and sunk into the chair like an infant cuddling to mother, her head back as far as it could go, her eyes staring blankly at the ceiling, her arms wrapped around herself. She turned her head towards me.

"It's a good thing you didn't marry me for my brain, Morgan."

"What's that supposed to mean?"

"Morg, I have cancer. A rare form of…"

"What?" I began to rise from my chair.

"Wait, let me finish." I slumped down.

"I didn't want to scare you. I'd been feeling poorly; headaches, the shivers, my vision was getting blurry, I lost my appetite and was losing weight, not much but enough to notice."

"I thought you had lost weight, but I didn't…"

"I went to three doctors, they all said the same thing: nothing they could do, it was far too advanced. Spread all over. My brain is like a map of the London Underground."

"That's crazy, there's always something!" I shouted and jumped up. I was angry and upset, but at who or what I wasn't sure: myself, Erin, the doctors, God, science?

"I can't believe you wouldn't tell me? And so you left?"

Erin stood up and came to me and put her arms around me. Her head rested on my shoulder and her words were soft and nearly muffled.

"I didn't want to ruin things for you. Your retirement, your plans."

"Our plans," I corrected.

"Yes, our plans."

"So what good would running away do?"

"I heard of a treatment in Europe. Something I couldn't get here. I didn't think you'd let me go."

"Oh, Erin, some quack doctor?"

She stepped back and looked at me with those eyes that now twinkled, not from joy but from tears.

"It was desperation, yes, but my only hope. I told you, Morg, the doctors said there was nothing to do, not chemo, nothing; the cancer had spread too much for surgery. I only have a few weeks to live."

She didn't shout, she was too tired to raise her voice, but the exasperation was as obvious as the despair on her face.

"A few weeks?! But you've been gone longer than a few weeks? Did you get any treatment?"

She turned away and walked back to her chair, her back to me, embarrassed by what she was going to tell me.

"You're right, it was some quack doctor. An entire quack clinic, on an island off the coast of San Marino. They gave me this special diet, a mixture of vitamins and herbs and proteins and nutrients, they said, to go along with hours of basking in the sunshine. It was supposed to cure me.

Funny thing, at first I felt better; mind over matter, I guess. I wanted to believe the cure was working, but after a while the headaches got worse and I got dizzy every time I stood up.

"They blamed me. They said I came to them too late. That's when I realized I'd been had. By then I'd spent most of my mother's money."

"Erin, the money doesn't matter. We'll go see someone. I'll make some calls and we'll get the best doctor. Tomorrow. I'll call…"

"You'll get the same answers I got, Morg."

"You said they told you a few weeks, and here you are, still kicking, and you look fine…"

She walked back to me with a big smile that said, thanks for the kind words, you liar.

"I've been back since Thursday. I went to see Dr. Evers again, to see if there was any change, you know, just in case the junk they gave me at the clinic had done some good."

"And?"

She shook her head.

"I want to talk to him. And damn it, how could these doctors treat you without letting your husband know what's going on? I'm going to call the insurance…"

"I didn't use our insurance, Morg, because I didn't want you to find out unless there was a cure. I used my mother's money and told the doctors I was a widow."

I looked at her left hand. She followed my gaze.

"Lots of widows wear their ring for a time after losing their husband. I went to a doctor in Indianapolis, one in Terre Haute, and one in Louisville. I told them I didn't want to tell anyone until I got their opinions."

"When did you do this? Where was I?"

"You were at the university, dear, where else? I can do a lot in ten hours, which was how long your day usually lasted."

I felt criticized, accused, as if my long hours at the university had caused her illness, as if I hadn't actually been working all that time. Maybe I had neglected her to the point where she allowed her system to retaliate by malfunctioning. The last months, there were articles to complete, meetings to attend to assure the continuation of the programs I'd designed; yes, I'd spent an excessive amount of time at the university but I truly intended that once I was finished, we, Erin and I, would have all the time in the world.

"I want to call Amy and ask her about the doctor she went to. He's Kenny and Amy's close friend and maybe they can convince him to see you quickly."

"Amy's cancer wasn't as advanced as mine is."

"Erin, I insist."

"What about your project?"

"Oh, hell, Erin, I told Janice that if...when you came home I'd drop the project."

She looked at my dirty clothes again. "Even after doing the field work?"

I shrugged and said, "I should change; be right back, then I want to hear more about where you've been, after I call Amy."

Kenny answered and he reminded me that Amy had had a spot on her breast that had been caught early. He said he was glad Erin had returned but devastated to hear of her illness, but I didn't have time for small talk and cut him short.

"Tell Janice tomorrow, but not anyone else, and tell her I don't know when I'd be able to work on the Bisseau papers again."

"I'll call Carl right now, Morg."

I let out a deep breath, said thanks, and put down the phone, sorry I'd been abrupt but too late to apologize.

Erin told me about her travels, that she'd stopped in London and Paris because she wanted to send me postcards from there so I'd think she was seeing the world.

Then when she reached San Marino for her treatments, she couldn't think of what to write me.

"I imagined that in a few weeks I'd be cured, and I'd call you with the good news and ask you to meet me in Paris. I was such a fool."

It wasn't long before Erin yawned, kissed me on the forehead and went to bed. A few minutes later Kenny called.

"Carl was out but I left him a message and he called back. He said for you to call his office in the morning, and give the receptionist your name, and he will have left a message to get Erin in somewhere, as an emergency patient. So be ready to go see him tomorrow. And good luck, pal. Our love to both of you."

My hopes were raised. If Erin had been naïve enough to consult a cluster of flakes on some island, maybe the doctors she saw here hadn't been any better. Maybe Kenny's friend will be able to do something.

Mindlessly I walked to the front window and looked out. Across the street a dark car was parked, one I didn't recognize as belonging to any of the neighbors. It gave me the creeps and reminded me of the stolen goods in my car.

I peeked in on Erin—she was asleep. I went outside and moved my car into the garage. The black car was still there. I lowered the door, shutting off view into my garage. I took the canisters I'd pilfered out of the car and carried them into the house and put them in the hall closet. As eager as I was to see what was in those canisters I restrained myself. Forget Bisseau, think of Erin.

I went to the window again and looked out, and at that moment the headlights of the car popped on, then the high beams, like fiery spouts of flame from a dragon, and the vehicle sped off.

I checked on Erin again; she could have been dead already, unmoving, her breath barely noticeable; I trembled.

I undressed and showered, poured a brandy, sat in my favorite chair, and remembered those days of shear happiness, when the kids were young and playful, and we did things with them; I wasn't always giving lectures. We played and sailed on the lake and flew kites in the parks, and we got puppies for the kids and I played ball and threw the Frisbee and we watched fireworks on the Fourth of July and then they grew up and began to date and drive their own cars and I began to feel old and then they were married and gone and Erin and I became grandparents and we were so happy and thrilled and I felt as ancient as the people I read about and taught my students about and talked about and wrote about.

I began to cry; tears rolled down my cheeks, my throat ached, my nose ran, the brandy, rather than soothing, burned and curdled in my gut, until finally, barely able to breathe, I lay my head back against the headrest of the chair, tried to think of a prayer to say, and fell asleep.

The last sound I remember was the glass thumping on the carpet.

11. LIFE AND DEATH

Illikaria Island, Eastern Mediterranean Sea

The ocean shimmered in the bright light, the sun flaunted its brilliance in the soft blue sky, the snow-white sand on the beach delicately merged with the lapping waves, and the man and the woman reclined on the veranda above it all, under a blue and white umbrella, sipping iced drinks from tall glasses dripping with condensation. They both wore sunglasses, a visor, and bathing suits, the woman's a floral pattern two piece that showed off her stylish figure, a skimpy suit she never wore without a coverall unless the only man around was her husband.

The man set his glass down on the round table between the lounge chairs and turned to the woman.

"Someone broke into my cache."

"Really? Which one?"

"The one in the Midwest."

"Do you know who it was?"

The man nodded. "I do now. He activated the alarm and was followed until he could be identified."

After a moment the woman asked, "Are you going to tell me or am I supposed to guess?"

"The gentleman is a professor at Lyman Wilson, would you believe."

The woman shrugged. "Why wouldn't I believe? Did you know him?"

"No, not really, but I think I ran into him a time or two. It was just before I left for the last time."

"So what does this mean? Is he on to you?"

"I'm not sure, but it does clear up something about what Jay did with my papers. I suspected he stored them at the university but it wouldn't have been safe for me to go back there as long as there was anyone around who might recognize me. And it's not like I can go prowling around the halls as if I still belong there. Colin Bisseau is dead, you know.

"At the last Rendezvous, which you didn't go to, in twenty-ten, I met a man who had a message for me. He said Jay had given it to him back in eighty, just before Jay died in the car accident, and Jay told him that if he ever ran into me to ask if I'd gotten the papers Jay was holding for me. But he said he hadn't been able to get to any of the Rendezvous since then and didn't know how to contact me.

"I played dumb at first, but eventually we came to trust each other. I told him Jay had been killed and I had no idea where he had stored the papers. He said Jay had told him to tell me,

'Thrice there
and thrice gone,
thrice deep,
and one more'

"And you know what this means, Colin?"

"Why do you still call me Colin?"

"I got used to it. It was you who insisted I call you Colin, then you wanted me to change. I'm tired of changing names; it gets confusing. You don't expect me to call you Cosmo, do you? I hate that name."

The man laughed. "Yes, it is confusing, as you may recall from when we first met."

The woman laughed and shook her head. "Oh, my, that was funny, now, as I look back. Then, I was so flustered."

"A pleasant memory."

"So, do you know what Jay's poem means?"

"Surely he refers to Lyman Wilson. Three times I taught there, and three times I left."

"And what's 'thrice deep and one more'?"

"The buildings are only two stories, but there is a basement in the main administration building. That would be thrice deep. Under that is a sub-basement, which dates back to when there was a limestone quarry. It was abandoned and a warehouse was built over it in the late nineteenth century. The university received the land in a grant and they built right over the sub-basement, shoring it up with the intention of using it for storage and labs, and what became the basement would have been the first floor, and so on. Apparently it was too difficult to design heating and plumbing, so while it was used for storage, it was never practical for offices or classrooms. Eventually it was forgotten, like on of those ancient repositories in the depths of New York's Museum of Natural History. I believe that's where Jay stored my papers."

"And this professor found them?"

"I guess so. I dug up what I could on him. He's not anybody famous, but he's apparently sharp enough to have published respected textbooks and numerous articles and papers, mostly on nineteenth century American History. So he's the kind of person who would find the papers interesting; in fact, Colt Boston's and Cade Bunyan's even more so than Colin Bisseau's.

"Among the material I left for Jay was a folder which he was not supposed to file with the papers, but maybe he forgot to remove, that hinted at where my cache was. This professor was smart enough to figure it out, so he bears watching."

"Are you going to go see him?"

The man shook his head. "No, I'll let him come to me."

"How's he going to find us here? I don't even know where we are."

"You constantly downplay your intelligence, dear, but I guess that's how you survived so long, by never letting other people, especially men, know how sharp you are. Not even me."

"I must admit that by now I probably know the history of the islands of the Adriatic, Aegean, and Ionian Seas better than anyone who ever lived, except for you, of course."

"And the Mediterranean, don't forget."

"Yes, I know, your history sold well, didn't it, the one published under your silly Cosmo Ballantrie name?"

"Yes, it did. By the way, my novel is almost finished."

"You've been saying that for years."

"I keep revising it."

"Are you really going to publish it? Do you think anyone will believe it?"

"I don't want anyone to believe it, it's just my way of coordinating the information I've kept in the journals all these years; more for my own purposes than anyone else's. And now that I know that at least one of my caches isn't as safe as I thought, there is more reason to do it."

"Won't the others get upset?"

"Possibly. I have to think on it. I might wait till the next Rendezvous and get some feedback."

"That won't be for five years."

"There's no hurry, but I will send an advance copy of the manuscript to one Professor Morgan Miller, at Lyman Wilson University."

"Hmm, I think you're asking for trouble, Colin."

He chuckled. "Maybe so, but I've been getting bored."

"So am I. I want to go back."

"Soon. This professor, he could be just the person we've been looking for."

"You think so, eh?"

"By the way, speaking of books, your book of photography is popular, I notice. I knew you'd find something interesting on these islands."

"I should write a real book."

"What about?"

"The true story."

"Of?"

"Ha! You know what, you're the historian."

"Truth is always more fascinating than fiction. I think you should."

"Okay, but I'd like to re-visit some of the places first."

The man sat quietly for awhile, his mind having leaped to a place in the niche where he kept a jumble of unconnected ideas that he sensed were important but couldn't always understand why.

The woman waited, at first wondering if he was ignoring her comment because he wasn't interested, and then realizing, as she had learned during the years they'd been together, that he had drifted off somewhere, as good as onto another planet, and when ready he would return to her.

After a minute or more he turned to the woman and said, softly, almost as if he was in a library, "I'd like to wait and see if Professor Miller takes the bait. If not, we'll go to him. Okay?"

"Whatever you wish. But let's not wait much longer. We've been here eight years already."

"There are lots of islands."

"Yes, as you've shown me. Still, sometimes I miss the big cities. I can't even go shopping out here."

"What do you need besides a bathing suit?"

"I'd want reasons to wear a dress: go to the opera, sip champagne at Emily's…"

"It was only a few months ago we went to Athens for an entire week."

"I want to see New York again, Colin, and San Francisco. I need new clothes."

"Okay, soon; I don't want to bother him yet."

"Why not, if he's becoming a nuisance?"

"His wife is ill."

"Ill? How so?"

"She has inoperable brain cancer."

"Oh, God, how awful. How old is she?"

"Fifty-seven."

"A mere child. It's so unfair, I…"

"Let's not go there again."

"Aren't you worried he'll find out everything about you…about us?"

"What do you propose I do? I've had him watched carefully; he hasn't gone to anyone; he's been involved caring for his wife. He hasn't even opened the canisters yet. The kind of man I think he is, he'll want to confirm his suspicions—he'll come to me, not anyone else. Besides, who'd believe him?"

The woman lowered the backrest of her lounge chair, then closed her eyes. "Wake me in an hour, please," she said, her voice level but leaking irritation.

"I will. I'm going to walk down and take a swim."

"Colin?"

"Yes?"

"Do you think Jay was killed on purpose?"

"No…I had the incident investigated. It was an unfortunate accident."

The woman patted her stomach and said, more to herself than him, "Need to lose a pound or two."

"Don't be silly; you're perfect."

"Thank you, dear. But I'm still an old-fashioned girl at heart; I can't get used to these skimpy bathing suits that show off so much skin.

"That's progress," the man said with a big grin and a wink.

The man rose from his chair and began to clamber down the uneven stone steps, fifty of them, that led to the beach and to the sea.

"Be careful," the woman called out to him. He waved backhanded.

The woman raised her head, took off her sunglasses and watched her husband as he eased down the stairs. He was tanned, muscular, his physique belying the gray hair that covered his head, gray, she knew, from dying it to make himself look older, odd she thought, since she always wanted to look younger. She rubbed her stomach and said to herself, "Need to lose a pound or two."

A week had passed since Erin's return, and six days since she and Morgan had gone to see the cancer specialist recommended by Kenny. To Morgan's dismay the doctor's diagnosis was the same as what Erin had received from the other doctors she'd seen. When he had a moment Morgan spoke to the doctor alone.

"Would it have made any difference if she'd come to you three or four months ago?"

The doctor shrugged. "I don't like to deal in speculation Mr. Miller, but based on what I see, not likely.

Even had it been caught early I don't think a cure would have been possible. Yes, the two of you would have had more time to prepare. If she'll give me permission to look at the records of her other doctors, I could tell you more, but what good would that do now? There's no sense in dealing in what-ifs. Actually I'm surprised she's able to get out of bed anymore. She hasn't got long, to be blunt, but you said you wanted it straight. All I can do is give her something for the pain."

"Will she be in much pain?"

"Oh, she is already. She holds it in well, I suppose, if you haven't noticed. I'm sorry, I don't sit with soft-coating the facts."

"That's the way we want it. So...what should we figure on? What can we do in the time left?"

"If you love her, and I can tell you do, be with her every moment you can. Soon she'll sleep more and more, and when she's awake she'll be in pain and need medicine, which will make her drowsy. She'll get weaker, won't want to eat, and you'll have to carry her to the bathroom. So get ready for it. Once the pain gets unbearable, even with the pills, if she's lucky...I'm sorry, but she'll get to where she hopes she doesn't wake up from the next sleep."

"Are you talking weeks, days...?

The doctor nodded; despite his reticence to give false hope it was always difficult to estimate how much time someone had to live because it was almost always wrong, either too optimistic or overly pessimistic, but always an answer the patient, or more likely, the patient's spouse or child, didn't anticipate. They always thought in terms of months or years, when doctors knew the reality was that the sand was rapidly running out of the hourglass, and turning the glass over was not an option.

The doctor put a hand on Morgan's arm. Though his face showed no emotion, his voice oozed compassion.

"Enjoy every hour you have with her, Mr. Miller. I doubt there'll be reason to bring her to me again, but do call, if you need me to see her, or need more pills."

Morgan teetered where he stood, the twin faces of life and death hitting him like a kick in the groin. He sucked in air trying to offset the tears forming in his eyes.

"Let it go, Mr. Miller, don't be ashamed to cry. You can stay here in this room until you're ready. I'll have a nurse take your wife to the waiting room in back; you can meet her there."

The days dragged and Erin spent more and more time in bed or in the recliner, sleeping or too weak and drowsy to stand up. I felt helpless; I would have kicked holes in the walls if it would have helped Erin. I'd have taken her pain, hell, I'd have taken her disease if I could.

I insisted we see yet another doctor. She resisted, said it was too difficult for her. In my anxiousness to help her I was actually making one of her few, priceless days more painful. The answers were the same. The doctor told me the only thing holding her together was grit and my presence in her life. It was as if Erin, to pay back for having left me on her search for a cure, now felt she owed me to stay alive as long as possible, yet in my darkest moments I wished for her to not wake up the next morning so her pain would be over and I, selfishly, could get on with my life. And then I would feel disgust with myself.

It distressed me that she had gone off on this wacky escapade without me. We were supposed to be a couple, a team, a family. We do things together, but maybe too often we did things that left her feeling alone: conventions, dinner parties where the talk focused on scholastics and history, the ways in which history might have taken a turn if one key person had not had an upset stomach on a particular day, gabfests I found fascinating but Erin found tiresome.

I had been inconsiderate, thoughtless, preoccupied, and selfish the past thirty plus years, I concluded. It was mental flagellation; I clawed at my faults like a steam shovel ripping coal out of the womb of the earth, and with a metallic screech the shovel dumped my faults into a pile for curious gadflies to cull through.

Each night after I'd aided Erin to bed, earlier and earlier each evening, I lambasted myself for having failed her. Then each morning I'd put on a happy face because the worst thing for her was to sense that I was despondent.

So I filled the days waiting on her and helping her move about; she insisted we eat our evening meal at the dinner table, like civilized folks, she said, not that she ate much. She wouldn't even let me serve her breakfast in bed. I'd help her out, get her to the bathroom, then to the kitchen for coffee, which was all she wanted. I gave her a sponge bath every other day, read to her, and we watched old movie favorites, except she usually fell asleep before it was over and I would carry her to bed. Then I'd return to the movie, fall asleep myself, and awaken two or three hours later.

I still hadn't looked at the canisters I had pilfered. They were in the hall closet, ticking away, I thought at one time, like a time bomb. But I figured by now a bomb would have exploded so I laughed off that concern. Still, I was reluctant to open them when Erin was around, lest she got curious about them. Likely I could spend hours with the metal boxes while she slept, but I felt I'd be hiding something from her, which I was, but not as much so as if I actually pored through the contents. In effect, I was waiting for her to die until I could continue my investigation into the mystery of Colin Bisseau.

Then one day Janice called, apologetic for bothering me.

"No, it's okay, it's good to hear your voice. I'm just sitting here doing a crossword puzzle."

"Any change, I, I mean, for the..."

"Better? No, that's not going to happen. I've already made all the arrangements, Jan; I'm not expecting any miracles."

"This may not be the best time, but, I wanted to tell you that a package came for you, delivered to the university."

"What kind of package? What is it?"

"I don't know. It came by UPS, from Greece."

"Greece? From whom?"

"I don't know, Morg. It's a small box, addressed to you, and it appears to have originated in Athens, Greece."

"I can't imagine who..."

"What do you want me to do with it?"

"I...damn...I'm sorry, Jan...I don't know...please put it on my desk...I'll come in some time next week..."

Why Janice's call reminded of something, I'm not sure, but it did: I suddenly realized I had totally forgotten about the helicopter and the strange car parked in front of the house the day I'd returned from my grave-robbing episode.

I grinned, and then laughed at myself for being concerned. If no one had approached me by now, surely the alarm that had been activated had long since lost its connection to whomever had installed it.

I had laughed too soon; the next day, when I was out running errands while Erin napped, there it was: the shape and the color, black, were the same as the one I'd seen outside the house, and I, quick as Thomas Magnum to spot a tail, was positive the car was following me. I began to sweat and missed my turn into the parking lot of the pharmacy. I made a U-turn and the black car followed me. It was there when I came out of the store and it followed me home, though I took a circuitous route, but it passed the house and kept going.

If whoever was tracking me wanted the canisters, they could take them anytime. Walk up to the house, point a gun at me, and ask for them. I'm a retired history professor, I'm not going to fight an armed thug. They could break in when I'm gone and rip the house apart; who's going to stop them, a dying woman? No, they weren't going to take them by force; they were observing me so that I'd *know* they were observing me.

When Erin slept in the afternoon she was out for two or three hours. I called Janice and said I'd come by tomorrow to pick up the package. The next day I told Erin that if she took a nap after lunch I was going to go to the university to pick up mail.

Erin smiled. "You know I always take a nap, Morg. You go and don't worry about me."

"If you wake up and need anything, call me, okay?"

She smiled and nodded. I wondered if she was

estimating how long after her demise I would start seeing Janice. More guilt for me to pile up, like a tower of Lego blocks reaching higher and higher into storm clouds.

So once Erin was asleep I went to the university. I had no reason other than a sneaky suspicion but I bet myself that the package Janice told me about was connected to my new hobby of grave robbing.

The door to Janice's office was open so I stepped in and almost shyly said, "Hello", while tapping on the doorframe.

"Oh, Morgan," Janice said, surprised, excited or unhappy to see me, I wasn't able to discern. She looked like she'd forgotten I was coming by today.

"Did you forget?"

"No, no, it's just, I, I guess I don't know what to say, Morg. I mean, 'I'm sorry', doesn't seem to cut it, does it?"

I shrugged, and sat down in the chair on my side of her desk. I shook my head, agreeing there wasn't anything meaningful anyone could say. Of course people say they are sorry, or can they help, it's so sad, how am I doing, how is she (or he, depending on the situation) doing. Well, of course, she, or he, is dying, that's how they are doing. But it would be rude to point that out to someone who is trying to be sympathetic.

"She sleeps a lot," I said, "which is probably good. Less time to think about what's happening."

"And you, Morg, how are you holding up?"

I frowned and looked at my hands, for no particular reason other than I didn't know where to look. Again I shook my head, but I looked up at Janice.

"You know, Jan, I can't even answer that because I don't know how I'm doing. I think I'm running on stored energy, not that I'm doing much physically. But waiting and thinking, worrying if she's in pain, how will it end, when will it end; it takes up more energy than I would have thought, had I ever reflected on being in this situation, and who does? I'm a few years older than Erin, so I've always assumed I'd go first, and she'd be the one who'd have to deal with the grief of losing a spouse. I guess that's kind of selfish, isn't it?"

I didn't expect an answer and didn't get one other than for Janice to open her mouth, than close it, as if she realized anything she said would be the same banal comment that anybody could give, but she, being a special friend, wanted to express special words, words that the lesser friends couldn't express with real conviction, but at this point she didn't have those words. She gasped and put a hand over her mouth.

"Hey, no need for you to cry."

For a split second I wondered if Janice was contemplating that she would never have the chance to feel the grief of losing a loved one, and the realization caused the tears.

"I feel so helpless, Morg," Janice said, sniffling. "I want to say things, but I don't want to sound trite, so then I'm back to not knowing what to say."

"Hey, a smile and a hug, or just a quiet moment together with a special friend is far more important than a thousand platitudes from others."

She smiled and wiped her eyes with a tissue.

I looked at my watch and shuddered.

"What is it?" Janice asked

"The time; I've been away longer than I should have. She may have awakened by now. Sorry, Jan," I said as I jumped up. "No time for coffee, I need to go."

"Kenny didn't come in today, anyway. He called, said he'd call you at home."

The way she said it, it was as if she felt it would be inappropriate for she and I to go to the cafeteria for a cup of coffee ourselves, though we had many times, considering 'the situation.'

"Your package…" she went to the bookshelf and pulled down a brown box covered with shipping and address labels, about the size to hold a manuscript.

"Do you have any idea what it is, or who it's from?"

"No," I said, a partial lie. "I'll take it with me and look at it at home. I suppose it's a manuscript from a former student who has a new slant on some historical era, and wants my opinion."

"Hey," she patted my arm, "take care of yourself. I know, it's what everybody says, but I mean it, and if you need any help, anything…ah, there I go with the clichés."

"I know, Jan, thanks." I gave her a weak hug and left.

I drove as if on automatic pilot, expecting the car to know the way home without any help from me. The box lay on the seat next to me begging to be opened. I looked at it, then in the rear view mirror, watching for a black car. Traffic was heavy and I couldn't keep track of all the cars around me so soon I gave up worrying and paid attention to driving.

I pulled into the garage, then stepped onto the driveway and looked up and down the street. If a neighbor was watching surely they would ask, 'what is Miller feeling guilty about?'

Back in the garage I lowered the door, then took the box out of the car. Once inside the house I went to the bedroom: Erin was asleep.

I went into my den and set the box on my desk. Goose bumps rose on my arms. I had an itch of an idea, a suspicion, a gut feeling…that I'd been probing at, like scratching at a scab that isn't ready to slough off yet, so I had to rub around the scab, near to it, but not so near that it tears off and causes new bleeding.

As I was opening the box a voice behind me said, "What's that, Morg?"

I flinched, as if caught red-handed looking at a neighbor's mail, having been invited to wait for him in his study.

"Jumpy, aren't we?" Erin said, a wan smile on her face, a smile as thin as the nightgown she wore. I was startled by her voice and by her body as she stood where the light shone through the diaphanous gown, revealing a body that was once so beautiful but now was skinny and weak.

"Oh, Erin, you surprised me. I just looked in on you; sorry if I woke you."

"That's okay. How was your meeting?"

"Nothing much; I wanted to pick up this package. I think it's a manuscript from a former student."

I stepped away from the desk and came to her. "I can look at it later. You want something to eat, or hot tea?"

She shrugged, as if eating was a chore done by other people, and not worth the bother.

"Maybe some soup, or whatever."

Guilt again reared its hideous matrix as I wished Erin had not awakened yet, so I could see what was in the box. So I reminded myself that this could be the last day with her, the last meal we shared, the last time I would talk to her.

She grimaced as we walked to the kitchen; it was time for another pain pill, and I said a speedy prayer to let me take her pain for a day, or even however long she has to live. But I don't think it works that way.

I heated up vegetable soup I had made earlier in the week, we chatted about the kids, both of whom were scheduled to come this weekend to visit, code for, 'to say their goodbyes,' and I prayed again, this time that they got here while Erin still had the strength to get out of bed. The grandkids don't need to see their grandmother lying haggard in her bed, death gnawing at her like rats on discarded telephone cable.

As had become our ritual we put on a DVD of an old movie, one of her favorites, to watch for the last time. I always let her chose. This time it was *Far From the Madding Crowd*, the Julie Christie version. Erin winced when the sheep went over the cliff, she groaned when Bathsheba married the dreadful soldier, and she sniffled when Bathsheba finally realized it was Gabriel Oak who truly loved her, and she him. I watched dutifully, and occasionally Erin commented on some detail that I would need to handle, 'when the time comes', as she put it, words gentler than, 'when I'm pushing up daisies'.

I hemmed and nodded, acknowledging her but reticent to talk specifics.

Maybe it was a surge of energy—it is often said that just before death, cancer patients have a few days when they feel and look better, raising false hopes that they are recovering—but Erin made it through the entire movie without falling asleep. But then she needed me to assist her to the bathroom, and to bed.

"I just need an hour or so, dear. Wake me."

"Sure," I said.

I poured a glass of iced tea and went back to my den, the contents of the box having been on my mind throughout the entire movie.

As I had suspected, once I unwrapped the thick cloth that enclosed the contents, it appeared to be a manuscript of at least two hundred typed pages. I searched for a note or letter, or anything to suggest who had sent this, but there was nothing.

I read the title page:

"IN THE MIST"

a novel by

Cosmo Ballantrie

"For what is your life? It is a mist that appears for a little while, and then vanishes."
James 4:15

I was immediately struck dumb and deaf. I knew this quote; at least, I'd read it recently. It was one of the last entries Colin Bisseau made in his journals before his disappearance.

Before reading further I went to the computer and checked the quote. I found it exactly as Bisseau wrote it in one reference, and in another it was slightly different: "You are no more than a mist that is here for a little while and then disappears."

I slumped back in the chair and felt goose bumps crawl up and down my arms. I scratched at them, as at the imagined scab. I shivered and covered my mouth with both hands as if to lessen the shock of the words in front of me. Again I looked at the title and the author's name. Why does he always use the initials, 'C.B.' I wondered: Colin Bisseau, Colt Boston, Cade Bunyan, and other names mentioned in the journals. Now it was Cosmo Ballantrie, and he, whoever he really was, knew I had robbed the grave of Martin and Wilma Bisseau, he had helicopters and black cars following me, and he wants me to read his story.

So I would comply.

12. DEATH AND LIFE

I began to read…

An Introduction

There are some who swear that the sunlight at the eastern end of the Mediterranean Sea—in some places called the Aegean Sea, in others the Sea of Crete—is brighter and more soothing than in any other part of the world. It is a light that glows and disperses warmth that some say is regenerative and invigorating.

(Maybe Erin should have gone there for her cure, I muttered aloud, not that I believed it would have done any good.)

Scattered like rose petals blown loose by a warm breeze, there are speckles of tiny islands, some no more than a half-square mile in size, with populations numbered in the hundreds, where a person living past one hundred years is not uncommon. The locals banter with each other, 'Now it's on to my second century!' Anyone less than ninety years old is considered a youngster.

These tiny islands, like the one called Illikaria, do not appear on any but the most detailed, specific maps of the region. Even then, one would be hard pressed to find transportation to these rocky isles, which before the GPS were difficult to find in the vast waters of the Mediterranean even for an experienced navigator. But if one did have a boat, the beaches to which one could sail would be as inviting as a Siren's song.

To the approaching traveler the sand is as white and bright as if bags of sugar had been deposited for the length of the shore and fifty yards deep. One might think the beach was layered with new snow, if it weren't for the temperature, eighty to eighty-five degrees most days, hardly varying year round.

When you step on the sand you want to take your shoes off and let your toes mingle with it. The sand is soft, and one thinks this may really be powdered sugar used to sprinkle over fresh pastry.

A few steps inland and the island loses its friendly attitude: the slope up to the village is too steep even for a mountain goat. Here and there—and one either knows where or needs to find a friendly resident who knows— there are steps that have been laboriously carved out of the side of the hill, still a challenge but not as formidable as thousands of years ago when the island was an ornery, lava spouting volcano.

Atop the slope lies the village—there is only one on this island. The buildings are as white as the sand on the beach, as if only yesterday given a new coat of whitewash. Old women—they are all old—scrub the steps every other *day to maintain the virgin appearance, steps so glistening one is reticent to walk on them, but one does, as the old woman smiles and beckons you to enter and enjoy a cup of tea or grappa, depending on the time of day.*

When grappa is offered, one passes slowly and quietly through the home, as if in an art museum, to the back porch, where an old man sits, sometimes by himself but more likely with two or three of his friends, their faces and hands wrinkled and brown from decades of sunshine, men he has known so long the years have been lost in memory. He gestures to a table where glasses and a carafe of grappa sets; you help yourself and sit while admiring the view.

The yard is an array of colors: red flowers and sunny yellow ones, purple, carnelian, white, and one or two shades you can't name. The vista is endless: the blue waters extend to the horizon, and from up here they look calm and serene, and one would never believe that thousands of ships lay on the floor of the sea, some put there by the merciless forces of nature, others by warring navies. But now, from these heights, the sea is peaceful and even if you cannot converse with the old men, they will greet you happily, smile and share their grappa, make a toast before drinking it, and laugh some more.

The old woman might return with a plate of cheese, olives and bread, the latter freshly-baked and trailing an aroma straight from heaven, and you won't be allowed to leave without a taste of every item.

Food is either grown on what little farmable land exists; olives, grapes for wine, a variety of vegetables, or caught in the sea. A few sheep and chickens provide an occasional piece of meat. Cheese is made locally or on nearby islands, and it and other necessities are brought in as requested by the island magistrate on the monthly ferryboat from Rhodes, Kos or Tinos by way of Athens, or from Crete. The magistrate is generally the eldest man, or, if he is at the point in his life where decision–making is difficult, his son, who may be a kid in his eighties.

As the population ages the only young people remaining are the fishermen or farmers who sell to the older residents who are too old to do much physical work. (But it is not unheard of for a doddering centennial, as part of a dare on his birthday, to take his boat out to catch dinner for his birthday celebration.)

Fresh-caught fish with home-baked bread and olive oil, plump green olives, several types of cheese, and a glass (or two or three) of homemade wine; what more could one ask?

Eventually even the hardy old-timers will die out, the younger people will move to the larger islands or to the mainland of Europe, and the buildings will bake in the sun, silent and empty, until the ceaseless pounding of the sea *washes away the edges of the island and then attacks the whitewashed stone homes and other structures.*

It is likely, though unproven and unaccepted by the residents of these isolated islands, that the longer than normal lifespan is due to a fluke of genetics mixed with a lifestyle that is virtually stress-free and calm, and a diet that eschews the junk absorbed by people of more developed societies.

But what if a person knew he would live over one hundred years? Or maybe two hundred years; three, even more? Would you plan your life differently? Maybe not, as the fact is that few people plan their lives in detail; they sort of take things as they come and try to survive against the vicissitudes of Mother Nature and an unforgiving society.

It might depend on one's health: who would wish to live another century if the body was so frail that rising from bed each morning was a chore, and the joints ached and the eyes and ears failed, and finally the mind forgot who it belonged to. Death would be welcome.

Is this why Colin Bisseau hid from society, to write science fiction? He disappeared in 1980; now it's 2015 and he would be ninety-one years old. Nothing wrong with that, but what has he been doing for thirty-five years? Does he believe that certain places on the planet enable people to live longer, so he exiled himself to a tiny island thousands of miles from anyone who ever knew him, or heard of him?

Curious if there were any other publications under the name Cosmo Ballantrie, I did a search and came up with a history of the eastern Mediterranean, published in France a few years ago, but not translated into English. There was no picture of the author and the brief bio said Ballantrie resided "among the islands of the eastern Mediterranean."

There was also a note crediting the book's photographs to one E. Parker.

I went back to where I had stopped and began to read again.

Death would be welcome.

As it might be for someone virtually confined to bed, their brain wasting away as they slept, not only waiting to die but praying for death, so the pain would be gone and the hopeless feeling would vanish with one's last breath. Like Erin.

Ah, but what if one did not get old, or sick, or frail? What if one regularly regenerated? What if the people around you, family, friends, and co-workers, all aged, turned gray, became frail, needed knee replacements and hearing aids, while you romped like a twenty-something stud? How would you explain it to people who have known you for thirty years? What are you using to get rid of the wrinkles, Joe? I never had any. You dye you hair? Did you make a pact with the devil?

Ah, the devil! Is it he, in his mischievous way playing games with mortals to see if he can run the old scam of trading immortality for one's soul?

Does God let Lucifer try again, as he did with Jabez Stone, claiming the man's soul in exchange for material riches, but even more--promising everlasting health, youth for eternity, with the trade-off to come much later, when the mark has become used to a endless life of wealth and health and luxury? Will the sucker think he can outlast old Beelzebub?

But if it is Lucifer running the scam, eternity might not be as delightful as he promises. The immortal still has human emotions, so he (or she) falls in love. A few years pass and the loved one begins to age; the immortal doesn't. You tell her she looks as young as when you met her, and she smiles at your lie.

At fifty you give her a party, and by then you have been dying your hair to make it gray. You wear plano glasses to blend in with everyone else whose vision is weakening. You try not to move with the agility of a twenty-eight year old, but it's difficult to fake. When you met her you told her you were twenty-eight, and twenty-five years and three children later you can jog for miles, play basketball with the youngsters, and oh, yes, what exactly is

it you do for a living, other than handle our—your—
investments?

So the Immortal has to disappear. He has to
abandon the one he fell in love with, abandon children,
friends, his job, because no one would understand that he
doesn't age, or if he does, so slowly that the growing of
grass would be like a shooting star flashing across the sky.

How can the Immortal explain it? He can't, and
would be treated with scorn and disbelief, and eventually
hatred by some, for pretending such a preposterous idea;
by others because they wonder if this person has truly
discovered the fountain of youth and they are envious,
green beyond the most intense emerald, desiring their
chance to dive into the fountain.

If this was the writing of a ninety-one year old Colin
Bisseau is was not the type of fiction I would have
expected. If he'd wanted to try his hand at fiction I would
have thought historical fiction. Yet, I was not convinced;
had someone usurped Bisseau's identity, killed him and his
wife, and absconded with their wealth? If so, why send me
this book, teasing me with it, practically telling me where
he is?

I was born in the year…

I scrunched the page in my hand as I was startled by the tiny voice at the side of my head. I hadn't heard Erin get up, much less sense her movement to within inches of where I sat. Her voice was less than a sparrow's peep.

"Is that from the package you went to get?"

"Erin, are you okay? I didn't hear you?"

"I got up to go to the bathroom. I didn't want to bother you."

"Can I get you something?"

"No, yes, a glass of water. Can I see that?"

She took the page I was reading out of my hand and as I rose to go for the water she sat down and read.

When I returned she said, "What student of yours wrote this? Doesn't sound like history to me, Morg."

"No," I forced a chuckle. "I don't know who it's from. There's a name but not someone I know. I think it might be a joke, or was sent to the wrong Morgan Miller."

Erin's awareness and energy level, even her appetite, surprised us both, though I simply smiled when she mentioned it.

"I think I'm getting better, Morg. I feel good. Maybe all I need is lots of rest."

"Maybe," I said, remembering stories of the surge before the crash landing. I hoped with a passion Gerald and Connie got here in time. They were scheduled to arrive Saturday, two days from now.

For the rest of this day I forgot about the mysterious Cosmo Ballantrie, left the manuscript on the table next to my chair, and enjoyed sitting in the yard with Erin, soaking up the soft sun, warm, not too hot, sipping iced tea, and watching birds splash in the fountain, occasionally sharing an old memory from our years together, ones that made us smile.

Erin smiled more today than she had since she'd returned home. I watched her face and the movement of her lips and her eyes, even the movement of her throat when she swallowed the tea. I sensed they were actions I wouldn't see anymore and I wanted to memorize them, as I wanted to memorize everything that happened in the few hours we had left.

"I'm sorry, Morg."

"For what, Erin? You can't help it you got sick."

"No, I mean that I didn't tell you, didn't let us enjoy that time together, you know, the time I was gone. Even If nothing could have been done, we could have spent those weeks together. I'm so sorry."

We both teared up, harboring thoughts about what we each could have, should have, would have, done differently. It's spilt milk, so we hugged each other and I assured her I held no hard feelings and she made me promise I'd not fall into depression when she was gone, that I would go back to my project and enjoy the work and not to forget our friends and visit the kids and grandkids; it was like a general giving his final orders before the big battle.

"It has been a good life, dear, it really has."

I didn't say anything; the fact that she felt she needed to tell me it'd been a good life indicated to me---my mind already beset with self-induced pangs of failure—that she had had doubts, that she had been disenchanted with our life, that she had fantasized what her life might have been had she taken another path; married someone else.

She prattled on and I didn't interrupt, her voice fading as she recalled special moments we'd shared as a couple and as a family. I knew she felt the same disappointment as I did that our kids had moved away from us, too far away for frequent visits or to afford us the opportunity to spoil the grandkids. But as she reminded me, we had grown closer once Gerald and Connie were two thousand miles away and we had, despite my selective memory spent much quality time together, to use a cliché I abhor.

Our trips to see the kids and grandkids, once both Gerald and Connie had begun families, we stretched into visits to parts of the country neither of us had seen before. Yeah, as usual I tended to point us towards historical areas, but Erin insisted she'd enjoyed every minute of every hour we'd spent together, and even more so once we were relieved of our parenting duties.

"You became more romantic, Morg, did you know that?"

I was almost embarrassed to hear her say it, but what guy wouldn't be pleased?

She clasped my hands in hers and smiled and in her eyes I saw real love and it made me think that maybe I hadn't been too bad a husband after all.

The afternoon of the funeral service friends gathered at the home of Kenny and Amy. Janice stayed in the background as much as she could, helping Amy in the kitchen most of the time. I noticed and appreciated it, but towards the end of the event, when most of the guests had departed, she came up to me.

"Haven't had a chance to talk."

I smiled. "Yeah, lots of people want to say something, I figure I have to let them."

"And me?"

"You're my friend, Jan. I know how bad you feel. You don't have to say anything."

"Thanks, Morg, but I have to say it, I am truly sorry, you know I am..."

"I know you are, Janice, thank you..."

"It was good that Gerald and Connie arrived in time."

"Yeah, they cut it close. At least this way they didn't have to make two trips," I said, smirking as if to show my sense of humor hadn't died with Erin.

Kenny walked over.

"Everyone else is gone, Morg. Sit down and have a drink. You deserve it; you probably need it. I've got an unopened eighteen-year old sitting here, and we want to toast Erin."

"Sounds good, Kenny. Amy, thanks for putting this together. Erin and I had talked but, when the time came...when it happened, I suddenly forgot what to do."

Kenny took me by the arm and led me to his lounge chair where I plopped down. I'd been standing for hours and now I realized how tired I was; for a second I felt dizzy. He stepped away and returned with a glass of Scotch, handed it to me, raised his glass, as did Amy and Janice, their glasses filled with a hay-colored wine, and said, "Here's to Erin, a great lady, a wonderful friend."

"Here, here," Amy said.

"Thanks, guys," I said, and downed the drink.

"The words you had me read, Morg, where did you come up with them? Beautiful, but kind of chilling."

"Something I came across recently, Amy. I wasn't looking for anything specific."

"Yes, Morg, they were wonderful, and sad." Janice said. "I guess sad is okay at a funeral."

Amy stepped away for a second and returned with one of the pamphlets we'd hurriedly printed up for the service.

"Here it is: 'For what is life? It is a mist that appears for a little while, and then vanishes.' "

We stood silently for a few seconds, each, I suppose, contemplating the words, taking them to heart or perhaps thinking them trite I couldn't say, nor did I wish to discuss it.

"I need to go," Janice said, setting her glass down. "Work day tomorrow."

I stood up. "I may need a few days, Jan."

"No problem, Morg. I don't expect you to come back immediately."

"What else would I do, sit around, go to movies? Play golf? Hell yes, I'll be back next week, count on it."

"Morg, if there's anything I can do…"

"Not now, Janice, there's nothing."

We exchanged gentle hugs and I think Amy and Kenny's eyeballs clinked as they watched us. But unbeknownst to them, maybe not even to Eros, I think it was at that moment, irony be damned, that I realized that the possibility for a romance between Janice and I never had existed, and never would. When our eyes met I saw in hers the same understanding, blended with acceptance and disappointment. I hope now she opens herself to a relationship with a man who can love her the way she deserved to be loved; the way Erin and I had loved each other.

I wanted to leave, too, but discretion suggested I should dally. So I asked Kenny for a refill and sat down.

13. CANISTERS

The house I awoke in the next day wasn't any quieter than it had been in recent weeks, but it reeked of gloom. My eyes hurt and my mouth was as dry as the sands of Trinity Site, but I didn't want to get out of bed and face my new world.

I opened my eyes, rubbed them, and stared at the ceiling, thinking about what to do. Paperwork, messages to people who didn't know Erin had been ill, going through her…things; where to start? Why start; why not just lay here until I also die?

I thought about loneliness, whether I understood what it was. I was lonely when Erin first left, but I found something to occupy my time, so when I was busy, my mind occupied, I didn't miss her; when I came home and she wasn't there, I was lonely; or was I just *alone?*

When Erin was away on her flight of fancy I always felt, deep inside, that she would come home and everything would be copasetic. Now, that could never be.

When she returned I was devastated because she was a shell of the woman I had loved and lived and shared my life with. Even then, for those few days, she was always there, nearby. Three weeks ago I was in denial concerning Erin's condition, not knowing how to accept the inevitability of her passing, yet behaving with the understanding that these were our last days, our last hours together. So on that final afternoon when I went to wake Erin, her nap having lasted longer than usual, and she was gone, I was torn between a gallery of emotions, pulled at and tugged and tossed, my head swirling but my body doing nothing but sitting on the edge of the bed, my hand combing her hair.

I remembered something I'd read, about how the room felt like the life had been sucked out of it, and I strained to recall where I had read or heard that. Then I remembered: it was Cade Bunyan describing Etta's apartment when he returned and she wasn't there, and I wondered if I was confusing fiction and reality and whether I knew the difference anymore.

Finally I cried, weeping at first, then a torrent, so when there were no tears at the memorial service it wasn't for lack of feeling, as some observers may have assumed, while others conceded that I was in shock, too shattered to show emotion, it was because I was spent, too tired to think to express pain. The death tableau of the past few weeks was like a drawn out, bloody murder scene in a movie, on and on, gruesome, the audience wanting it to end, and it does, and you are glad it's over, even though you rue that the creator killed off a character you admired. A sudden death, shocking at the moment, is over quickly, leaving time for grief and tears and hand-wringing; I'd been carrying out that performance every night, lying awake next to Erin, listening to her breathe, wondering if this was her last breath, then this one, then the next one, until I'd fall asleep, and awake with a start listening again for a sign of life.

I wallowed in the bed, embracing the feeling of desolation, accepting that I deserved to be miserable, that I needed to acknowledge a huge chunk of blame for Erin's escapade, for the creep I must have been for her to believe it was better for her to fight her condition by herself.

Then survival instincts overwhelmed my malaise and I allowed myself the luxury of a few more moments in bed to process the hours Erin and I had shared the last few days, especially our conversations, so I could lock them in a safe in my brain, subject to my own secret combination, more secure, I mused, than the safe in the grave in the woods. There was this male thing that made me want to hang tough, show the world that I was OK, that I was dealing with the loss and no one need concern themselves about my emotional state of mind. What an ass.

Erin had given me a soft kiss and a delicate smile when she went off to her nap, and insisted she didn't need me to help her to the bedroom, and I didn't say anything, maybe knowing she would not waken but didn't want to frighten me by saying 'Goodbye'.

The kids and their families had arrived; I called them at their hotel and Gerald gallantly offered to accompany the body to the crematorium, a task I was glad to hand off.

There were the calls that had to be made; I was frozen in uncertainty for an hour or more, then Kenny and Amy arrived and helped shake me back to awareness. I insisted certain calls I would make on my own; they handled others.

Two days later there was the brief but affecting service, attended by more people than I'd expected; followed by the gathering at Kenny and Amy's.

I brushed away the two tears that had formed, one in the corner of each eye, possibly the last two tears I'd ever be able to fashion, and swung out of bed, the call of nature finally rousing me from ennui. I took care of that, then gargled until my mouth became unglued, splashed water in my face and looked in the mirror to see a stranger.

When had my hair gone to silver? My eyes were red and my skin the gray of a dead fish. Too much drink, too much crying, not enough sleep.

I had not finished a cup of coffee before the phone began to ring. Each time I answered I figured it was someone, Kenny or Janice, checking on me to see if I 'was all right'. It was neither of them but it was other well-wishers and sympathizers. I wanted to say, no of course I'm not all right, you ninny, my wife just died. But I was polite and thankful and gracious, I think.

I dumped the remaining coffee, lukewarm now, and poured fresh, hot coffee from the carafe. I sat quietly and sipped the brew, knowing what I wanted to do but putting it off long enough to cement in place certain impressions.

Even before the end I was trying to pretend that Erin's futile effort to sidestep death had never happened, her escapade an episode to be wiped away, erased as if it had been no more than a sweat-induced dream. I would save in memory only the years we had together, and the last few days, and consign her absence when she challenged fate to the realm of a fantasy to be disregarded.

I changed the voice mail message to something bland and lowered the volume. The rest of the morning and afternoon I spent on practical matters--if hassling with getting Erin's name off credit cards and banks accounts, contacting the lawyer, the insurance agent, the investment counselor, and casual acquaintances and relatives (too distant in geography or emotion to have been instantly notified) that at some time or other would want to know about Erin's passing, can be called practical matters. If I was going away I needed to arrange for Kenny and Amy to take care of things at the house, handle the mail, and so forth.

I checked e-mail, something I hadn't done lately. Most messages were quickly deleted, typical junk, but there were some from people who lived too far to have attended the service for Erin; there were electronic sympathy cards—it's come to that—others I saved for later. Then there was one that jarred me.

I didn't recognize the address but the subject line jumped out: 'In The Mist'. I opened it.

Professor: the manuscript recently sent to you is in novel form a summary of my journals, some of which I assume you have been studying, the ones you retrieved from my cache, and others that I have been missing for many years. I know you found files of mine at the university. The journals are more detailed than the manuscript, but I decided, mostly for my own amusement, to summarize centuries of notes into one volume (not yet completed), although I am not certain yet whether I will, or should, publish the book. I remind you again, for you own safety, to not share my possessions with anyone else until we have had the time to chat. Enjoy, and again I look forward to our meeting; make it at your convenience, but if in reply to this message you send me the details of your arrival, I'll arrange for someone to meet you in Athens.

My wife and I express our deepest sympathy to you on the loss of your wife. I know the feeling.
C.B.

So he has helicopters, shadowy observers, secret caches, knows who I am and knows my e-mail; so why am I not surprised at this point? It was time.

I went to the closet where I'd stashed the canisters, and dragged them out and lugged them one by one to the den; it was time to see what was important enough to bury in a safe, deep in the woods, guarded by an alarm which brought out helicopters and men in black cars, but which no one seemed eager to recover. Then I went to the garage and put a new blade in the hacksaw and returned to the den.

Before opening the canisters I went to the front window and examined my surroundings. I was paranoid that faceless men in funereal suits would know that now that Erin was gone, I'd turn my attention to the canisters. They would be right, but there was no one in sight.

Back in the den I hesitated. I began to wonder: since the safe appeared to have a silent alarm that I had activated, prompting the helicopter and the occasional sinister-looking car outside my house, though no one had made an effort to get the canisters, maybe they'll explode if opened, or set off another alarm. That must be it: that's why no one has broken into the house, or confronted me, because they *know* I haven't opened the canisters. Opening them will activate another alarm and then I can expect either the gendarmes knocking on the door or thugs knocking down the door.

I am not the kind of person who feels there is nothing to live for just because a tragedy has struck. But at this moment, two days after my wife had been reduced to ashes, I felt cavalier and madcap, if not rash. I took a deep breath and cut the locks off each canister, then randomly selected one and undid the latch.

No smoke poured out, nothing exploded. Inside the canister a green light blinked on, identical to the one inside the safe. I expected it and was undaunted by it. It told someone that I had finally opened the canisters. Whether they cared or not I guessed I'd fine out soon enough.

Inside the canister were packets wrapped in leather, which in turn were sealed in waterproof bags. The bags were so tightly sealed I needed scissors to cut into one. Then I unwrapped the leather to find another tightly sealed bag, which I also cut. Inside was a stack of one thousand…no, I gasped as I realized they were $10,000 bills of United States currency. Such high-denomination bills were taken out of circulation around 1970, and a mere few hundred have been unaccounted for. Well, here are some of them. I counted them out: one hundred, or one million dollars cash, probably worth even more to collectors.

I ripped open the three other packets: more common, one hundred dollar bills, old ones by date, but in excellent condition. Each packet was the same size, one hundred bills per, I assumed, so the packets of one hundred dollar bills each totaled $10,000, and there were a dozen packets.

There was one other packet, larger, similarly wrapped. I opened it and past being surprised anymore could only grin and shake my head as my eyes beheld dozens of silvery diamonds, glistening like tiny chunks of ice reflecting the high noon sun, even here in my den, where no sunlight shone. I don't know the value of diamonds very well; the ring I gave Erin for our engagement had belonged to my grandmother, because I couldn't afford to buy one, but I laughed out loud as I realized that for weeks a king's ransom in cash and diamonds had been sitting on the floor of the hall closet. The biggest surprise was that no one had made an attempt to claim the treasure.

I replaced the packets in the canister and shut it. If the other three canisters contained the same thing I could not even contemplate what I would do with this fortune. Return to the woods and put it back in the safe in the ground?

I sat on the floor of my den and tried to inspect my life of the last few months as if I was an uninvolved observer, a voyeur, if you will, into a person's life. How did I get myself into this?

I retired from my lifetime vocation, my wife left me, I'm invited to delve through the papers of a famous man who had infamously disappeared 35 years ago, I am led by those papers to a secret hiding place in a forgotten cemetery in the deep woods, where I commit a crime, my wife returns, dying, men in black cars follow me but do not interfere with me, my wife dies, and I find the items I stole from the grave that have been sitting quietly a few feet from me for the last three weeks are worth more than I earned in my entire life.

If Erin had not left, I wouldn't have taken on the project Janice offered me, at least not yet. I would have put it on hold. I wouldn't be sitting on the floor contemplating what would happen if at the next moment the police knocked on the door with a warrant, or men in black wearing hats pulled over their eyes and gloves to avoid fingerprints, burst in, killed me and took the canisters. But Erin would still be gone.

I refilled my coffee cup in the kitchen and returned to the den to see what was in the other canisters. I opened another one, a green light blinked on, and I saw similar packets as in the first canister. I opened one packet to find it contained stacks of Euros in 500 Euro denominations, which equates to, if my math was correct, about $60,000 dollars in US money. I didn't open the other packets.

The next canister also contained packets, similarly wrapped, but of varying sizes. In one I found a batch of passports, some for the United States, some for other countries. The older ones didn't contain a photograph, as photos either weren't yet possible or not yet required at the time. In the ones that did contain a photo the man always bore a strong resemblance to a gentleman I had seen many years ago, Colin Bisseau.

In some photographs he wore glasses, in others, he did not; in some his hair was gray, others brown or black, sometimes cut short, in others longer, and sometimes barely any hair. In one picture he actually wore a crew cut; this passport, in the name of Conrad Barnett, had expired in 1955. No matter the shade of his hair, or its length, the man could not hide his youthful mien.

I flipped through the passports: United States, Great Britain, France, Germany, Canada, Greece, Italy, and Monaco. Various names were used. I found two in the name Conrad Barnett, expired, one in which the man is completely bald. The names in every one I looked at carried the initial 'C' for the first name and 'B' for the last name.

I found one issued in 1906 to Cade Bunyan. This would have been shortly before he traveled to Europe in 1907, searching for Emily. My memory as a historian was that passports weren't universally necessary yet in 1907, but having one facilitated movement in foreign countries. There was no picture, just a description of Bunyan, which indicated he wore a long mustache.

There was a British passport, issued in 1925 to a Clive Barton, merely a folded piece of paper, not a booklet, with a picture of a man sporting a long, dark mustache, wearing a three-piece suit and holding a hat in front of his chest, a barely perceptible smile on his face. The almost identical picture appeared in a Canadian passport, issued in 1946, also to Clive Barton, except in this picture the man was wearing a monocle. Both Bartons, even with mustache and monocle, looked suspiciously like Colin Bisseau. Had Bisseau been collecting memorabilia of ancestors? If so, why bury them? Why, a better question, bury millions of dollars worth of cash and gems?

A notebook about the size of a contemporary passport contained names of banks, account numbers, what appeared to be passwords or codes, a name associated with each account, and dates of activity, none of which were recent.

Finally, there were journals similar to the ones in the file cabinet found in the university sub-basement, except more compact. There were about a dozen in this canister and more booklets than that in the final canister, all enclosed in sealed waterproof bags. There was also a smaller notebook, which stood out due to its bright red cover, so I opened first. In the book was written this:

Over time most of my earlier diaries and journals and notes have faded, been damaged, or thoroughly destroyed. The ones still readable I have copied verbatim into these books, which I believe, will hold up over time.

(A note printed in the margin, obviously entered at a later time, said:)

(Later I had them scanned and saved in a digital version, two copies, which are kept in bank safety deposit boxes, two different banks.)

Notations in poor condition I have copied what I could and in some places added to them as best I could based on my recollections. (I was nearly one hundred years old before I started to keep written records.)

There are two sets: one here, one in a cache in Europe. Only my wife and I, and Marcus, know the location of the one in Europe.

I implore whoever finds this cache, other than someone authorized to retrieve it, and they know who they are, take care of the contents and not be too eager or impatient to share the information before considering the following:

If you have found the cache, but were not authorized to do so, you would not have known how to prevent the alarm from activating. So I know, or persons authorized by me know, that you have been to the cache and have opened the canisters. You will quickly discern that there is a treasure stored in the canisters and you may be tempted to abscond with it.

Trust me, these bills are marked and their serial numbers recorded, and if you use them you will be identified and probably go to jail. In fact, you will be safer if you do go to jail. The diamonds you will similarly have a difficult time selling or using without being identified as a thief.

If you have found this cache as a result of legitimate research, congratulations. In that case I think you will be more interested in the source of the contents of the canisters, and the author (or authors!) of the journals. You will shortly, or already have, received something (I'm not even sure myself at this point in what manner) that will tell you where to find me. I look forward to making your acquaintance.

Sincerely, C.B.

I remember a movie, with Michael Douglas, where for his birthday the Douglas character's brother organizes an elaborate game that puts Douglas into seemingly precarious situations, ones that appear to threaten his life. It's all a ruse; in fact, the story is preposterous. It's an entertaining movie, as much a fantasy as a thriller. So now I began to wonder, would people I know have put together this scheme to liven up my retirement days? Are my friends sucking me in to doing something incredibly silly, something that they'll laugh at while I turn beet red with embarrassment, until I break out in belly laughs of my own?

I sat on the floor for at least ten minutes trying to fathom whether this was a sophisticated, complicated joke, and decided no way would anyone have made up these journals, all the papers, bury fake money and glass baubles in the ground, hoping I'd figure out how to get to them, and be so crass as to not let me in on the prank even after my wife returns home, days from death. It was impossible, just as the other ideas that had been evolving in my mind were equally as impossible.

I decided it was not a childish prank, nor could I accept that there is an island somewhere in the Mediterranean where people live to be three hundred years old. And to prove it, I'd go to Illikaria—if I could find it.

In the evening I went back to where I'd been reading *In The Mist.* It took awhile to find the manuscript—it was on the table next to my chair, where Erin had put it, four days ago, now hidden by the newspaper several days old. Wouldn't it be fun, I mused, if she were going with me on this adventure?

"I don't want to go there anymore; it's overrun with tourists."

"It used to get like that only in the summer."

"Did you know that Hippocrates came from Kos?"

"Yes, dear, I read it in your book."

"Did you know Professor Morgan has opened the canisters?"

"Why did you wait until now to tell me?"

The man shrugged and looked upon the sea where he spied flying fish leap out of the water, reflecting the sun off their bodies, sparkling as if Neptune was strewing diamonds from his underwater home. The man pointed at them and the woman cried out with glee and laughed as the fish crashed back into the water, elegant dives that barely raised a splash.

"We're almost home," the man said, pointing at the island that suddenly appeared on the horizon, so small one had to be almost on top of it to see it.

"These GPS devices are a miracle. I never would have dreamed something like this could be invented."

"You didn't answer my question."

"Oh, I didn't think on it much today, Liz. And when I did remember I didn't want to talk about it. I just wanted to walk around Kos and enjoy a lunch prepared by someone else."

"Are you tired of my cooking?" Liz said, a smile on her face that could have been a squint caused by the bright sunlight.

"Give you a day off from cooking and you tease me!"

"It was a nice lunch. What about his wife, did she die?"

The man nodded.

"What are your people doing?"

"Just observing. I instructed them to leave him alone, as long as he doesn't do anything foolish."

"Like?"

"Like going to the police. Now that he's opened the canisters his every move will be followed."

"Don't you have money in those canisters?"

"And diamonds."

"You're not worried?"

The man chuckled. "He tries to spend the money he's likely to get arrested. It will be interesting to see what he does, but I think he'll come here."

"It's not easy to find Illikaria, even for people who live on the islands."

"Then we'll find out how clever he is."

I read from the beginning to the point I had stopped:

I was born in the year 1520, give or take a year; I was never sure and we didn't keep track of dates as carefully then as we do now.

My birth took place on a farm in the fall, when the air was crisp and the sky muddy, at least that's what I was told. It rained on the day I was born and the roof of the house leaked and my father had to climb up and put a blanket over the area that was dripping water down onto my mother as she gave birth to me.

My given name was Casmir Baczynski, or so I was told, though I'm not sure of the correct spelling of my surname as I never saw my name written out.

Our home, a wooden structure near a forest, a kilometer from a village of any size, was in an area near where the borders of Poland, Hungary, and the German Empire met. My father said he was born in Russia but his mother was French. My mother was Polish, she thinks, but isn't sure. So I am an amalgamation of several ethnicities, as were most people I knew when I was young.

My father worked several trades: at times he was a farmer, then a tanner; he was also a builder (of houses, barns, fences). He drank heavily, a type of vodka made from potatoes. All the men drank heavily, most evenings, but especially so at the end of the work week when they gathered to drink and tell stories, mostly exaggerations, to laugh and eventually to stagger back to their homes or fall asleep in the house where they were meeting.

Occasionally, one of the besotted men would attempt to walk home during a winter storm, get lost, fall and freeze to death. Sometimes their body wasn't found until the thaw. That may be what happened to my father, but his body was never found, so we assumed he simply tired of us and left. That was when I was twelve or thirteen years old. Six months later my mother died in childbirth, along with the baby.

My surviving brother and two sisters, all younger than I, continued to live in the house and we managed to grow enough food and make enough money from doing odd jobs to keep ourselves alive, until one day, while I was at a village trying to find work as a tanner, bandits came to the house, killed my siblings, took what food there was, and burned down the house. I buried my brother and sisters, retrieved some tools that I dug out of the charred remains of the house, and began to walk.

I can't say much about what else was going on in the world at this time from personal knowledge—my world consisted of poor villages, woodlands, farms, peasants like myself, and spending most days looking for work and food. Later, however, in trying to put my life in perspective with what else was happening in the world I became a ravenous reader of history. So for example, at the time my siblings died in the mud of what is now either Slovakia or the Czech Republic, in England Jane Seymour died, somewhat like my mother, of complications following the birth of a son who would become King Edward VI.

Since I was nearly always hungry I assumed that was the normal state of affairs. Later I learned that in the 16th and 17th centuries southern and Eastern Europe suffered from frequent famine. As I made my way west I came upon larger towns and found that food was more plentiful for anyone willing to work hard, as I was.

I grew to an adult but instead of looking older the process of aging seemed to come to a stop. I remember one morning, when I was around twenty-five years old, waking up feeling so refreshed and strong and healthy it was as if I'd been given a new body. Scars I had accumulated were gone, bruises, sore muscles, all gone. I remember the morning but I didn't understand if it meant anything; years later I would realize what had happened to me.

In a town near Paris I met a pretty French girl and received my education in the differences between men and women. Soon she was pregnant and we made a home together, me working as a tanner in Paris at the shop of a man who called himself William Tanner, who had been kind enough to give me employment. Nicole, who I considered my wife though we were never formally married, tended the house and the farm, growing vegetables to go with the meat I was able to purchase in Paris, or the chickens we raised.

Nicole and I had six children, three of whom died before their first birthday. Of the other three, one, a daughter, married when she was fourteen and her husband took her to Lithuania, where he said he had family. I never saw her again.

My two surviving sons both learned to be tanners and eventually we opened our own business, making a living for the three families, my sons having married and become fathers by this time.

Nowadays people read or hear that the life expectancy during what is called the Middle Ages, was shockingly short, an average of around thirty years. That is true to a point, because of the high mortality rate for infants and children. Even by the early 17th century, in England, two-thirds of children didn't survive to their fourth birthday.

But it is estimated that a male of the English aristocracy, having survived to his 21st birthday, could expect to live another 50 years. Of course, for the working class folk who toiled day in and day out and didn't always have the best food and lived in conditions of sanitation that today would be consider appalling, life rarely lasted much past the half-century mark.

Eventually people I had known for years were dying all around me; my friends and wife aged, but I didn't.

By the time my wife was an estimated forty years old she was always tired, often ill, her hair was gray and her hands wrinkled and bent from years of farming, cooking, cleaning, and chopping wood. I, on the other hand, was never sick, always felt rejuvenated in the morning on awakening, no matter how hard I had worked or how spent I had been the day before, looked as young as the day I'd met Nicole, she claimed, and I could not agree or contend, my hair still thick and brown, and my hands strong and young-looking. Even my sons began to look older than me.

By the time I was slightly over fifty years old (I remember this because I knew the years now; it was 1574, the year Henry, who had been elected King of Poland, returned to France to succeed his brother on the throne); people began to talk about me: why does Casmir look so young? What does he do to keep himself looking so good, younger than his sons? Does he have a magic elixir?

When some began to ask, "Has Casmir made a pact with the devil," and crowds gathered near our home, mumbling and cursing, and business at the tannery began to suffer, I knew it was time to leave. I bade my sons to take care of their mother and, cowardly as it may seem, I left my family, as my father had done. At the time, and most times even centuries later when I think back on those days, I felt I was doing the best thing for them by leaving, else they might experience tangential wrath from the uneasy mobs.

I had accumulated a small amount of money that afforded me passage to England. By good fortune I met a man who was investing in shipbuilding, as there was a growing demand for ships for explorations and colonization of the land called the 'New World', or America, in honor of the explorer Amerigo Vespucci, an Italian explorer. (Years later when I studied history I read that Vespucci actually

242

explored what became known as South America, but not the northern part of the continent that now includes the United States.)

At the moment we exchanged greetings I decided to call myself by a different name: I chose Charles Barrett, a name that popped into my head. From then on I always chose a name that used the same initials, a quirk developed for no other reason than it helps me to remember names I have used.

The man I met, name of Carver, convinced me to invest with him in a shipbuilding enterprise. A bit leery—I was actually thinking I should go to this new land across the ocean—I decided to take the risk, figuring if I go bust I can still travel to America. Carver, a man of my same age, but of much older appearance, said that a young man like me will have plenty of time to go exploring, but now I should work hard and make money and find a wife and start a family. I invested all but what I might need for passage to America, if it came to that.

And so, good reader, if you have made it this far I hope you do not think of me as a hallucinating madman, or a pedestrian fiction writer with a bizarre imagination. I don't intend the story of my life to be a history lesson—there are thousands of good books you can read for that purpose, but rather a story of how myself and others like me (we call ourselves Immortals, or IMs, though whether we are truly *immortal is not yet known), and how we deal with this strange and wonderful, and at times demanding, gift of long life. The Fountain of Youth does not promise happiness, but it does provide surprises.*

I did not think the writer mad or hallucinatory, but he certainly has an active imagination. I smiled and read the chapter listings...

1. *Birth and Early Life*
2. *Learning About Ships*
3. *Learning About My Gift*
4. *Learning About Wealth*
5. *Traveling Across Europe*
6. *My First Visit To The New World*
7. *I Meet Other IMs*
8. *Learning About Money and Economics*
9. *My Second Visit To America*
10. *Travels in America*
11. *Friends and Lovers*
12. *Living History*
13. *Rendezvous*
14. *Wars and More Wars*
15. *Meeting, Losing, and Finding Her*
16. *Fame Can Be a Burden*
17. *Meditations: The Gift That Keeps on Giving*

18. How Long The Future?

I jumped to the chapter entitled, *Living History.*

I don't mean to boast about note-worthy historical events I have experienced, or famous people I have met. Any such occasions would not have seemed historically important to me at the time, any more than knowing a person in high school who later becomes famous.

So in 1605 when I met William Shakespeare and saw a production of "Macbeth" (maybe the first, I don't recall), it did not enthrall or fascinate me anymore than meeting other writers, artists, politicians, etc. of the era. Many common folk met Shakespeare without thinking he would, five centuries later, be regarded as one of the greatest writers, arguably the greatest, in the English language. In fact, I saw several of his plays at the Globe Theater and more than once shared conversation and a pint or two with him and others after a performance. Looking backwards in time I am impressed, not by anything I did, but by my good fortune.

I smiled and skipped to the chapter, *Meeting, Losing and Finding Her.* I was startled to find that the first few pages were a virtual repeat of the journal entries of Cade Bunyan in 1907, when Bunyan met the woman who at first said her name was Etta Place, then quickly amended that to Emily Parker. Once I was over my initial surprise I began to put the pieces of this jigsaw puzzle together.

Colin Bisseau had been working on his novel long before he disappeared in Alaska. The manuscript must have been given to someone to proof read, or Colin's friend Jay had it and someone else came across it after Jay's death, and it lay around for decades, until now, when that person learned I was going through Bisseau's papers.

That still didn't explain the safe buried in a forgotten cemetery in the woods, stuffed with money and diamonds. But that could be explained as part of Bisseau's eccentricity. Maybe the treasure was somehow related to his parents or other ancestors; maybe Bisseau buried it and later couldn't locate it, or maybe he intended to retrieve it after the Alaska trip. Or it might be part of the mysterious 'resources' mentioned in Bisseau's journals.

In any case I decided I would amuse myself by reading how Cosmo Ballantrie describes the reunion between Cade Bunyan and Emily, that is, Etta…or is it between Colin Bisseau and the woman he married, and disappeared with, Elizabeth?

14. REUNION

As the Governor's Special Advisor on Stqte Education I traveled frequently to every corner of the state. As someone who has traveled all over the world, more than once, in fact, and by virtually every device invented by humankind, moving often and rarely having reason to unpack everything in my suitcase, hop-scotching from city to city, hotel to hotel, was not a burden, though I could see my assistant wearied easily and would not be long for this position.

On this particular trip to the far northwestern section of the State, I made plans to meet Marcus in Chicago, to dine and review our mutual financial situations, which we had not had opportunity to do so in over three months, my fault entirely.

We met at Maximilian's Steak House, in one of the suburban cities, which Marcus assured me served the best steaks in the Chicago area.

The food was excellent, the wine equally so, and Marcus and I enjoyed pleasant conversation. We arranged to meet in the morning at my hotel suite so we could complete our business.

We were sipping cognac when my eye caught the movement of people rising from their table. A woman who had been seated with her back to me, so I had not had the chance to see her face, turned as she stood and I saw her straight on, and she saw me. Both of us gaped in astonishment; I almost dropped my snifter, which still contained about twenty dollars worth of fine cognac.

The woman put a hand over her chest, as if to steady herself, while her companion, a white-haired gentleman who looked much older than she, gently guided her by the arm towards the exit. I started to rise from my seat, then slumped down, confused about what to do. The woman looked back at me as she went through the doorway.

"What is it, Colin? You look like you've seen…"

"It was her, Marcus, and I'm sure she recognized me."

"Who, Colin? Who was it?"

"Emily, Marcus. Remember, I told you about her."

"Emily? Oh, that was, what, Colin, fifty years ago!"

"No, it was 67 years, Marcus. Sixty-six years and seven months actually."

"Who were you then?"

"Cade Bunyan. She is one I especially remember. There was no one like her, and no one since."

"She left you, didn't she? And you went after her, to Europe."

"Now I know why she left me."

"Because…?"

"We were in love, Marcus, truly so. And we didn't recognize each other as IMs. Given more time I think we would have, but she left me rather than prolong our affair and have to hurt me later. I'm sure she felt it would be easier to do sooner instead of later, when our emotional tie had swelled."

"I do remember. You were in New York, I was here, in Chicago. I kept waiting for you to join me and you kept saying you were delayed. So now you're going to dump me for her again, aren't you," Marcus said, but at least he was smiling.

I rose to leave. "Don't worry, I'll still meet you tomorrow. Emily won't leave me this time; I could see it on her face."

"Maybe the old gent's her husband."

I shook my head. "I doubt it, but even if so, he's much older than… you know what I mean. If I have to I'll wait for her, we just need to know that we are both alive and well."

"You sound giddy, Colin, I've never seen you like this."

I smiled broadly and realized that the other diners were staring at me; I hadn't realized I'd been talking so loud. "Don't let the rest of this cognac go to waste, Marcus. I'll see you in the morning."

Emily and her companion were standing in the lobby conversing with the couple they had dined with. She saw

249

me, smiled and kept glancing at me, as if trying to match my face with her memory of someone from her past. I knew I looked slightly different as by now I was tinting the edges of my hair gray, to look more like the nearly fifty-year old man I was supposed to be, not the twenty-six year old Cade Bunyan at the time he met Emily.

She, on the other hand, looked exactly as I remembered her; it's my story so I can plagiarize from myself, using the description from Cade Bunyan's 1907 journal:

'She had light brown hair, shoulder length under a hat that, like most ladies' hats, does more to distract from a woman's good features than adds to them, was fairly tall, slim and sported a very fine figure. She was striking.'

This time she wasn't wearing a hat, so I could see her face clearly. It is indeed a strange sensation to feel one's heart palpitate in excitement; fear, yes, I'd experienced fear, but astonishment, illogical emotional longing—no, never.

I nodded to her and with my eyes motioned towards the ladies' rest room. She excused herself from her group and I moved to accidentally, as it were, intercept her near where a large plant was placed aside a sofa, unoccupied at the moment.

"It is you, isn't it, Emily?"

"And you are, sir?" She said coyly.

I smiled. "I'm Colin Bisseau now, Emily. I was Cade Bunyan in 1907." I fanned a hand in front of my face. "I've tried to make myself look older for my present circumstances."

I could see from her eyes she was nearly sure, her mind working out how anyone else could have know the name Cade Bunyan, but she needed one last bit of proof.

"We first met in New York, outside the office of Mr. Carswell. You dropped your handkerchief, the one embroidered with the initials, E.P. for Etta Place."

She stared wide-eyed now, her eyes as bright as the high beams of an oncoming vehicle in the deepest woods at the darkest hour of the night.

A hand at her throat, she said, haltingly, "And I lived…?"

"At the Dakota." I said, triumphantly, as if I'd answered the $64,000 question.

"Cade!" The woman's eyes widened and a hand went to her throat. "I would never have left you had I known! How could I have known?"

"I understand. I worried myself, getting involved with you. I had vowed never to get involved with a mortal again, but I couldn't help myself. I began to think, could you be like me, but it seemed so unlikely…" I nodded my head towards where the man she was with still stood talking to two other people.

"I have to get back. He's only a friend, dear…oh, he's a dirty old man, but he's rich."

"You don't need him, Emily. Money is not an issue. Get rid of him."

"I don't want to hurt him. I need to get back. I'm in room 309. Give me a few moments; oh, I go by Elizabeth now."

She returned to her companion just as he was ending his conversation. He smiled at her and she smiled back, took him by the arm and they moved towards the elevators. Emily turned her head and smiled at me and blew a kiss. I copied her actions and was mortified to find Marcus standing next to me.

"I'm glad no one but me saw the Governor's special envoy blow a kiss at a young woman strolling off with her sugar daddy."

"Hmmph. It's her and I will see her later. But since you're still around, let's go finish our drink, and I'll tell you more about her."

For reasons I can't even explain to myself I was reticent to make journal entries regarding Emily other than the notation that we had found each other. It is so personal with her, more so than with any one I've ever known.

We were awake until dawn, talking and laughing, believe it or not, about what had happened in our lives these last sixty-seven years.

There was no escaping it now, what I had suspected since the first few days of reading the journals found in the file cabinet: the author was claiming he was all three people, Colt Boston, Cade Bunyan, and Colin Bisseau—and who knows how many other identities; I'd lost count of the aliases I noted on the passports, but I would make a list of them and research the names.

Acknowledging that I was probably being foolish, I decided I was going to obey my gut feeling and seek out the author of *In The Mist,* and, likely, the fabricator of the journal entries mixed in with the legitimate Colin Bisseau papers. I went back to the e-mail from the enigmatic C.B. The part about someone meeting me was unsettling. Not that I had any idea how to get to Illikaria on my own, but I didn't want to be kidnapped and never heard of again. I mused that if I were in danger, I'd have met it already, close to home, so I sent a reply:

"C.B.

Will send travel arrangements as soon as I have made them. In the continuing interest of my safety, your possessions will be placed with a trusted friend who will be advised to take them to 'proper authorities' if I have not returned by a certain date."

I hit 'Send'. I was bluffing because I was unsure what to do with Bisseau's papers, and especially, the money and diamonds. Best idea I had was to store them in my home safe, built into the floor under the carpet in the main closet. A determined burglar would find the safe given enough time, but I don't think I'd be upset if I was relieved of what was becoming a burden. If I die on this trip, my trustee (Kenny) will get the shock of his life when he opens the safe. The journals won't fit in the safe so I'd take those to the university and store them in my office in the new file cabinet, the one with a working lock. Some of the less vital Bisseau-Bunyan-Boston documents I'd put back in the file cabinet from the sub-basement, that long-lost cabinet which had pulled me into this mystery as much as if it had come alive and sprouted tentacles and dragged me across town.

I went online to make plane reservations. The price gagged me but what else am I going to spend my money on now? That done I searched for anything on Illikaria Island. There wasn't much.

I learned that it is an island of the Dodecanese Islands, the southernmost chain of Greek islands. It is situated in the general area of where the Sea of Crete meets the southern end of the Aegean Sea, about midway between the islands of Crete and Rhodes, roughly seventy-five miles from either. Illikaria is about one-half square miles in size with an unknown population, but in the neighborhood of two hundred.

Based on the introduction to *In The Mist* most of the population must live on pensions or savings or help from children, though I doubt there's much to spend money on.

One problem in my quest is that there is no regular transportation to and from the island. Re-reading the introduction again I noted that the writer said there are monthly ferries, so I might get to Athens and find out I have to wait a week or more for the next one. Or I could send C.B. my ETA and see if he follows through on having someone meet me.

Industry, what there was of it, include olives and olive oil, grapes and wine, cheese, wool from a small heard of sheep, and fishing. The women knit clothes from the wool and send them to Crete or other islands where they are sold to tourists. Some of the old fishermen, if their calloused hands are not too bent from a lifetime of tangling with nets and other tools of the fisherman's trade, still make or repair nets. Some produce is grown for local consumption. The website info indicated that cheese and fish are sold to residents of equally tiny islands in the vicinity, or bartered for other goods.

The phone continued to ring in the evening. People meant well, I appreciate that, and it was a good element of the grieving process to talk to people and to let them express their empathy. I didn't want company, but on the other hand it's good advice that a person not be alone if they get depressed after the loss of a loved one.

Janice was one of those callers. Don't worry, I told her, I'm not going to do anything foolish. Had I hinted that I hadn't eaten properly for a few days I'm sure she would have rushed over and fixed me a gourmet meal.

It is also good, I reasoned, not to ignore what has happened: life isn't the same anymore; I hurt, I am close to depression, and I miss Erin now more than I did when she was traipsing around the world trying to find a quick fix. I doubt I'll ever get over the regret that I hadn't been more forceful in preventing her from going, or insisting that she explain exactly what she was thinking. At the time I thought I had been as insistent as I could be, but now I wondered. So I was going to allow myself to hurt for awhile, but I was determined not to let it absorb me.

I knew about the so-called stages of grief one can experience. Sipping a glass of chardonnay, I reconsidered how I had dealt with those stages.

Certainly I had at first denied that Erin's illness was fatal, but the doctors and Erin's weakening condition soon convinced me. Though my emotions bounced around, angry, depressed, fright and acquiescence, all over the board, I hadn't had time to wallow in my feelings while Erin was still alive; acceptance is what I felt I was dealing with right now, this day, this minute. I did wonder if my lack of intense outward show of emotion indicated I was not as struck by the loss of my wife as I should be.

I called Kenny, but more to speak to Amy, who had experience in dealing with people suffering traumatic personal losses.

"Do you think I loved Erin, Amy? From what you observed?"

"Yes, Morgan, I always thought you two loved each other very much. I have no way to measure love; no one does. It's so…personal."

"And do I act the way a person should act at this time?"

"Oh, Morg, there's no correct way to act, to show your grief. No one knows how he or she'll respond to what you've been through until it happens. Don't think you have to cry and throw a tantrum and curse God and the world, make a show of it so people will say, 'Wow, he really loved his wife'

"At the same time, don't ignore the pain you feel; if you try to pretend that you don't hurt, it'll pop up later, on some day like an anniversary, and you could topple into depression."

"I must admit I do find myself thinking about what I could have done, or we could have done."

"Don't go too far with that, Morg. Have you got any plans?"

"Yes, actually, as soon as I take care of a few things at home I'm going to go back to working at the project on the Bisseau papers, which will involve some travel, so I'm

257

hoping you and Kenny can pick up my mail and keep an eye on the house."

"Okay, as long as you promise to stay in touch daily."

"How about I promise to try?"

"Do, don't just try."

The next morning I gathered up the journals from the canisters, took them to my office and locked them in the file cabinet along with the other Bisseau-Boston-Bunyan papers. Then I picked up cups of coffee and brought them to Janice's office at about the time in the morning I knew she was headed to the café for her second or third cup. I didn't need to see Janice or ask permission, I didn't even need to tell her I was going to Greece, but that would be rude.

"Morg, how nice, I didn't expect to see you so soon."

"I got a lot done yesterday. Here," I set down a cup of coffee, no cream, one sugar, the way she always takes it, on her desk, and I sat down, holding my own cup with two hands.

"Are you coming back to work on the papers already?"

I shook my head and I felt a droll grin break out on my face, as if I knew what I was going to say would cause her to look at me as if I'd grown a third eye.

"What is it, Morgan?"

"I'm going to Greece."

Her mouth dropped.

"Greece? Just like that? When?"

"Friday. I've made the reservation."

Janice's frown expressed her confusion.

"I can understand wanting get away for a spell, but how did you set on Greece...oh, the package...does that have anything to do with it?"

I nodded. "Yes, everything. In fact, it's related to my work with the Bisseau papers, so if you chose to have the university fund pay for my trip, I won't argue."

Janice leaned back in her chair and laughed. "Morg, I'd have a hard time explaining that, unless you have a rock-solid reason."

I drank from my coffee, stalling, deciding how much to tell her. I definitely was not going to tell her about the cemetery, and certainly not about the contents of the canisters.

"The box from Greece contained a manuscript of a novel. I don't know who wrote it, but from what I read so far, I'm sure it was written by the same person who authored the journals in the file cabinet. In fact, I'm sure it was Colin Bisseau."

"So who sent the manuscript to you? And why from Greece, after all the years Bisseau's been missing?"

I shook my head. "I'm not sure but I'm curious to find out. The name on the manuscript, Cosmo Ballantrie, is also the name of an author of a book on the history of the Mediterranean, but I don't know anything about him. And seriously, I don't expect the fund to pay for this. I'm probably on a wild-goose chase and will make a fool of myself, but a visit to the Greek islands sounds like a nice getaway; it may help get my mind clear."

An alluring smile blossomed on Janice's face. She looked at a paper on her desk, as if what she was going to say was of no real importance, that she was humoring me while she kept on working.

"If you could come up with some solid evidence to indicate a trip to Greece might explain what happened to Colin Bisseau, I might get the fund to pay for two tickets."

I chuckled, and drank again from the cup of coffee.

"Janice, I can't even give myself a logical reason for going, much less for you to join me. Besides, it may be weeks before I can find who I'm looking for. The fund can't cover two of us gallivanting around."

"Besides," she added before I could get to it, "it wouldn't look good, the two of us tromping off to Greece only days after…" She didn't need to finish the thought.

I nodded. "Yes, but I'll keep in touch; promise."

She switched to the tone she uses for business-like discussions, the flirting over. "Morgan, deep inside your gray matter is there a somewhat fuzzy idea, not quite a certainty but a hunch, that Colin Bisseau is still alive, living on some remote island in whatever sea they've got over there?"

"He'd only be ninety-one years old, Janice. You know, some of those people in the Mediterranean live a long time."

"Ninety-one…and Erin got fifty-seven years; hardly seems fair, does it Morg?"

"You could fill an encyclopedia with things that aren't fair."

"Does it make you angry?"

I put my coffee cup on her desk and rose from the chair.

"I haven't thought of it that way; if you care for someone it doesn't matter how short or long their lifespan, they're gone too soon."

I picked up the cup, swirled the remaining coffee and took a sip, but it had lost its flavor.

"If I could figure out where to direct anger, I'd be downright pissed, Jan. It hurts, it's a hurt I've never felt before; I suppose no one can gauge how something like this will hurt until it happens, and then it's not something you can rate. Like love, or any emotion, you can't put a caliper on your feelings and measure them. How was it for you when Dave left?"

"Dave didn't die, Morg. He stood up one day and walked out of my life with nary an explanation. I was stunned and demolished, too blown away to be angry. I got

angry later. I threw some of his things against the wall."
She laughed. "Had to get the wall fixed and painted."

"Sorry, didn't mean to bring up a sore subject."

"It's alright, it was a long time ago."

"I'm going to go find Kenny; why don't you catch up with us later and we'll go to lunch?"

Janice nodded and allowed a semi-smile. "Sure, later."

I decided not to e-mail C.B. with my arrival plans. I had a hunch he'd know anyway; he seems to know my every move, so if he wants to have someone meet me in Athens, I can't stop him. If not, getting to Illikaria might present a problem. But then, I've got nothing but time.

15. ILLIKARIA

The most convenient flight I found out of Indy was one that stopped in New York City and from there direct to Athens, arriving at 9:30 in the morning. I landed in Athens hungry, grimy, and tired. Fortunately I didn't have to wait for luggage: I had packed light, bringing only a carry-on bag.

I spent much of the flight reading *In The Mist*. The novel had a clever idea: a man claims that there are people who for no known reason stop aging when they are young and live for hundreds of years. The writer claimed to have been born nearly 500 years ago, and described his life from the 16th century up until the 21st. Some of the stories were expanded renditions of the incidents I'd read about in the papers of Colin Bisseau, Cade Bunyan, and Colt Boston.

The author, Cosmo Ballantrie, wrote, in the chapter, *Learning About My Gift*:

...every twenty to thirty years I would pick up from where I was living and working and move to another city or country, change my name, and start over again. I did this because as everyone I knew aged and I didn't, superstitious minds began to shun me, just like the first time, when I left Nicole, or worse, I'd feel threatened. I

learned to live frugally and save money because when I had to move, or make a 'change', it often took weeks before I could find work and a place to live. More than once I was assailed by highwaymen and robbed of all my valuables. Thus, I began to set up caches where I would hide a portion of my money. As I grew older and as civilization became more sophisticated, so did my methods of earning and hiding assets and changing my identity, and holding my resources in several places under multiple guises.

As I will describe in more detail in Chapter Seven, eventually I met another person like myself, one who continues to be my most trusted friend, up to this day in the 21st Century; and then another, maybe one every fifty years. They, like me, were cautious to a fault, wary of revealing themselves, all having had the experience of being thought of as an evil or dangerous person because they never seemed to age, or even get sick.

As a way for people like us, who began to call ourselves, jokingly at first, 'Immortals', or IMs for short, to meet other IMs and to gain from each other's talents and experiences, gatherings were planned, eventually referred to as The Rendezvous, held every ten years somewhere in the world, a different place each time, secluded from common tourist traffic. This enabled IMs to meet other IMs and talents could be exchanged when needed: we were a diverse force of engineers, doctors, financiers, teachers,

*tradesmen, nurses, accountants and, as important as any
other profession, forgers.*

The writer went on to explain that once it became
necessary to carry identification, such as driver's licenses
and passports, to acquire credit cards, or identify oneself
for any of a hundred reasons as society became more
complicated, an IM could not honestly obtain what he
needed whenever it was time to make a change. Most, like
the author, maintained more than one identity at a time.
The author claimed that some IMs tended to stay in the
same country and not risk carrying a forged passport, but
even they needed to move and get new credit cards,
licenses, and so forth, even a new, professionally forged
birth certificate, every few decades, and it necessitated
knowing people who could help them obtain items vital in
modern society. In effect, every thirty or forty years they
had to manufacture a new identity.

The author claimed he had been Colin Bisseau (and
before that Cade Bunyan, Colt Boston and numerous
others) and had fallen into a trap that IMs all advised
against: becoming too prominent. By 1980 he had been in
public view for nearly forty years, ever since his actions
during the Battle of the Bulge earned him national acclaim,
and he still looked as young as he did at that time, except
for dying his hair gray, using makeup to age his skin, and
wearing glasses although his vision was perfect.

Rather than just disappear, as he used to do the first few centuries of his life, Colin Bisseau wanted to convince people he had died, and then he intended to lay low for a lengthy spell. I guess he found a hideaway on his own little island. I was eager to meet this creative person, whether he be a ninety-one year old Colin Bisseau or someone else who had carved out an interesting book idea.

The first thing I did on arrival was to go to a restroom to splash cold water on my face and brush the old-socks taste out of my mouth. Then I stopped at an airport shop and purchased underwear, socks and toiletries, which I stuffed into my bag.

The airport was bustling, or more accurately, it was a hectic scene of international travelers dashing around as if they urgently needed to find a toilet. The babbling of multiple languages might not have been irritating if I was in a familiar environment, but not knowing where I needed to go now that I was in Greece, I was apprehensive and for a few seconds I wondered if I should hop on the first plane back to the US without setting foot outside the airport.

As I made my way, flowing with the crowd, like salmon fighting the rapids to advance upstream, trying to figure out where to find local transportation, my head and eyes flitted left and right and around, as I felt I was being watched and followed by C. B. or his minions.

So when a man approached me and said my name I almost dropped my bag and ran. But he gently took my coat sleeve between two fingers and said my name again, with a question mark at the end.

"Yes, I'm Professor Miller; who are you?"

"Mr. Cosmo sent me. He asked me to help you find your way, if you wished me to help."

"You know where I want to go?"

"Si, oh, no I mean yes, sorry, sometimes I get my languages mixed up. You wish to go to Mr. Cosmo, he is far away, it will take two days."

"I'll need a hotel, and I don't have any reservations."

"No, no, you come with me." He waved his arms in the air, beckoning me to follow him, the rosary-like worry beads he held in one hand swinging around his head as he gestured.

To simply accept a stranger's offer of transportation in a foreign country where one not only can't speak the language but can't even decipher the signs, Greek being a language of its own, would on first appearance seem crazy, but my life was not the same one it had been for its first sixty and a few more birthdays. My life was turned up and over and out, it was taking on, or being taken, on a E-ticket thrill ride, so I dutifully followed the man.

"What do I call you?" I shouted, straining to keep pace with him.

"Come quickly, we need to get taxi; I have one waiting."

Then he turned and said, "Zorba, you know, like the movie."

I laughed and lengthened my stride.

As Zorba explained it, we would take the taxi to Zea, a section of the port of Piraeus, which serves Athens, and from there a hydrofoil to Iraklion, which is the largest city on the island of Crete.

"How long?" I asked, meaning to get to Crete.

He shrugged, "Ah, five hours," he said, shaking his head and waving the hand that caressed the worry beads, meaning, I interpreted, five hours, give or take an hour.

The one other time I'd been in Greece the main method of island hopping was by ferry, always crowded and slow and suffused with the odor of sweaty bodies.

"Why two days to get to Illikaria?"

"We have to spend one night in Iraklion, then we will get a boat, from a friend of Mr. Cosmo. There are no boats, most days, to Illikaria. You have to find someone, a good sailor, to take you there."

"And you found a good sailor?"

"Hmm, yes, Mr. Cosmo told me where to find him, tomorrow, no hurry, today we go Iraklion; you will like it."

The taxi ride to the dock at Zea, bumpy, with jolts, sharp turns and skids, amidst horns beeping, brakes squealing and drivers and pedestrians cursing each other, did not take long.

"Hurry, hurry," Zorba urged me. "Boat leave soon."

I grabbed my bag and trotted after Zorba, who was already ten yards ahead of me. I glanced at the taxi driver but he seemed satisfied so I assumed Zorba had paid him in advance.

I ran to catch up to Zorba and we joined a mass of people inching along until we were on a gangway that led to the hydrofoil. Zorba handed me a ticket, which I presented to a young lady when she asked for it and Zorba shoved me with his hand on my back.

"Get inside," he ordered.

As best he could in his broken English, Zorba explained that the hydrofoil goes much faster than the old ferries, which are still much in use, and it can be exciting and people like to go outside to better experience the speed and the rush of the wind and to take pictures. But he cautioned that it was dangerous because the ride isn't always as smooth as one might expect, and a sudden bounce on the waves can send cameras, hats, and even people tumbling to an injury, or worse, overboard.

We claimed seats and I decided I wouldn't leave my seat except to use the facilities. Other than that, I dozed through most of the trip, though the nodding of my head and the noise from the boat and the jabbering of passengers made for an oft interrupted and unsatisfactory nap. It wasn't exactly the travel I had envisioned for Erin and I in our post-retirement years, but it was all I had.

Near as I could figure it was about four o'clock local time when we got to Crete, to the city of Iraklion, spelled Heraklion on English maps.

Zorba waved down a taxi, spoke to the driver in Greek, and in a few minutes we were at a hotel. Again Zorba spoke in Greek to the desk clerk and we were led to our rooms. No sign-in, no passport, no credit card.

"Who is taking care of this?" I asked.

"No worry, Mr. Cosmo, he takes care of his friends. You rest now, I will come for you at nine o'clock, we will go have good Greek food."

Like a sheep I followed Zorba and the bellhop to my room and waited while Zorba tipped the young man.

"Is room okay?" asked Zorba, his hand and worry beads waving in the air.

"It's fine, thank you."

He bowed and said, "I will be back for you."

I felt like I'd been on a Ferris wheel or the teacups at Disneyland. I stood in the middle of the room, a nicely decorated one: over the bed was a picture of a beach scene with waves slapping the shoreline, the shadows indicating a setting sun; a filled ice bucket was on the desk, and next to it a chilled bottle of Rosè wine in a bucket of its own; a vase with yellow and white flowers; a Queen-sized bed with layers of plush pillows neatly stacked, and a large screen television.

I stripped off my clothes and went into the bathroom. I let hot water stream down my back and head for five minutes, then scrubbed and shampooed. Contrary to the best advice for dealing with a time change of several hours, I lay down on the bed after the shower in the thick, soft robe I'd found in the closet; I only intended to rest my eyes for a few minutes. I was asleep instantly.

When I awoke a dusky yellow light, filtered by the curtains, flowed into the room. Dust particles flit through the rays like mad amoeba under a microscope. Soft music was playing outside and for a few seconds I didn't know where I was. I could have been anywhere in the world but I grinned inwardly when my mind settled and I remembered that I was on the wildest goose chase of all time; maybe I was 'finding myself', as Erin had said, her excuse to run away from home—for me or from me I still struggled with.

The clock read 8:57 so I rose from bed and hurried to dress, assuming Zorba would be prompt. He was, as a knock on the door before I was finished dressing proved. I let him in hoping he wouldn't be in a big rush to get moving. He wasn't; in fact, when he saw the wine, he glanced at me with eyebrows raised, and I nodded. He picked up the corkscrew and opened the bottle while I finished dressing.

"We have time," Zorba said, "it is early for dining."

So we sat and drank the wine, the Rosè a pleasant variety I was not familiar with. I tried to make conversation with Zorba but his answers were evasive. When I asked about Mr. Cosmo, he seemed wary, only saying, over and over, that Mr. Cosmo was a good man, a nice man, rich, who takes good care of his friends. I asked if Mr. Cosmo came to Crete on occasion and Zorba seemed unsure how to answer. He shook his head no, and then he said, "He comes when he not tell anyone, and he do nice things for people; spends lots of money."

"Is he an old man?" I asked.

Zorba recoiled in confusion. "Oh no, no, he is a young man, handsome young man."

As an afterthought he added, "He has a pretty wife, American lady, very pretty."

Zorba downed his wine and suggested we should now go to dinner. I was starving so I eagerly followed him.

We dined at a restaurant that specialized in meats, especially lamb, grilled or roasted on a spit. I don't recall the name, but it was a lively place inside a covered meat and produce market. At least it seemed lively, but Zorba claimed it would be more fun and noisier later in the evening.

I let Zorba order and we started with ouzo, the traditional Greek anise-flavored liqueur, which was served with appetizers of small fish, olives and feta cheese. We then enjoyed a Greek salad and wonderful warm bread on which I poured a generous dose of olive oil.

Zorba ordered a chilled white wine and he suggested we get a variety of foods so I could sample the local cuisine. Our main course consisted of bits of lamb, a square of moussaka, four or five types of cheese, olives, fish, calamari, and a variety of roasted vegetables. It was delicious and I insisted on paying but Zorba said it was taken care of; he spoke rapidly in Greek to the waiter, who bowed and backed away, as if he'd discovered he was in the presence of royalty.

"Mr. Cosmo take care?" I said. Zorba grinned and nodded.

I slept like an innocent child that night, the boom of jet lag lowered on me, but was awake before dawn, a bit light-headed. I dressed and went for a walk.

The horizon was unveiling the first hint of a new sun, the air was clean and the odor of fresh pastries wafted through the air and enticed my senses. A few people were scooting about, setting up produce stands or sweeping down the sidewalk in front of their stores. Dogs sniffed at the doors of the cafes, on the lookout for an easy touch who would throw them a piece of bread or meat left over from last night. A café open to the street was serving coffee and the aroma was strong and sweet and I realized I had yet to acquire Euros. I didn't think I could tell the vendor that Mr. Cosmo would take of it.

I kept walking until I found an ATM and knowing I'd pay a heftier fee than at a bank, I purchased Euros; the coffee was too tempting to wait for the banks to open. The way Greece was going these days I wondered if the banks would open at all today.

Zorba found me a few minutes later and he smiled but scrunched his mouth in a way that scolded me for going out alone.

"I would have come for you, Professor. You should have waited."

"I'm a big boy, Zorba."

"You wish to have breakfast?" I nodded.

"Come with me; I know the best place."

We walked for a few minutes until we came to a café where a man was setting up tables and chairs on the sidewalk. He and Zorba greeted each other with hugs and air-kisses and the man offered menus that had been stowed in his apron pocket. Zorba grabbed mine from me and set it and his on the table.

"No need, I will order."

"Okay, but I want to read it."

The menu included an information section in Greek, Italian, and English about the island of Crete. It claimed that the life expectancy rate in Crete is the highest in the country, which contradicts what C.B. had written in his manuscript. The menu went on to mention that the olive groves, vineyards, herbs, and wild weeds provide products for a delicious and healthy breakfast. Whatever Zorba ordered for us, I think it included all of those items, plus a quiche made with feta cheese and spinach. It was indeed sumptuous, washed down with tea generously flavored with honey.

"When do we go?" I asked.

"Soon, when the man comes for us."

"The good sailor?"

"Si, si, the good sailor. He will come around noon. Then we'll go."

"How long will it take us to get to Illikaria?"

Zorba wiggled his hand up and down as he pursed his lips until he said, "We go five hours or so, maybe six, the sailor, he will know; he is a good sailor."

"I'm sure he is."

"We can go to the museum this morning, if you wish."

It sounded like a command, so, after a leisurely walk in the town and along the waterfront, we arrived at the Archaeological Museum, the key cultural attraction of Iraklion, an old city, the port of Knossos in prehistoric Crete. At the museum we viewed its treasures of pottery, frescoes, and rhytons, ancient vases used for pouring libations.

As a historian I should have been more impressed and fascinated by these works of Minoan Bronze Age civilization, ancient before Julius Caesar died or Jesus

Christ was born, but I was more interested in getting to Illikaria and learning about old people.

A little before noon we hiked back to my hotel (I never did learn where Zorba had spent the night), collected my belongings, and walked to the wharf.

"Hallo!" Zorba cried out, waving his arms, worry beads swinging in the air. A man on the boardwalk, standing in front of a sleek, blue boat, a yacht by my thinking, but more properly an ocean-going sports-fishing boat, waved back, his deeply tanned face smiling under a black beret. On the side of the boat was the name, 'Mist of the Mediterranean,' and below the name was its port of call, Kos, which I knew was one of the larger of the Dodecanese Islands, but not where I expected to go.

"Whose boat is this?" I asked.

Zorba said, "Oh, it is Mr. Cosmo's, and the captain is Tony. He is a good sailor, he will get you to Illikaria."

We walked down a ramp to the boardwalk, met Tony, which I suspected was short for Antonio, hand shakes all around, and the two Greeks spoke for a minute in their native language. Then Zorba grabbed my hand and shook it vigorously.

"You aren't coming?" I said.

"No, no, I have work on Crete. You go with Tony. Goodbye."

I stepped aboard the boat, by my guess at least fifty feet long, large enough to hold a good sized fishing party.

Another man appeared on the dock and he jumped aboard.

Tony nodded to him and said, "Dion, this is Professor Miller."

"Please, call me Morgan."

Dion smiled and we shook hands. He was a younger man than Tony but looked enough like him for me to guess he was Tony's son. He didn't say anything but went to work, beginning to untie the lines.

Tony's English was not as good as Zorba's but he managed to explain to me that I could use one of the bedrooms if I wanted to nap, or I could relax on the aft deck, under the overhang that provided shade.

I stood around while Tony and Dion hustled about getting ready to move out to sea. Tony climbed to the top deck and Dion went around to the bow. There was nothing for me to do, or if there was I didn't know it, so I sat down with the sun on my face, which felt good for a few minutes, the warmth a contrast to the chill from the breeze as the boat began to move faster and faster. Soon I adjusted to get the sun off my face and pulled C.B.'s manuscript out of my bag. I had finished reading it on the plane but decided to scan through it again. It was an astounding work of a vivid imagination.

The men hardly spoke to me; in fact, they hadn't been around except when Dion brought food. He sat with me and also ate some cheese and bread, but he said nothing other than comments about the weather. Later Tony came by and asked if I was comfortable.

Hours later, most of my time spent gazing out at the sea, napping, drinking cold beer from a cooler conveniently set next to my chair, and enjoying the lunch of cheese, bread, and olives, the boat began to slow.

I stood up to see what was happening and felt the boat continue to slow and begin to bob. I went to one side and looked to the east. Land appeared, the only land we'd seen other than occasional specks on the horizon, since we'd cleared the Crete harbor.

From this distance it was hard to discern where the shoreline began, and in most places the beach was totally obscured by large rocks that reminded me of the Oregon coast. Waves crashed against these rocks and soon we were close enough to hear the sound of the water relentlessly attacking the rocks. Where there were openings between the rocks the waves smoothly rolled up to the beach, bubbly foam unfolding as the water slipped over the sand, then retreated. The sun, now to our back, hit the white sand and the shimmering reminded me of the sparkling diamonds I had found in the canisters. As we came closer I could identify where the beach began and where it ended, hard up against a dark wall that from here looked inaccessible.

We had come to a stop and I examined the island while Tony and Dion lowered the small motorboat that had rested atop the aft5 overhang. Tony called to me and lifted my bag into the motorboat, then gently held my arm and motioned for me to climb in. He followed and within a few seconds we were motoring towards shore.

As we neared, the waves seemed larger and rougher than when observing them a hundred yards away. And the entry to the beach between the boulders seemed tinier, no bigger than the eye of a needle.

Tony alternately gunned and reversed the engine in response to the force of the waves and the angle at which they smacked the boat. I swayed and felt the strength as the water toyed with us. Without the power of an engine a small boat would have a tough time navigating to safety.

Tony, a good sailor, took his time; we moved forward a few meters and than back one, but in a few minutes we glided onto the beach. Tony jumped out, pulled the boat to secure it on the beach, then climbed back in, took my bag and bade me to follow him.

"Illikaria," he said, when I had stepped ashore.

The sand was clean and white, the sun soft and warm, the air fresh and pungent with the aroma of the island's flora, and I knew I was being influenced by what I'd read in C.B.'s manuscript.

"Now what?" I said.

Tony gestured with his hand to follow him and we walked across the sand towards a wall of black, a monolith of rock graced with strands of greenery that hung down a good thirty feet. Tony walked us directly to the wall and we were only a few feet from it before I noticed steps cut into the rock, the dark slits blending in perfectly to make them nearly invisible. The steps were uneven and narrow and there was no rail.

"You go first, " Tony said. "If you fall back I will catch you."

I suspected that if I fell backwards we'd both tumble to the bottom but I gingerly stepped up and carefully, at a pace that must have tested Tony's patience, continued upward, one slow step at a time.

I hated to impede progress but I had to pause twice before I could complete the climb. I felt Tony's eyes burning into my back while he waited for the old guy to catch his breath. It was warm and I was sweating profusely. Finally, I reached the top and gazed on a grove of olive trees on one side, a pasture as green as any in Ireland on the other, home to a flock of grazing sheep, and a stone path lined with purple, yellow and white flowers that trailed to a white house that from this distance appeared to sprawl over an acre of ground.

Tony moved next to me and pointed at the house. "Mr. Cosmo will meet you. I will be back when you are ready to leave." He handed me my bag, nodded and turned, and I watched as he disappeared down the cliff. Walking down looked like it'd be more hazardous than coming up.

For a moment I felt like Dorothy on the yellow brick road, except this road was made of tiny white pebbles, though it might lead me to a land as odd as the one Dorothy found.

It was a walk of nearly one hundred yards to the front yard of the villa. The house was built on the extreme northeastern edge of the island, perilously close to the edge of a cliff, and from where I stood there was a 180-degree view of the Aegean. To the south, numerous rows of olive trees stretched out as far as I could see.

The white pebble path ended and became one of reddish wood chips that circled behind the house towards a hip-height fence. I took the path, came to a gate, which swung open easily, and continued on the path to the rear of the house. From here the view of the Aegean was supreme, cobalt waters shimmering with flashes of silver where the sun kissed the tips of the waves, serene and seemingly endless. There was no land in sight, but specks representing small boats danced and bobbed on the waves.

The yard was mostly hardscape where I entered, and to my left a satellite dish, raised on a concrete pad several feet off the ground, pointed at the sky. A few yards from it, extending to a concrete wall that appeared to be a safety feature to prevent one from slipping over the cliff, was a granite top, state-of-the-art barbecue area posh enough to make any aficionado of outdoor grilling drool. To my right was a small swimming pool and farther to the right, amid shrubbery and a variety of flowering plants, a fountain issued a pleasing rhythm of running water cascading down three levels, the only sound at the moment. Past the fountain there was a bunch of olive trees and what looked like a vegetable garden. Two blue and white striped lounge chairs were placed at the edge of a tiny pond formed by the water spilling from the fountain. A table and four chairs occupied the center of the patio; a shade umbrella poked out of the center of the table. The pads on the chairs matched those on the loungers. Everything was bright and pristine. I bet myself that if I lifted the lid of the barbeque, the grill would be spit-polish clean.

I sauntered around the pool and to the edge of the yard where another gate prevented a careless person from stepping over the precipice. I charily peeked over the edge and saw a cliff that led to a snow-white beach. The slope was as steep as the one Tony and I had climbed, and though I scanned the cliff side I couldn't spot steps cut into the rock similar to the ones we had used to climb up, but I suspected they were there because on the beach I saw a woman on a blanket.

"Don't lean over too far," a voice behind me cautioned.

I turned and saw a man dressed in white shorts and a pale blue shirt, the top half unbuttoned, sandals, and polarized sunglasses. His thick hair was brown with silvery sideburns and his skin was tanned, head to toe. He took off his sunglasses and either smiled at me or grimaced against the sun, and said, "Welcome to Illikaria, Professor Miller."

I had only seen him a few times, never knew him well, but I'd studied the photos of him in the Lyman Wilson yearbooks from the seventies. He could have been a clone. We each took a step forward and shook hands.

Colin Bisseau; looking as young and healthy as when I last saw him over thirty-five years ago; he looked nowhere near like a nonagenarian.

16. C.B.

My host—I wasn't sure what to call him; Colin? Cosmo? Casmir? led me inside the house to the guest quarters, where he suggested I might want to freshen up. I wanted nothing better at the moment. I tarried in a lukewarm shower, shaved, and changed clothes.

My quarters consisted of bedroom, bathroom, sitting area, and an alcove with a kitchenette, I guess in case I didn't want to dine with my hosts. The sitting area contained a large screen TV, a bookshelf along one wall, filled, at a glance, with an eclectic mix of fiction and non-fiction, particularly European-oriented, and a butler's pantry with a wine rack and other paraphernalia endemic to the well-stocked bar. A small sundeck opened to a garden of flowers and a birdbath and statuaries of a squirrel, a turtle and a sleeping dog. In the distance the sea shimmered.

I returned to the main patio and joined my host at the table.

"What can I get you?" he asked as he waved a hand at a drink cart a few feet away, which boasted a variety of choices, alcoholic and otherwise.

"First, a glass of ice water, then a chilled white wine would be fine."

I had expected there would be someone to serve us but my host got up and prepared what I'd asked for and brought it to the table. The villa looked like it would be a huge task for two people to care for by themselves.

"We are alone for a few days, that is, you and I and my wife, who will join us shortly. I gave the staff a holiday off so we could have this time alone. I hope that is acceptable to you."

"Does that mean I have to make my own bed?" I said, in a way I hoped would be taken as a joke.

The man grinned and nodded.

"What do I call you?"

"My wife still calls me Colin, the name I was using when I met her."

"The time you met her as Colin Bisseau, you mean?"

Another smile.

"The resemblance is uncanny, I must admit."

"Resemblance? You mean you doubt I am Colin Bisseau?"

"The Colin Bisseau I met at Lyman Wilson some forty years ago would be over ninety years old by now. Of course," I added, with a grin of my own, "on Illikaria people tend to live a long time, don't they?"

"I'm glad to see you have kept up with your readings, Professor."

"You don't really expect me to believe that *In The Mist* is other than fantasy, do you, or believe that you're five hundred years old?"

"No, I don't expect you to, in fact, it would be better if you didn't believe me. I am torn myself as to why I brought you here. For centuries I have expended massive amounts of time and energy to keep the secret of the Immortals from the rest of the world, as have my colleagues. Yet, sometimes I feel I'd like to share the story with someone I could trust with the secret. And, the fact that you are here indicates you are curious."

"Why me?"

Colin shrugged his hands. "Serendipity, I guess. You found my papers, and then my cache—I congratulate you—so it falls to you, maybe."

"Depending on…"

"Depending on how well we get along the next few days."

"And if I chose not to stay?"

"Professor Miller—may I call you Morgan?"

I nodded.

"There is no boat scheduled to call on Illikaria for a week, so please, be my guest and let's enjoy ourselves."

I didn't remind him that he had his own boat; why be an inconsiderate guest?

I picked up the glass of wine, a Pinot Grigio the label of the bottle revealed, and tipped it to Colin as an affirmative response, and sipped the wine.

"Nice choice."

I heard the sound of footsteps and looked up to see an extremely pretty woman walk onto the patio. She was dressed similarly as Colin was, except her shirt was a pale yellow dabbled with white flowers, the yellow shade of her shirt matching the flower in her hair above her left ear. Her hair was light brown, almost an ashy blonde, and reached farther down her back than as described in Cade Bunyan's journal. Her skin was tanned but not as coppery as Colin's, and she displayed an exquisite figure.

I rose to greet her and she removed her sunglasses as she stretched out a hand. She smiled and her eyes fixed on me as if we were former lovers finding one another after a long separation, but in a situation where we had to disguise our joy.

"Ms. Place, I assume."

"Misplace?" she said, a quizzical look replacing the smile.

"I guess that didn't come out too well, did it? May I call you Etta?"

The smile returned, even broader. "Oh, please do; no one has called me Etta in years."

"I only know of one picture of you, Etta; it doesn't do you justice."

"Is that the one with Harry?"

I nodded.

"That's the only one I have of him. I was surprised you would have heard of me, but Colin explained that you are a professor of history."

"Ms. Place, I mean, Etta, if you're truly who you suggest you are, you know that in American culture..."

"Yes, Professor, I saw the movie."

"Is it accurate?"

Sadness washed over her and she looked away for a second, then back at me. "I wasn't there when they died."

Colin stood up and raised his glass. "We need a toast," he said, scuttling my trifling and Etta's reminiscence. He filled a glass with Pinot Grigio and handed it to Etta.

"First, let us toast to your wife, Professor; I'm sure you have many fine memories of her and I was deeply saddened to learn of your loss."

We drank, and then I said: "Ironically, if she hadn't gone away in search of a cure for her illness I probably wouldn't have worked on your papers, Colin."

We sat down again and Colin proposed another toast, this to a relaxing and enjoyable week on Illikaria.

"Tell me, please, how this all came about, your finding the papers and what led you to my cache."

I took a deep breath and thought for a moment; where to start, what was the sequence of events, why had I come to this island. I was surprised that Colin had not asked about the money and diamonds. I began with Erin's sudden departure, then to Janice's phone call, and from there through my readings of the papers and the journals, researching the names, the Grant letter (at which point Colin chuckled in a way that made me think that in retrospect he realized he'd acted recklessly, a notion which made me wonder if I was slipping into belief of his claim of an extended lifespan), the enigmatic clue that led me to the cemetery, and finally here, half way across the world to Illikaria. By the time I finished we were on a second bottle of Pinot Grigio and the last curve of the sun was dipping into the sea.

"The green flash," Colin said as he nodded towards the vanishing sun. I caught a millisecond of the phenomena.

We sat without speaking and took in the sea, which like a chameleon began to change color, from azure to navy blue, purple, then black. A slight breeze passed over the patio, pleasant on the skin.

Etta rose and said, "I'll be in the kitchen getting the food ready. I hope a simple meal will be fine with you, Professor?"

"Yes, of course, and please, not so formal."

Colin and I continued to sit quietly while the sky darkened. I had so many questions for him I didn't know where to start, and I still wasn't convinced of his claim, or was it his game? Some of my questions felt foolish as I thought of them. So I started with more practical ones.

"What do you want me to do with the money and the diamonds?"

He grimaced and looked at me dead-on, the stare giving me the answer.

"Your people, the ones following me, they've recovered them, haven't they?"

Colin nodded.

"I understand they had to do some damage to get at your safe, but then, I owed you one, didn't I?"

I grinned.

"When your floor is repaired I will pay the bill."

"No need, I had it coming. But why did you wait? Your people could have taken the canisters anytime. I wasn't going to fight over them."

"Believe me, Morgan, my secret is not so important that I would risk someone's life. There was a time, I must admit, I wasn't so solicitous, but I have seen too much death, known many people who have died in wars, and I know how sacred, and fleeting, life can be. I didn't want you to get hurt; now, with no one in your home, it was easy."

"Five hundred years and no one has figured out your secret, and of others like you, and threatened exposure?"

"I haven't been personally involved but I know of a few incidents."

"What happened?"

"What I heard is that the people were forcibly taken away and isolated in a place unbeknownst except to the IMs who took care of the matter, until they lived out their lives."

"Kidnapped," I said.

"Yes, a grave crime," Colin agreed. "But it seemed sensible. There is so much at risk."

"You don't have people killed, do you; I'm not going to be dumped at sea, am I?"

Colin shook his head. "If I was going to have you eliminated, it would have happened long ago."

"The note in the canisters was rather threatening."

Colin grinned and swished a hand back and forth, a gesture I took to mean that the note was to cause concern, but was not a serious threat of bodily harm.

"There were two times that I know of where one of ours, an IM, did take matters too far."

"And had someone killed?"

Colin nodded. "Yes, then we had to deal with them."

"How did you?"

"We have a Star Chamber," Colin said, using the term for by a 15th century English court that dealt with cases affecting the Crown.

"And is it as arbitrary and oppressive as the original Star Chamber?"

"No, of course not. We use the term to remind ourselves that what we do is off the books, as we say, basically an illegal application of justice, and we do it with considerable circumspection. And as far as I know, no written records of the incidents exist."

"And these people were executed?"

Colin shook his head. "Let's say they were isolated, and to the best of my knowledge, still are."

"How..." He raised a hand as a stop signal.

"And nothing was ever learned about what happened to these people?"

"I only chronicle my own life, not the history of all the IMs, though I wish someone would write such a history."

"That could be an interesting undertaking."

"You're starting to believe me?" Colin said, his eyebrows rising up and his eyes smiling at me.

I laughed at being caught, feeling silly at accepting what he was telling me.

"Let's say I'm trying to go along with you for now. I'm still not convinced. You could be Colin Bisseau's son, or grandson, and you prepared those journals as a gigantic practical joke, and..." I lost track of where I was going.

"You seemed to believe Liz, or Etta, as you call her, immediately, but not me? A pretty face can be persuasive, yes?"

I think I blushed.

"And my cache? The money, the diamonds, the passports?"

I shook my head; I had no answer but I still expected he would eventually explain everything to me, and it would be like a Jack popping out of the box with a wicked grin on its face, smacking egg on my face.

"I can't explain them, but they don't prove you've lived five hundred years."

"That's true; they don't."

"You use the term, Immortals; so can you die at all?"

"Of course we can die. If you read my manuscript I'm sure you remember me writing that we believe IMs can die a natural death at a young age, say, from disease, before the regeneration takes place, which seems to occur in the early to mid-twenties. And of course, like Jay, we can die in accidents or be killed by bullets, knifes--any number of ways."

"According to your journals, you took some big chances with your life."

He nodded and his mind went somewhere for a few seconds, his eyes viewing long-ago events, maybe back to Bolton Depot, or to the frozen forest in 1944.

"Yes, I must admit that some of us, myself included, while we are not truly immortal, do seem to have an inordinate amount of…what should I say, good luck or kismet, saving us for a destiny that awaits in the future, so we seem to skirt danger."

He hesitated and chuckled. "When I was younger…younger, that is, two or three hundred years old, I tended to take more chances than I do now."

"In your journal you wrote that you were eager to get into World War Two. You took remarkable risks during the Battle of the Bulge."

"I felt a great obligation to fight in that war, even if it killed me. I had managed to avoid duty during the First World War, except for serving in the medical corps, away from combat. The Great War, they called it, as if a war can be great. Like the first, this Second World War started in Europe near where I was born, and had spread its horror to the entire world. I felt I needed to contribute. But now…I have come to abhor violence and am astounded that after all these centuries the human race is no closer to world peace than it was on the day Cain killed Abel.

"I also wonder if it is reckless on my part to take unnecessary risks, because of this gift of long life."

"Yes, I remember such a comment in the journals, more than once, I believe."

"It may sound selfish to you but I do wonder if there is a particular reason I, and the others, have been given this gift, and do we have an obligation to take special care of it."

"Colin, I think most people believe life is a special gift."

We were interrupted by Etta, who returned pushing a serving cart laden with a tray of food, plates, and utensils. Colin rose to fetch more wine.

We dined leisurely on cheese, vegetables, olives, warm bread, fish and roasted lamb.

"I also seem to have an unrivaled capacity for alcoholic beverages without being adversely affected," he said, chuckling as he refilled our glasses.

We talked about Lyman Wilson University, and what my years there had been like; we talked about the Greek financial situation, the country appearing to be descending into an economic chasm; we talked about Colin's vegetable garden, about his book on the history of the Mediterranean, and about Etta's photography book.

"How long have you been on Illikaria?" I asked

"Going on eight years. It has been sinfully relaxing here."

"It's getting boring, Colin," Etta opined.

"Liz is eager to go back to the States. I believe we will do so soon."

"Aren't you afraid someone will recognize you?"

"I'm thinking of trying the bald look again. I haven't used that disguise in a long time."

"What about you, Etta, are there people who might know you?"

"Oh, I doubt it. We haven't been in the United States since we left Alaska."

"Thirty-five years ago," I said.

"Where else have you been all these years?"

Colin waved an arm high above his head and pointed at the sea. "We have visited dozens of islands in the Mediterranean and the other nearby seas; the Aegean and Ionian Seas, the Black Sea; we have traveled widely in Greece, Turkey, North Africa, and other countries. We lived in Sicily for three years, on Rhodes for four, in Athens for a few, seldom more than three or four years anywhere, except here."

"Why have you stayed on Illikaria for eight years?"

"I got tired of moving," Etta said, the exasperation obvious.

Colin laughed and shrugged. "I fear I drag my wife around too much. However, we both love this house and the view is unmatched."

"Hmm."

"Meaning what, Morgan?"

"Meaning sometimes I think I dragged my wife around to places she didn't care to go. You at least, if you're telling me the truth, have plenty of time to make up for it."

"More and more you believe me, don't you?"

"Look, I'm an historian; I deal in facts."

"Yes, but a historian may know what happened but not the why or the how, isn't that true?"

"Yes, often it is true, which is why many books are written about an event, the Battle of Waterloo, for example, and the authors come up with different interpretations as to why the battle developed the way it did."

"And the ramifications," Colin added. I nodded.

"Does it make you angry, Professor, that your wife lived such a relatively short time?"

"My friends call me Morg, Etta."

"Morg, do you resent us, as others have?"

"You mean when they began to wonder why you never seem to get older?"

Etta nodded. "More than resent, as Colin mentioned. They look at us with both fear and rage. I was nearly torn apart by a group of women who thought I was the devil himself, in the guise of an evil women bent on stealing the bodies and souls of their men."

"Where was this? When?"

"I made the mistake of returning to the Texas town where I first met Harry. It had been a long time since I visited and I was sure there'd be no one who remembered me. But there was, an old man who had courted me when we, when he was in his twenties; I was over one hundred years old by then, and just coming to accept I had this…situation of long life; I wasn't sure what it meant or how to handle it. At the time I had not yet met any others like myself. I tried to dissuade this man from pursuing me but he insisted, until I insulted and embarrassed him. He was angry, and I was sorry, but it was for the best.

"This man was amazed to see me and that I looked the same as when he had pursued me all those years ago. He made a scene, demanding I explain why I looked so young, accusing me of being a witch. I pretended I was someone else, but my eyes gave me away, the look of recognition, I guess. Soon a crowd gathered and the women began to throw clods of dirt at me, calling me 'She-devil', and 'filthy whore', and even worse.

"It was fortunate for me that a man came by with a buggy and scooped me up and rode me out of town. He didn't know what was going on, but he assumed they were accusing me of being a prostitute. For a second I feared he was going to demand I pay him for saving me, if you know what I mean.

"He spoke to me as if preaching; he said he was a married man and that he hoped this incident would cause me to re-think my ways. I thanked him and he drove me to the next town where I could catch a train."

"Those were more primitive times, Etta. I don't think..."

"Morgan, be serious," Colin cut in. "What do you think normal people would do if they found out that people such as us existed? They'd put us in the laboratory and cut us open to find what is different about us. They'd kill the golden goose to get the last golden egg."

"What is different about you? Is it in your DNA?"

"I know of at least two doctors who are IMs, and they have worked, when they can access facilities, to try to find an answer, but so far they have no explanation. It is a mystery."

"What about children, or grand-children? Do they inherit this trait?"

Colin shook his head. "There is not one documented incident. Maybe it has happened, but if it has, no one has admitted it. That is why Etta and I refrained from having children."

"We'd outlive them," said Etta. "I couldn't stand that."

"Yes, I can see it would be difficult."

"You didn't answer my question, Morgan."

I hesitated for a few seconds, not that I wasn't sure of my answer, but I wanted to express it in a way that would make them believe me.

"I don't resent you Etta, and Colin, because for one thing I'm still not sure about you."

"You recognized me, Etta said, "from one old picture."

"Maybe I was seeing what I wanted to see."

"You're still avoiding the question."

I shook my head as If I didn't know how to answer; but I did.

"Recently a friend asked me the same question you asked, Etta."

"And…" Etta said, softly, a heap of compassion entwined in one little word.

"I said when someone you care for dies, it's always too soon. The older I get, the more I pretend I'm not yet old, but it creeps up, at least, for us normal people. You know the feeling of losing someone who is dear to you, Colin, if the incidents in the journals are true."

"Yes, that's why until I met Liz, or Emily as she called herself at the time, I had vowed not to get involved with a woman again unless she was like me, an IM."

"But you did get involved, dear."

"And so did you."

"And Etta, you ran off because you didn't want the heartbreak that would have to come, right?" I said.

Etta smiled and nodded. "Yes, and it wasn't long before I questioned myself but after a few months I was sure he had forgotten about me."

"Never did I forget."

"Right, you were a virgin for the next sixty-seven years, sure!" Etta said, laughing loudly.

"In spirit I was," Colin said, and Etta laughed so hard she began to cough.

"Seriously, I was starting to get the feeling that you were an IM, Liz, but it was too late; you were gone."

"You're older, Colin, maybe your senses are keener than mine."

"As my old pal Will used to say, all's well that ends well."

"I'll drink to that," I said.

Etta excused herself then. She leaned over to give Colin a kiss and I stood when she did. I reached out to shake her hand but she stepped closer and gave me a hug.

"I think we will be friends, even if you do know our secret. Let me know if you need anything in your room; good night."

"Good night."

"Now that you've found us, we'll have to leave Illikaria." It's a shame, I've come to love this villa," Colin said, in a grumble that sounded forced, after Etta was gone.

I sat down. "I can keep a secret."

"I trust you would intend to, but you tell your closest friend, because you have to tell someone, and he tells his wife, and so on."

"You yourself indicated you want to tell your story by writing *In The Mist*."

"More of an ego thing, Morgan. I'd honestly do want people to take it as a novel, that is, if I publish it at all."

"When will you decide?"

"I'm still thinking about it; we'll discuss it later, if you don't mind. Maybe I should wait and discuss it with some of the others, but the next Rendezvous is not for five years."

"Where will it be held next time?" I asked, trying to make the query as plain as any other question, wondering if I could get Colin to slip and reveal a big secret. He didn't, just looked at me with a wide grin while he pursed his lips to form a solid 'No, no!'

"I would be ostracized if I revealed that."

I chuckled, knowing he knew I was testing him. What a story that would make, if I could crash a Rendezvous and learn about these people: real or kooks?

"Can you tell me this," I asked, "Are you in contact with other IMs, other than Etta."

"Only Marcus on a regular basis these days, a few others once a year or two. It depends on how we can assist each other. My specialty is advising on issues to consider when making the change; trouble is, even I am having a difficult time as the world evolves."

"The man you called Marcus, is he the one you mentioned in your journals, under various guises?"

Colin nodded. "He now goes by the pedestrian name of Walter, though I still call him Marcus, out of habit. And please, don't try to squeeze his current last name from me."

"Wasn't he also known as Kittredge and…"

"He's had several names, as have I."

"He handles your financial matters?"

"For the most part. It gets complicated, having accounts under several names in different places; New York, London, Geneva, Rome, Chicago, and more. But I, and other IMs I have known, are convinced it is necessary. We don't know how long we will live, maybe indefinitely, so we must prepare for whatever comes: wars, revolutions, economic chaos, social changes."

"A man who's lived five hundred years would have witnessed many such events."

"Tell me. When the telephone and airplane were invented it seemed like the height of technological achievement, but it was nothing compared to the scientific breakthroughs of the last half century."

"So you have legitimate holdings in the usual places, like banks and brokers, under a variety of aliases, all over the world, plus, what, more caches, like the one I found?"

"Banks can fail, stock markets can crash, and currency can be devaluated."

"So what do you keep in your caches, gold?"

"Mostly gold and gemstones."

"Aren't you worried they'll be found, like the one I found?"

"Believe me, Morgan, my other caches are hidden so well even I will have a hard time accessing them when I need to. The one you found was not designed properly; it was sloppy work on my part, but I intended it to be temporary and would have had Jay send me the contents."

"Why didn't you go back for them?"

"It was too soon to chance being recognized. The years went by, no alarm had been raised, and I figured the cache was safe."

"Who do the alarms alert?"

"Don't concern yourself. I have people on retainer."

"You must have sources of regular income, don't you? Sorry, I guess I'm being nosy."

"No, no, you have a right to know, since I have, in effect, dragged you away from your home. Yes, I have income coming to me, or my aliases, in several countries, to numerous accounts, from dividends, commissions, a considerable amount from real estate rentals, the shipping industry..." He twirled a hand as to indicate there were more sources.

"Yes, you mentioned you got into shipping when you first realized you were...different, and left your family."

Colin nodded, his eyes reflecting old memories. "Despite Greece's financial problems Greek companies are a powerful force in international shipping."

"And you are involved?"

"I have holdings."

"Over four hundred years in the shipping business, you must…" I stopped trying to calculate how wealthy this man might be, assuming he wasn't a crazy lunatic.

He grinned at me from one side of his mouth, and winked. I changed the subject.

"Colin, you implied that those people you retain had gone to my house and recovered the canisters. What about the file cabinet contents?"

"Oh, I'm sure they could handle that, but if those items go missing from the university I assume it would be noticed. And I wouldn't want you to get into trouble."

"Oh, thanks. So what do you want me to do with the papers?"

"The Bisseau papers, my letters, articles, all the boring reports, you have my permission to publish if you wish. I suppose they have some minor historical relevance. The journals, Morgan, what do you think?"

"Colin, there are some fascinating first person accounts of historic events there. Why not let me publish them? I could say that Colin Bisseau was doing research on Colt Boston and Cade Bunyan. I'd be careful. However, I'd like more than the journals in the file cabinet."

"Let me think on it." He answered so quickly I got the impression he had already thought on it, and had made up his mind, and withholding his answer was a habit of control.

It was late by now—I had no idea what time it was, having left my watch off after showering—and the only lights were a single candle in the center of the table, exuding a lemon scent, a dozen or so solar lights outlining the shape of the yard, and thousands of stars decorating the black roof endless miles above us. I stared at the sky until my neck hurt, realizing I seldom saw such a brilliant display other than on a TV show or at a planetarium.

"There are electronic lights in the yard, but I often leave them off so we can enjoy the sky. Wonderful, isn't it? A sight that is lost to most people these days, in the cities, at least."

"It must have been something to live under a sky like this every night, in years past."

I could almost hear Colin's smile.

"Funny thing is how little by little I got used to the loss of the stars. I moved to the cities, to Paris, London, other places, and one day a long time ago I looked up and it was as if a cat burglar had snuck in and stolen the stars. I felt sad, almost as if a friend had died."

We sat quietly and bathed in the light of the stars until I felt my eyelids began to droop.

"You must excuse me, Colin, I think the travel has finally caught up with me."

"Of course, take your rest now and sleep as long as you wish. Tomorrow I will give you a tour of the island."

I went to my room and poured a nightcap of brandy from the carafe in the bar. After one sip I decided I'd had enough to drink. I eased into the bed and instantly fell sound asleep.

17. A BILLION DOLLARS

I awoke once during the night for a few seconds. The red digits on the clock read 2:33. The world was silent except for a slight breeze, which ruffled the curtain of the door that was open to the garden deck. I could smell the sea air, and even a faint hint of lemon, from the candle that must have been left burning, and as my eyelids closed again my foggy brain made a note that I needed to text Kenny and Amy and Janice and Erin and the kids.

I slept for hours. I could sense it was light even though my eyes were still closed as they followed a developing dream. I was on the verge of awakening but wanted to see how the dream played out.

My feet shuffled through the powdery white sand as I approached the woman who lay on her stomach on a blanket nearly as white as the sand. It was like being in a movie and also in the audience watching one's self perform on stage.

I saw myself kneel down by the woman, who said, "Hello, dear."

"Hello, Erin," I responded as I unsnapped the back of her bra. I picked up the suntan lotion and spread a generous portion on my hands, then rubbed it into my arms and back of my shoulders. Then I began on Erin's back.

"Feels good," Erin purred.

When I finished with her back and shoulders I started on her legs. She sighed and said, "I'll give you an hour to stop that."

A few minutes later I said, "Turn over," and she did.

She had a smile on her face and even with the large sunglasses she wore I could tell her eyes were closed. And then it hit me like a slap across the cheek that this wasn't a dream, this was real. It was in a dream that Erin had gone away and then come home to die. There were no Colin Bisseau papers, no Immortals, no Kenny and Amy, no Janice; even Lyman Wilson University was a dream. My entire life had been a dream

I couldn't remember what I'd done since I'd met Erin but I knew it had been many years ago and now my life was near an end and what had I done and where had the years gone? How could life go by so quickly? Maybe I don't even exist except in the dream of someone else.

I looked back at my duplicate, the man in the audience, sitting in the sand a few feet away. He smiled, a sneaky, Cheshire cat grin, shrugged and held out a fist and grains of sand dribbled down and then he vanished as if vaporized. I was glad to see him go.

I began to rub lotion on Erin's legs but she reached a hand to me and pulled me towards her. I leaned forward and she said, "Kiss me", and I brought my lips to hers and when she took off her sunglasses it was Etta, not Erin, but that was okay and ours lips touched and I heard a high pitched noise and my eyes popped open and I was awake. The bird on the deck chirped again and waves of emotion washed over me: frustration, depression, and guilt. I threw the sheet off and rolled out of bed.

The clock showed 8:52, the latest I'd slept since I was a child. But what time was it really? Here, on this tiny island it was 8:52 in the morning, but what time was it for me? Like the Yogi-ism, you mean, Now?

Fully awake, the last frames of the dream fading like the ghosts in *Field of Dreams* as they return to the corn field, slipping away to wherever it is that dreams go to die, I calculated the time in Indianapolis: it must be near 11 pm or midnight; a good time to send messages as there won't be a reply for several hours.

I stepped into the shower and stood under a stream of tepid water. I didn't need to soap up, I just wanted the water to spray over me and wash away the imaginary sand I'd accumulated in my dream on the beach.

When I went to dress I noticed a package on a chair. I opened it and found a pair of shorts and two shirts similar to the one Colin had worn last night, and a pair of sandals. My wardrobe for the week was complete.

"He thinks of everything."

I noticed one other thing that I was sure had not been there last night. A gold chain hung from the bedpost and on the chain was a cameo locket. I took it in my hand

310

and strained to recall where I'd seen it before. I pressed the tiny button on the side and the locket opened to reveal a picture of Etta. I smiled; no, I hadn't seen it but I'd read the description of it in Cade Bunyan's mournful journal entry after Etta had abandoned him back in 1907.

Dressed in my new clothes—tan shorts, a light blue shirt with the logo of an egret, sandals, and with locket in hand, I went to the backyard in search of my host and hostess. No one was there so I walked to the edge and peered down at the beach. Two figures were trotting along the shoreline, ripples of water slapping at their feet. They, Colin and Etta, stopped at a blanket to retrieve sandals and Colin picked up a towel and wiped his face and head. He looked up and waved at me; I returned the gesture.

They walked towards the cliff until out of my view. A minute later I saw them as they edged up the cliff on the steps carved in to the side that from my vantage I could not see.

They wore bathing suits and I stared at Etta and wondered if this was how Europa looked when her beauty mesmerized the Greek god Zeus, and for a second the last vestige of my dream was rekindled. Etta dropped her eyes and put on the coverall she had carried with her.

"Good morning, Morgan, did you sleep well?" Colin asked.

"Yes," I said, "quite well. Sorry I'm so late; I was bushed."

"Of course, no problem. Perhaps tomorrow you'll join us for a jog on the beach."

"Yes, I will," I said, fearful that a jog of more than a hundred yards would leave me breathless.

"Help yourself to coffee, Morgan. We'll be back in a few minutes."

"I think this is yours," I said, holding out the locket to Etta.

She smiled coyly; "Thank you. I wondered where I'd left it."

They went to rinse off and change and I poured a cup of coffee from the carafe on the table and sat down to wait for their return.

After breakfast Colin showed me how to get an Internet connection and I sent texts to Kenny and Amy, to Janice, and to the kids. Then Colin suggested—more of an order—that we take a tour of the island.

It was a walking tour and the exercise felt good after hours of sitting on the plane and then the boats.

"Do you ever get tired, Colin? Or is unlimited stamina one of the factors of your…condition?"

"Condition? You make it sound like an illness."

"Sorry, I don't know what else to call it, this supposed longevity of yours."

"Hmm, still the skeptic. Yes, I get tired, Morgan, but I do have more stamina and strength than most people. I'm not super-human, by any means. And I'm not immune to nature."

"Meaning?"

"Meaning sometimes I shiver from the memory of those days and nights in the forest in Belgium during World War Two. I was never so cold, and never so afraid."

"Do you ever get tired of living, of having to make the change, as you call it, giving up friends, and starting all over?"

"Making the change was never easy emotionally, but until recently it was fairly simple to quit one's identity and create another. Now, society has become so technologically complicated with computers, IDs, passwords, and so forth, and hackers stealing personal data; it is difficult and tempts me to drop out of society, which I have basically done these past few years, but…I can't do that forever—then life would become dull.

"So no, I'm not tired of living. One gets used to it, doesn't one? I do get tired of dealing with things I can't control, but who doesn't, I suppose? Perhaps the day will come when I've visited everywhere, read all the great books, learned all that I wish to learn, and then, who knows? More than a few IMs, it has been reported at the Rendezvous, have cashed it in."

"You mean, suicide?"

Colin nodded. "Yes, apparently some do get tired, or discouraged, or they feel guilty when a loved one dies and they go on and on, not even getting sick."

"I know I'm repeating myself, but do you ever dwell on this…gift you have, this gift of long life, in the sense that you have a special obligation?"

"Yes, I do, Morgan. I wonder if we have a singular responsibility to use this special gift for some extraordinary purpose. As yet, I have not found what that purpose might be."

"Colin, I'm curious about the quote, about a mist, from the book of James, that you cited."

"Curious about what, Morgan, that I would read the Bible?"

"No, but it seems ironic that you—and for the sake of this conversation let's say I accept that you are 500 years old---"

"Actually only 494, but thank you, Morgan," Colin said with a nod and a grin that reflected victory.

"You cite a quotation that in effect is reminding the reader how short life is, yet you so-called immortals live many times more than the average person."

"Wasn't it you that said—let's see if I remember correctly: "…when someone you care for dies, it's always too soon."

"Touché," I replied.

"It's all relative, Morgan."

No one spoke for awhile as we continued to walk along a hard-packed dirt path that cut through a meadow of green. Fifty yards away on one side of the path thirty or forty sheep quietly chewed grass, on the other side the meadow fell off abruptly a few yards away at the edge of the island, and the view was comprised of the dark blue sea meeting the lighter blue sky at the horizon. While the walking felt good, I was starting to perspire as the sun rose and with it, the temperature.

After another minute of soaking in the view I asked Colin, "You read the Bible, so do you believe in God?"

Colin hesitated; his tongue slipped out and he licked his lips, thinking, as if he had to make a monumental decision at this moment, give the final answer with no further time to reflect, as if his answer would decide the issue for everyone.

"Morgan, just because one reads Conan Doyle doesn't mean he believes Sherlock Holmes existed."

"Do you ever give a straight answer?"

After a hardy laugh, Colin said, "I don't think reading the Bible requires, or implies, that one believes in God, but, yes, I do now."

"Now?"

"I have vacillated over the years, the centuries; sometimes I still do. There have been times I've lived where conditions for most people were so horrid, how could I believe?"

"There are still horrors for millions of people today," I pointed out, unnecessarily, obviously, as Colin ignored my comment.

"In my experience, Morgan, people who claim they always have been believers, in God as Creator if not as staunch Christians, grew up in a home where religion was practiced to some degree, even if they only worshiped at Easter and Christmas."

"What about in your home, your first home?"

Colin shook his head. "I had practically no exposure to religion until after my father disappeared and my mother and siblings had died, though I often heard people refer to God, the devil, or angels, and I took them to be speaking of spirits."

"So when did you get exposed to religion?"

"When I came to Paris I was astonished by the buildings. I visited many churches; magnificent structures, as I'm sure you're aware."

"I wish I had seen more of the great cathedrals; never seemed to find the time."

"It was amazing to me that people had expended so much time, energy and resources to construct buildings in which to pray; I mean, you could pray outside, or in your home.

"As I traveled I came across beautiful churches even in small towns. Not always gigantic edifices, but always the biggest and most beautifully decorated building in the village.

"Finally it came to me: faith; very powerful stuff. People have faith, often in spite of awful circumstances."

"And so you became a believer?"

"It didn't happen overnight. Remember, Morgan, in the 16th century every day was a fight for survival: finding work, food, and shelter took most of one's energy without much spare time for contemplation.

"Yet, I noticed that many people, poor people, downtrodden people, did take the time and did keep their faith. I was impressed that amidst such hunger and poverty, cruelty from the powerful, people still kept faith in their eventual salvation.

"It was a long, slow process. Often I went years without giving it much thought. Eventually, from lectures, conversations, reading, thinking, contemplating, study; I came to believe, albeit cautiously."

"Any particular reason why?"

"There are subjective and the objective reasons, at least for me."

"Educate me."

A few yards ahead I spied a bench, perfect for people like me, in less than the best physical shape and breathing hard.

"Let's sit a spell," Colin said, clearly for my benefit.

"I need to start an exercise program," I said as I plopped down.

"At one of the Rendezvous—70 or 80 years ago---a few of us had a long talks about Darwinism, Creationism, and so forth; stimulating and interesting conversation."

"And what did you and your friends conclude?"

"We didn't exactly conclude anything, and we didn't all agree. But here's my take: the way I see it, Morgan, and my acquaintances concurred on this point, is that there are three possible explanations for the existence of the universe, and by extension, of life.

"One, the universe always existed; two, it began from nothing, and three, it was created by a God who already existed. Actually one person suggested a fourth possibility, which is that our universe was expelled out of another universe, but that only passes the question of the origin of our universe from here to there, that is, to the other universe.

"Now, all three ideas are alien to human thinking: how could something have no beginning, or how could something be created from nothing? The first two ideas make no sense to me."

"Does an omnipotent God make sense?"

Colin pursed his lips and seemed to be thinking about how he came to his conclusion.

"No, for the same reasons I just gave, no beginning; it would be a *time* when time itself did not yet exist. How does a mortal being wrap his mind around such a concept? That conundrum alone kept me from believing in anything that I couldn't see or touch for many, many years.

"Time is intrinsic in everything we do, everything that happens. Where did time come from? The possibility of spontaneous creation from nothing never made sense to me; there must have been a pre-existing force.

"It also makes no sense to me that some poor fishermen, or a tax collector, would suddenly decide to write stories about a man who performed miracles and then came back to life after a gruesome death. Why invent such a person? Those people were not writing fantasies two thousand years ago, Morgan. What would be the purpose? I realize there are no journals, like I prepared, written at the time Jesus lived, the lack of which causes doubters to question the veracity of the Gospels. Recall that the Roman historian Tacitus mentions a man named Jesus as having been ordered crucified by Pontius Pilate."

"The Greeks were writing fiction, including about gods, long before Matthew, Mark, Luke, and John."

"Ha! Well, you've got me there, Morgan, but I don't believe the genre was the same as what we think of as the modern novel form."

"I don't disagree with you, Colin, just wondering how your thoughts developed. After all, you've had much more time than most people to ponder the question. Doesn't your own existence, you and the other Immortals, make it seem more likely that life is random?"

"Trust me, Morgan, I've mulled over that for more hours than you've been alive."

"Hmm."

"Sorry." Colin patted Morgan on the leg. "Don't mean to rub it in." He stood up and began to walk again.

"Like you, I tend to look for facts, for practical answers to questions. And from what I've read, and from what others have said and written, people who have studied the ancient writings with far more diligence than I have, I don't see where there was anything in it for Paul and the others except poverty and struggle and eventual death as payment for their preaching. Again it makes no sense to me."

"So was there one deciding factor?" I asked, trotting to catch up.

"Nothing I could point to, just a gradual acceptance of what I felt to be true, or at least, the most likely. In an impractical world, what is practical can be subject to individual interpretation. Like people since the Stone Age, I gaze at the stars and a magnificent full moon and wonder, what's it all for if we only live a few years and when we die the light goes off forever. Seems like a waste of a vast universe—no matter how few or many years one lives. I'm sure it's easier for those who are born into a faith, into a family that already has a religious structure in their life. They simply grow up as if it is part of their skin."

"Some people change from belief to atheism, and vice versa. People grow up and have to deal with a world riddled with corruption and cruelty and they…"

"Yes, horrors from the Dark Ages, I know, Morgan. Look, I can't explain everything; no one can. I can't explain why an all-knowing God would allow a baby to be born with a defective brain."

"But then, we mere *mortals* cannot know how God's mind works."

"I note the emphasis, Morgan, and I agree with you, which is why I choose not to dwell on the question of how God thinks. And understand me, I don't believe I'm truly immortal. Something, whether age, illness, or accident, will take me and the other Immortals, sooner or later. In fact, from the number of participants at the last couple of Rendezvous, we don't seem to be increasing. In a way believing in God makes life a bit more meaningful and gives me a sense of calmness whenever I begin to dwell on the banalities or the horrors of the world.

"One reason I started writing *In The Mist* is because I'm more at ease with my…condition, as you call it, and it is no longer an issue that uses up mental energy. I am what I am, as we all are, and it is useless to waste time worrying about things one cannot change."

He looked at me with a grin, "For now, anyway. Give me another five hundred years and maybe I'll understand the cosmos better than I do now."

"And Etta?"

"She doesn't think of herself as particularly religious, but when she was younger church services and Bible studies were a regular part of her life. She says she never questioned the existence of God, and she doesn't trouble herself trying to understand why He allows certain things to happen, good or bad. She takes life's occurrences in stride better than I do. There is a small church on the island; it was crumbling so I arranged for workers from Athens to do a major renovation. Etta is more involved than I am but I will accompany her to services occasionally."

I had more questions but Colin beat me to it.

"What about you, Morgan? What do you believe, if anything?"

"Neither Erin or I grew up in a church-going home, but for the childrens' sake we exposed them to church and to talks and readings about religion and God and Jesus. At least we tried to point out what Christmas really celebrates, other than packages under the tree."

"Were they impressed?"

"Children are always impressed by bright lights and colorfully-wrapped packages."

"Did it take?"

"Oh, a bit…I don't know. Erin and I were those people you mentioned who go to church twice a year, Easter and Christmas. We attended more when the kids were younger, to give them the exposure. For the last few years we spent Christmas with one or the other, alternating each year. Christmas services were always part of the festivities, but I don't know how active they are the rest of the year,"

"And now, Morgan, what with Erin dying relatively young, how do you feel?"

I leaned forward and folded my hands together. Colin's question was one I had been avoiding pondering.

"Colin, I honestly don't believe her death affects my feeling or beliefs one way or the other. Of course I admit I haven't absorbed all of what has happened yet. It may sound corny but if you believe God gives life, you have to accept he can take it, whenever he wants. Understanding it is another matter, and agreeing with it is impossible, but it makes it easier to deal with Erin's death."

"And if you don't belief in God you don't even have Him to be angry at," Colin suggested.

I nodded and shrugged.

"So when people die in man-made wars do you think it was a fated event on an irrefutable cosmic schedule?"

"Oh, Colin don't confuse me with sophisticated theological questions, I'm just an average historian…"

"Sorry, I was baiting you. Even with my four plus centuries over you I can't answer that question either."

"Back to my original question, Colin: do you feel you have special obligations?"

"I'm not sure, Morgan, but the fact is, these past years I have been feeling a bit guilty, because it's been one long vacation.

"My respite since I left Lyman Wilson is the longest I have avoided developing a new profession and, as I have always tried to do, contribute to society. I felt I needed to avoid the madness of the world for awhile and wanted to make up for the years Liz and I missed spending together.

"Oh, I have studied extensively; much of it home-schooled, if you will, honing up on economics and world politics and delving into scientific disciplines. Cosmo Ballantrie has also taken courses in pre-med in Paris and in London prior to settling on Illikaria.

"For decades, centuries even, I concentrated on acquiring wealth, paranoid that I'd live on and on and end up a street bum, begging for a slice of bread. Some IMs who did not plan well have found themselves in less than satisfactory situations. We try to help them, the other IMs I mean; we have a fund."

"Sort of like welfare?"

"Somewhat, but it is limited to a set period of time, until they get themselves settled and working. Better to teach one how to fish…you know."

"Sounds like a little world of your own encased in the bigger world of us mortals," I said. Colin made no reply.

"But eventually, and I'm there now, I think I need to become more active in society again. Yes, financially I support numerous charities, which do wonderful work all over the world. With my wealth I feel it would be a sin for me not to use those assets to help others. I am beginning to feel the need to get involved in some new profession."

"Like? What haven't you done?"

"Oh, my dear Morgan, many things. As I said, I have been studying various sciences, taking college-level courses, some on–line, and reading voraciously. Maybe in the future I'll get to travel to space, to other planets, should I live so long."

"Is that something Etta would want?"

Colin spread his arms in a shrug. "Hard to say. Lately she is into photography and writing. She wants to go back to the States, so we will, soon. Eventually, maybe it'll be a hundred years or more, humans will travel to other planets and moons of our solar system. I think we will go."

"In thinking of less-ambitious journeys; when you and Etta return to the States, can we meet?"

"I need to think on that, Morgan."

We hiked through a grove of olive trees; I say hiked rather than strolled because Colin set a rapid pace. A path wound through the grove and when we exited we were in the village of Illikaria.

The buildings beamed snowy-white and the streets looked as if they'd been air-blown and washed down.

"Is it always so clean?"

"The residents take pride in their homes. The stoops are cleaned often, and the streets and walkways are watered down at least twice a week."

"Are the people here really as long-lived as you say in your book?"

"Their longevity is slightly exaggerated, but not much."

"So are some of them like you?"

"Immortals? No, no, you will see, they look their age. There are pockets in the world where the average life span is greater than the global norm, and this is one of them. I'm positive none of the people on Illikaria are IMs."

"Maybe the young men move out when they find they aren't aging."

"It's possible, but virtually every IM I've ever met says they went through the same experience: they began to be ostracized before they realized they had this condition, as you call it."

"So that portion of *In The Mist* is fiction; so how do I know that parts to believe as truth?"

"Just ask me," Colin said, with a chuckle.

Colin slowed down and we ambled through the village for two hours, meeting and greeting people along the way. My host spoke to everyone for a minute or more, using the local dialect.

Just as I was looking for a bench where we could sit down for a few minutes, Colin accepted an invitation to the home of a man who looked younger than most of the other people we had met.

"He says he is a youthful sixty," Colin said. "He still fishes or repairs nets six days a week."

"So today he is off?"

"No, he starts as early as 4 a.m. He is done for the day and now he relaxes with a local brew."

"Home made beer?"

Colin nodded.

We were invited to the man's back yard where we sat and were treated to a view as good, if not as expansive, as the one from Colin's villa, with the sea gleaming in the distance, fishing boats that looked like flotsam bobbing on the modest waves.

The man, whose name Colin said was Petra, served us frosty glasses of an amber beer, made, Colin told me, in the basement of Petra's house, enough to keep he and his best friends in beer all year around. A woman who I assumed was Petra's wife set a platter of cheese and bread and olives on a table, smiled and with a hand gesture invited us to eat.

"It's a good thing I like olives," I said. "They seem to be a staple."

Colin and Petra conversed while I enjoyed the beer and the food and the view. They went on for ten minutes or so, after which Colin gave me the gist of their conversation.

"Petra asked about you and I said you were a historian and former colleague of mine. He said you must be much older than me, and I said, as I always do, that I look young for my age."

"Do none of them..."

"No, but don't talk of it here; I'm never sure how much English the locals understand."

After two beers we made our thanks and our departure. Colin showed me the rest of the village and pointed out the shops where women sewed clothes and one where a shoemaker made sandals and one where a potter crafted all sorts of vessels, vases and ceramic jars.

"The shoemaker has a monopoly; everyone on the island wears sandals made by him."

"If the population is composed of elderly people, none having children, what will become of this place in a few years?"

"It's a sad situation, but few young people come here because there's not enough work, just what it takes to support the older people."

"And when all these hundred-year old people do pass on?"

"Without meaning to sound pessimistic, it is possible that fifty years from now only Etta and I will live here."

"You said you'd have to leave."

"Yes, but I hesitate to give up this place. It is beautiful, it is isolated; I feel snug here, as if the entire island were a warm blanket, sheltering us from any disturbance."

"I recall you saying you couldn't trust me to keep a secret."

"I guess I did imply that but I meant no offense."

"Besides, in a few years I'll be gone and then you can return here without worrying about me showing up with reporters," I said.

"In some ways you are a realist, Morgan, even if your comment is glum. But yes, that is the reality, and I didn't want to put it that way."

"It's okay, Colin, I'm not bothered by the possibility that you will be around long after I am dust."

"One does have to accept certain aspects of life that are unique to the person."

I merely grunted.

Colin stopped walking then, put a hand on my shoulder and looked deep into my eyes.

"Morgan, I've never taken a normal person into my confidence as much as I'm willing to do with you. If you will swear never to reveal the link between this place and my existence, I will accept that and then I can keep this island as a sanctuary, a place to return to every so often when I need a respite."

"There are people back home who already know I came to Greece."

"And to this island?"

I shook my head tentatively. "No, I never mentioned any particular place other than that I was flying to Athens. Illikaria is not exactly on the cruise ship lists of favorite ports of call."

"Good, good. This is important, Morgan. No one other than Marcus knows of this location. You must keep it secret."

"On the memory of Erin," I said.

In the afternoon we swam in the pool, played three-handed cribbage, and then we each chose reading material and a lounge chair to recline and nap in; at least I napped. Colin appeared to be distracted and wasn't interested in conversation. I decided to let him set the tone. I had this notion that Colin's purpose in bringing me to him had not yet been revealed.

Early evening and after dinner we talked of everything except being immortal. I wanted Colin to relate tales of his adventures, of people he had met; his mood had turned sullen and he rambled about poverty in the world, wars that killed more civilians than soldiers, the inanity of global politics, and the continuing strife and conflict throughout the world.

His only reference to his claimed long life was when his eyes would glass over and he would comment on how much simpler life was when the news of the world wasn't so easily and quickly disseminated.

"What you don't know can't hurt you?" I said.

He shrugged. "We know that isn't true, and yet, sometimes I'd just as soon not hear about the horrors of the world. Do you realize that in this day, the 21st century, boys and young men are being shanghaied and forced to toil on fishing trawlers, working under deplorable conditions? Girls, young girls, are kidnapped and forced into prostitution. Often they are beaten and eventually killed."

"I'm not naive about the world I live in, Colin."

"It disgusts me. I guess that's why I've been away for so long—if the world is going to go up in flames, to use a cliché, why do I want to be a part of it?"

"Because you are a part of it, Colin. And with your experiences, maybe you can provide answers."

"Answers? Like what, how to bring peace to the Middle East? Moses himself, if he returned, couldn't achieve that."

"You're probably right. But you can't be retired for the next thousand years, should you live so long," I added, trying not to sound too critical.

"I understand that, Morgan. But I'm still at an impasse. I can't go into politics; how would I explain it when I didn't age? Even your president, no matter his age when he takes office, begins to go gray from the day of his inauguration."

"You've been dying your hair for years, Colin."

"So what have you got planned for your remaining years, Professor?"

"Well," I replied in a tone equally harsh as his, "I was going to travel and goof off for the rest of my life, but maybe I'll find something useful to do, rather than sit on my can for the next thirty-five years."

Colin dismissed me with a wave of his hand and didn't say anything and I feared I had irritated him. Etta, who had gone inside, now returned with a tray with a large bowl of fruit and smaller bowls and spoons for each of us. She set the bowl on the table and sat down.

"Have you asked him yet, Colin?"

Colin frowned and shot a ray at Etta that might have melted steel. Etta ignored him and proceeded to dole out the fruit.

"Even IMs have tempers and emotions, don't they Colin?"

"Of course, why would you think otherwise? You've read my book; do I sound like I am stoic, or unfeeling?"

"Quite the contrary."

He slumped in his chair and reached out a hand and touched Etta on the arm. "Sorry, dear, you prodded me a bit before I was ready. Not your fault."

"Ask me what, Colin?"

We ate the fruit while waiting for Colin to say something. When he was finished he pushed the bowl aside and went to the bar.

"What's your pleasure, lady and gent?"

"My usual," Etta said.

"A touch of that wonderful cognac would be great, Colin."

Colin returned to the table with two snifters and a glass of white wine for Etta.

"Morgan, I'm sorry; often when I think of something that bothers me it affects my mood."

"Was it something I asked about?"

"I'm sure it wasn't your fault, Morg," Etta said. "Colin gets sensitive at times. He can be a pain in the ass when he dwells on the barbarity of the world."

"Is that why you resist talking about your other lives?" I asked.

Colin shrugged but I didn't want to drop it.

"You must have seen a lot of wonderful things, too, Colin, in all the years you've lived."

Colin nodded slowly, as if reluctant to agree.

For a minute Colin appeared to be arguing with himself, his mind elsewhere than on Illikaria, as if a tiny red imp on his left shoulder was taunting the angelic figure in pure white sitting on his right shoulder.

"Sometimes…" he started, then paused and I thought he had changed his mind.

"Sometimes, Morgan, I look at the world as if disconnected from it, like a visitor from another planet, floating above Earth looking down at it."

"Like you aren't part of the human race?"

Colin only mumbled "Hmmm." I looked at Etta, throwing with my eyes the same question.

"Not as much as Colin, but I know what he means."

"Maybe we aren't human; with our condition maybe we belong to another species. Maybe we won't die but we go on and on and maybe our task will be to turn out the lights. Maybe we have no other particular function."

"Does the idea sadden you?" I asked.

Colin shook his head, slightly, as if he wasn't sure of his answer.

"I'm generally a content, if not a happy, person, Morgan. Most of the IMs I've met seem to be the same."

I glanced at Etta. She smiled and nodded.

"The point, if there is one, is that to ourselves we feel normal; living indefinitely is the way life should be, as we see it. It's the rest of humanity who are odd to us, yet we understand that since we are the minority it's we who have to adjust to the norm of human life. So we have to change every few years; we have to adjust, lie, and adapt.

"And maybe it's once we have lived several *normal* lifetimes we understand that things will always change— the good times will not last forever, but will come back, and the same for the bad times. We are more content with our lives, not that we don't suffer along with friends when bad things happen to them."

"Or when friends die," added Etta.

"I thought you try to avoid close ties," I said.

"In a way, yes, but in that sense we are as human as you, Morgan. We have feelings, we live, we get angry, we hurt, we hope. You've read my journals."

"Some of them, yes."

"Actually, now that the life span of people is longer than it was hundreds of years ago, we have to move on before the friends we have made in our particular identity began to notice that we aren't aging with them.

"Or you come and go, as at Lyman Wilson," I suggested.

"That worked quite well," Colin said with a smile.

"I think what my dear husband is saying, Morg, is we should be content with who we are, with what we have."

I stared at her and knew she was reading my mind as it asked, why wasn't Erin content?

"It wasn't your fault, Morg," she said.

"How can you know, Etta?"

"Trust my instincts." She patted me on the arm, a grandmotherly and sagacious gesture; she, this ancient woman who hardly knew me simultaneously chiding me and giving me comfort.

Colin stood up then and went to the bar. "Enough," he said, almost a shout. He returned with the water pitcher and set it on the table.

"You ask him, dear," he said to Etta.

She spoke to me like the teacher she used to be, in one of her guises over a century ago.

"Morg, I don't want this to sound insensitive...but, with your wife gone, and you already knowing about us, Colin and I think you are a person who can help us with some...issues."

"Go on."

She turned to Colin. "You can tell him better than I what you want done with your papers."

"You want me to destroy them?" I cried.

"Don't jump the gun," Colin said. "But, if you wish, that's okay with me."

"It's not okay," I said as firmly as I could manage, interrupting an attempted sip of my drink.

"Then fine, organize them, publish them, whatever you and the university want to do, as long as you..."

"Don't let anyone know you're alive."

"If there are any proceeds see to it that the university gets them for the History Department."

"I'm sure I can arrange that. And the university will likely want to keep the original papers in its library."

Colin gave his approval with the wave of a hand.

"More so, I'd like you to edit, add to, embellish, complete, and publish *In The Mist,* not under your name, naturally, and certainly not under Colin Bisseau."

I frowned, got up and walked to the bar and helped myself to more cognac, gestured to Colin, who nodded, and I brought the bottle to the table, poured some for him, and set the bottle down.

"Etta, more wine?"

"No, thank you."

"Why should I do that, Colin? Why don't you do it yourself?"

"Oh, dear me, Morgan, I didn't mean to imply I expect you to do this out of the goodness of your heart. I figured you'd enjoy the task and I expect you to be reimbursed for your efforts. I can arrange for, and pay for, publication costs, have no fears."

"Morg, he needs to get this story out of his system," Etta said.

"I need to justify the countless hours I put into writing my journals. Unfortunately I don't believe I can write the book with complete honesty."

"Because?"

Colin sighed, started to speak, stopped, shook his head, then said, in a near-whisper, "I have done things in my life that I am not proud of. I don't regret them, because at the time they seemed right and necessary, but I hesitate to put them in the book. Hence, it's not an honest accounting."

"You have these incidents written down in your journals?"

Colin nodded.

"Aren't you afraid your fellow IMs will be upset if they find out about the book?"

"Maybe, but no one could link it to me, other than Marcus or Etta."

"You don't think I should publish it under my own name?"

"If you insist, go ahead, but it might cause the friends you've already told about the Bolton and Bunyan journals to wonder where you came up with the idea for *In The Mist,* and that makes me a bit uneasy."

"How about I publish it as written by…"

"The late Cosmo Ballantrie," Colin said, a hand spinning in the air as a magician might while exclaiming, 'Presto!' His persona will be dead by the time you publish."

"Your other journals, the older ones you referenced in your book, and the ones in the canisters I found, would I have access to them?"

"Not the originals, but I have digital copies in a safe deposit box in the States, and one in London. I'd have to review them first, Morgan."

"I must insist you don't censor your journals, Colin. It would defeat the purpose of having me write the book instead of you."

"Only to check the names, Morgan. I can't allow anything that would identify anyone still living. That's not negotiable. And of course, though only the three of us, plus Marcus, will know it is true, you must clearly identify the book as a fantasy novel."

"That shouldn't be hard; no one would believe people living five hundred years."

"One other thing," Etta said. "You must keep my name out of it. The last thing I want is a bunch of grumpy old historians searching for what happened to Etta Place."

"I'm an old historian," I reminded her.

"Yes, and for you to know is enough."

"Okay, as editor I think I can arrange for a pseudonym."

"Those tasks should keep you busy for awhile," Colin said.

"There's something else, Morg," said Etta.

I felt a twinge, as if, here comes the gotcha.

"We, the IMs, have a foundation that distributes funds to a variety of organizations throughout the world, mostly to those involved in medical work, somewhat similar to the what the Gates' do, but on a much quieter basis."

"What's it called?" I asked.

"Simply "The Foundation," Morgan. Funds are distributed in an anonymous manner, handled by Marcus..."

"He seems to have his hands in a lot of things."

"Too many," Colin said. "He's overworked."

"It's not just that. I fear that my... our," Colin glanced at Etta, "viewpoint is not a typical one, because our outlook isn't the same as..."

"Normal people," I interjected, a bit cheeky.

"What's normal for some people isn't for others, Morg; my God, what century are you living in?"

"I am admonished," I said, the snideness evident."

Colin continued as if I hadn't so rudely interrupted. "I truly marvel at people who are willing to dive into projects that they know they won't be around to see to completion. It is important to think of the big picture, the long run, if you will, but I need the opinion of someone who sees things from the viewpoint of a mortal, Morgan."

"You mean someone who can point out to you what needs to be done now, for people who need help this moment, not far in the future."

"That's it. Not that I don't want to support projects that I think are important to the long term needs of the human race, like the space program, or clean energy sources, but people are dying daily from lack of proper medical attention, lack of clean water; basic needs that we take for granted."

"So where have your funds been going?"

"I am not the only one who contributes to The Foundation; there are others, and sometimes—frequently—we disagree on how to distribute the funds. Some of the others are big on, as I mentioned, long term projects, which is fine to a degree, but for the person who is uneducated and untrained, or too sick to work, what does it matter to him if the ice fields melt a hundred years from now?"

"So how does this concern me?"

"The others have agreed to let Marcus and I choose someone to…"

"Colin, are you asking me to run your organization?"

"I told you he was smart," Etta said.

"No dear, I told you."

"How much say-so would I have? And how much is there to distribute?"

"Between my resources, Marcus, and the others who contribute, it would be over a half-billion, maybe close to a billion dollars a year, give or take, depending on the generosity of my fellow IMs."

My mouth gaped and I thought my eyebrows would leap off my face.

"You want me to handle the distribution of a billion dollars a year, Colin? Are you serious?"

"I'm perfectly serious."

"I make all decisions?"

"Approximately ten per cent of the available funds would go to certain pet projects we each have. Otherwise, yes, you'd decide; you'd have full control of ninety per cent of the funds. Although, as I have made obvious, I am partial to programs that deal with relatively mundane issues, like the urgency of clean water and plumbing systems, availability of birth control, education, and so forth. And remember, I am a citizen of the world, I wouldn't want you to favor one nation over others."

"I understand. And if you don't like what I'm doing?"

Before Colin could speak Etta put a hand over his mouth.

"We, and the others, promise you a minimum five years to do it your way. After five years we mutually agree to either continue, or to make a change."

"What if I die before then, Etta?" I said, giving emphasis to the pronoun.

"Then one of your first tasks will be to choose someone to train as your successor—but, and this is also non-negotiable, he, or she, is not to know the truth about us," Colin said.

"You mean about the IMs?"

"Yes, only you shall know that secret and you must swear to take it to the grave."

"What I swore before should be good for this, too," I said.

Colin reached across the table and we shook hands.

"Will the others protest you using a mere mortal?" I asked.

Colin shook his head. "They have accepted the idea, a least on a test basis."

"I can be your liaison if Marcus is too busy with other things," Etta said.

Colin's eyes dilated. "I thought you wanted to shop for dresses and go to the opera?"

Etta ignored Colin's remark other than to smile and purse her lips in a cutesy kiss.

It's an enormous undertaking, Morgan." Colin's eyes drilled into me, suggesting I might not be up to the task.

"I'll need a staff, a place to work from, possibly legal advice…"

"I'll have accounts set up for your use before you are ready to start. You'll have an adequate expense account and of course you'll take a salary."

"Not necessary, but I'll need to pay my staff."

"Once you get set up let Marcus, or Etta---he gave Etta a look I couldn't interpret, but appeared to be one that said, 'you never cease to surprise me' ---"know what you need to cover expenses. The money is not an issue."

"It sounds to me that while you're saying I will decide where to distribute the funds, you are steering me in the direction you favor."

"I won't deny that; I claim the right since the others have allowed me to chose the person who will run The Foundation. But, I promise not to interfere with your decisions."

"He'll try to promise," Etta corrected.

"When do I start, and what about your papers?"

"You'll have time to work on the papers and *In The Mist* before Marcus and I are ready to turn over The Foundation to you. When you return home, work on those two projects. We'll contact you in a few months and if you are still interested in managing The Foundation, we will set up a meeting for the three of us and Marcus to work out the details."

"Here, I hope," I said, scanning the yard. "It's so beautiful; I wish…" My eyes clouded, but I quickly recovered.

"And what do I say to my friends who know I went to Greece? I hate to lie to them."

"You must; you can't tell them about us," Colin said firmly. "No deal if you do."

"I'll think of something, but…"

"What is it, Morgan?"

"I still wish you could give me some definitive proof."

"Would it really make a difference?" Etta asked.

She had me there. I stared at her, considering her question. If Colin truly wants me to handle a massive portfolio, what do I care if he's the greatest teller of tall tales since Paul Bunyan? Then I remembered the cameo locket and grinned.

"If you give me the job of parceling out a billion dollars a year to causes I feel most need help, no, it doesn't matter. Being a natural skeptic, it would be soothing, I guess, is all."

"Even though you can't tell anyone?"

"Yeah, even though."

"Marcus could regale you with stories for hours; he's much older than I. He claims he knew Michelangelo, and I have no reason not to believe him."

"If you were born when you say, you could have known Michelangelo, too."

"Could have, but didn't. The great artist died in Rome in 1564; I was still living in Paris."

"Marcus, or whatever name he went by then, can't prove it, can he?"

"Exactly, Morgan," Etta said. "We can't <u>prove</u> how old we are, although I think Colin's journals are a bit of proof."

"I must admit the idea that Colt Boston, Cade Bunyan and Colin Bisseau were one and the same was nipping at me as I poured over the journals, but it seemed outrageous. Yet, the idea gnawed at me, like a headache that lasts all day."

"Even I, despite keeping the journals, never thought of acquiring items that might later be used to prove my lifespan. I had to move too often to be slowed down by possessions. I have some original works of art, in some cases given to me by artists who are still revered hundreds of years after their deaths, as geniuses. But so what, other people have such items also. It's not like Rembrandt gave me a dated and signed invoice.

"Rembrandt, hey?"

"Just an example."

I laughed and shook my head. Maybe this is nothing more than an incredible dream; maybe I am dead, maybe I've never lived, maybe I'll wake up and Erin will be shaking me, worried that I was asleep so soundly and mumbling about a thousand year old man and his beautiful wife.

18. NEW FRIENDS

The rest of the week consisted of busy days of playing tourist—to Rhodes, Santorini, Karpathos—and in the evenings exquisite dinners in the backyard of the villa, (Etta and Colin are both excellent cooks), savored slowly and with good wine, card games, and conversation.

I kept trying to work the banter around to Colin's and Etta's memories of their lives, stories of the various identities they'd lived as, occupations they'd had, and people they'd known. I had hoped one of them would say something that I knew was historically inaccurate; catch them in a fib.

Occasionally one or the other would relate a vignette from one of their former lives: Colin spoke of working as a tanner in Colonial New England during the early days of the American Revolution; Etta, likened as a lawless moll in some history books, spoke of her days as a music teacher using the name Ethel Bishop.

I daren't ask about rumors that under various names she was the same person whose vocation at one time was a prostitute—I wasn't that nosy and it would have been pushing our new friendship.

Generally, they were reticent to talk specifically about the past, as if there was too much to remember, or unhappy moments they'd rather forget.

"Did you know any…" My question to Colin about his days in America in the 1770s was cut off by his ready answer.

"Not closely, but I met a few of them. Most of what I care to speak of you will find in the other journals I will send you, Morgan. That should be enough for you to chew on. Some incidents you may find a bit unsettling."

Though much younger than they, I understood: nostalgia is not all it's cracked up to be.

"What's it like in America now, Morgan? We haven't been there since we left in 1980."

"It's a lot different, Etta; especially since nine-eleven."

"I imagine that was traumatic."

"It still is. People are afraid of everything they don't understand. They're afraid of immigrants, Muslims, of course, not without reason, of vaccinations, of peanuts and gluten, of ISIS sneaking into their towns, of drones and black helicopters that represent some deep fear of the unknown, like the devil himself coming to snare their soul.

"Almost weekly there's a mass shooting, often on a school campus; some nut with enough guns and ammo to start a revolution blows people away, then usually kills himself. And people respond by demanding the right to carry guns on college campuses. Wonderful! Then we'd have the wild west all over." Involuntarily I glanced at Etta, who only winked without smiling.

"Movies and television reflect the angst to a disturbing and obnoxious degree. It's scary how scared people have become, and they respond by stockpiling guns and ammunition, or reveling in violent sports and TV shows. They even have women kick-boxing events."

"Really? What do they do, these women?"

"You don't want to know, Etta."

"And you want to go back?" Colin said to Etta with a smirk.

"We can't stay here forever, Colin."

"I agree, but I need a few more months."

Etta's sigh was purposely audible.

One evening, when Etta was inside preparing a dessert, Colin admitted he and Etta were at a slight impasse.

"I'm considering going to work at a medical facility in central Africa run by a doctor who is an IM, one I have known since I was an Ambassador. That's why I've been study various sciences, especially those related to medicine. Other than surgery I could probably practice as a physician. You're right, Morgan, I need to get back in the world again."

"So you do feel an obligation," I said, almost crowing.

"Morgan, as long as you are healthy don't you want to be doing something, whether it is physical or mental, but more than just lying in the sun or watching television?"

I bowed in acquiescence. I vowed to complete the Bisseau papers project, edit *In The Mist*, exercise more, eat healthier, and read a book a week.

"Etta wants to return to the United States and visit some of the scenes of her youth. She has this idea of writing the true story of, as she calls them, her halcyon nights and days."

"Has she spoken to you of those days?"

"Yes, and I think she's been honest and forthright with me, to a point. Still, all of us, all the Immortals I have ever met, tend to keep secrets. We've become that way in self-defense, thus, even with people we love and love to be with it's difficult to be one hundred per cent open.

"Quite frankly, Morgan, I don't need to know everything about Etta's life, nor does she need to know all about mine. There are events and deeds that didn't make it into my journals because I was embarrassed to write them; I want them forgotten, and no, don't ask me."

"Colin, you don't have to be exceptionally long-lived to have secrets."

"True words, Morgan."

"As an historian I want all the facts, even, or especially, the unsavory, little-known ones. If I am being persistent it's that tendency to want to claw out the meaty parts of a story,"

"As I said, there were deeds done that I don't care to talk of and they aren't recorded, just remembered, but there are some you will read that, in retrospect, I wish I hadn't recorded."

I started to interrupt but Colin stopped me with a pointed finger.

"I promise not to delete any entries, even ones I may find embarrassing, and will let you decide what to publish. If I censor anything it will only be names that might identify other IMs, and for your own good I think it's better you don't have that information."

"Fair enough, but I make the final decision on what goes into the book and when it is ready for publication."

"Agreed. I will endeavor to get the other journals to you by the time you return home. That should keep you occupied until we contact you."

"And what if you and Etta cannot agree on what you both will do in the near future?"

"Oh, we may go our separate ways for a time. We've discussed that possibility."

"It sounds so complicated to me. On Illikaria you are Cosmo Ballantrie, and Etta is who, Elizabeth Ballantrie?"

"Yes, and we have documentation of a marriage in Venice in 1980. And when we leave here I will arrange to sell the villa to myself, under another name, and Liz and I will get married again, under whatever names we decide."

"Which you aren't going to tell me," I said, trying to sound offended.

"For your own good, Morgan, but we will be in touch, both Etta and I. She and I discussed it last night. We both agree that you are a mortal we feel comfortable sharing more of our life with than we normally do. To you, we will always be Colin and Etta."

"Thank you," I said, with a slight bow. "I will make a concerted effort to maintain your trust." Then I added, with a swipe of a hand across my mouth, "I wonder how long it would take me to Google everyone with the initials, 'C.B.'?

Colin laughed; "You won't have time."

Etta returned with a bowl of red and purple berries drizzled with Grand Marnier and topped with whipped cream.

"Are you two done talking about me? Have you settled my future?"

"Now, now, dear, don't be derisive."

Etta served the fruit, sat down, and we dug in.

"Colin says you want to write a historical novel, Etta," I said between mouthfuls of berries.

"Actually, it would be as factual as possible, but I suppose I'd have to publish it as a novel."

"Under what name?"

Etta gave Colin a glare.

"You know, he is smart, Colin. How could I write the definitive history of my life before I met you, and keep my identity secret?"

"You'll use a pseudonym, dear, just as Morgan will do with *In The Mist*. You've written history, Morgan, maybe you can help Etta."

"How would you explain Etta Place's disappearance from history?" I asked.

"Yes, I guess I would have to fudge a bit; I can't tell the whole truth and nothing but without it soundly like a science-fiction take on the Old West."

"It wouldn't be far from the truth to write that to avoid publicity you changed your name and moved to Europe," I suggested.

Etta nodded and chewed her lip, already thinking, I surmised, how she would describe her flight to obscurity. After a moment she blinked and looked at me.

"I don't know why I need to say this, Morg, but I want to make it clear to you that I'm a different person now than I was...when I was younger."

She stared at me in a way that made me feel she'd been reading my mind. I returned her gaze and gave a slight nod.

"Fiction is different from the type of writing I've done, but if you want to make it historically accurate I may be able to render some assistance."

"You're going to be a busy boy, Morgan, organizing my old papers, cleaning up my own book, assisting Etta..."

I snickered; "I'm a young man, Colin, only sixty-three; I have lots of time."

"Here, here," Colin said. It was the same simple toast Amy had given for Erin.

"Sounds like we'll all be busy, and it sounds like we all need to be; I know I do."

My mind drifted away from the table, from the villa, from Illikaria, to the university and to home, and I was both amazed and ashamed that so little time had passed since Erin's death. But life goes on, for some a short while, for others, a little longer.

When I blinked my teary eyes and looked up Etta and Colin were staring at me; they knew where I had gone. I smiled, picked up a glass and suggested a toast.

"Wait, I'll get champagne," said Etta.

Etta hustled to get champagne and proper glassware, opened the bottle and poured, and since she still stood Colin and I also rose and lifted our glasses high.

"To new friends," I said.

"And to interesting days, " said Colin

"And to long lives," I added.

19. LIFE GOES ON

Colin wouldn't tell me when he and Etta would return to the United States, nor what names they'd be using, but he gave me e-mail addresses and cell phone numbers for both of them, which he made me memorize and swear I would never reveal to anyone or write down or save in my computer. He said it might be a few months but I would be contacted.

I could only grin when upon returning home I found that whatever damage may have been done to the floor of my closet, in order to dig into my safe, had been repaired. And I smiled broadly when inside the safe I found that all of my belongings were intact and there were two thumb drives, which I soon confirmed contained the other journals of the man I knew as Colin Bisseau and/or Cosmo Ballantrie.

"Did you find this guy, Cosmo Whoever?" asked Janice, after an exchange of courtly hugs.

"Yes, I did. An old guy who apparently got my name from some history magazine, learned that I had taught at the same university as Colin Bisseau, who was an old friend of his, and decided I was the person to critique his manuscript."

"So how does it connect with the journals in the file cabinet?"

"He said the journals were written by his great-grandfather and grandfather and he was using them as the basis for an historical novel. Bisseau was guiding him to assure that his proposed novel was historically accurate. Cosmo had sent the notes and journals to Bisseau to read. After he didn't hear from Bisseau he tried to reach him, and somehow, he didn't remember exactly how, learned that Bisseau had disappeared. Cosmo couldn't figure out whom to contact about retrieving the journals. Eventually he forgot about them and abandoned his plans to write a book. But he still had his draft from years ago. He came across it in an old suitcase he hadn't opened since he'd moved to Greece, over twenty years ago, decided he was past caring enough to finish it, but thought I'd be interested."

"And are you?"

"I'm going to look into it; I've chewed on the idea of writing fiction. But not till after I finish compiling the Bisseau papers."

"So you're back to work?"

"Yes, and Ballantrie signed a paper giving me all rights to the novel draft he sent me, and the Bolton and Boston journals, which he claims still technically belong to him."

(This was something Colin and I had arranged before I left Illikaria, in case the university insisted on maintaining possession of the papers.)

"Might have to check with the Board," Janice said.

"You're the Cultural Development Committee; can't you decide?"

I was being cagey, maybe a bit devious, and I wished I could take Janice into my confidence, but I had promised.

She sat back, folded her arms, licked her bottom lip, and I feared she was contemplating what she might get in return, like a proposal, and I spread my arms, pleading my case, but also begging for her not to ask for something I couldn't give. I had too much on my mind to think of her as anything but a friend. I briefly contemplated breaking my recent promise and telling her the whole story, but the urge left me in a nano second. She wouldn't believe me anyway. I waited.

"I suppose..." she hesitated. "No one knows what's in that file cabinet other than us little elves...there's no reason the Board needs to know about anything other than the Bisseau papers."

I smiled and thanked her and we went to get a cup of coffee.

Two months passed and I kept busy cataloguing and editing the Bisseau Papers, to be published by Lyman

Wilson University. At first I tried to work more at home, but there were too many memories. I teetered back and forth between feeling pleasure that I had found something interesting to do, something that for hours took my mind off of Erin, and pain and guilt when memories flooded back into my mind. So I dug in at my office at the university and put the house up for sale.

I ignored the Bunyan, Boston, and Bisseau journals and buckled down to categorizing and organizing the professional papers of the Colin Bisseau known to the world as educator, ambassador, and small-time politician.

At times it was difficult to concentrate on what I was doing and not stop to think about Colin's offer to manage his Foundation; how to decide where grants should go, who to help me, where to set up my headquarters; I frequently had to shake myself from daydreaming and get on with my present task.

I didn't see much of Janice. If I didn't take a coffee break she didn't appear at the door to my office with coffee mug in hand.

Kenny surprised me with the news that Janice was seeing someone. I must admit the slightest twinge of jealousy, but due more to male ego than any genuine feelings on my part.

"That's good, I'm glad to hear it."

"She didn't tell you?" Kenny asked. I shook my head.

"He's quite handsome, silver-haired and tanned; they play tennis. I saw him one day when he came to take Jan to lunch."

"Good for her."

"I guess I always thought…"

"Thought what?"

"Oh, nothing. Golf this week?"

"Sure, I know you need someone to beat."

The cataloging of the Bisseau papers was finished in time for Janice's board presentation. I then I attacked the thumb drives I'd found in my safe. They contained a wealth of data---Colin's tales, ones that had survived the centuries. They made for fascinating reading even if most weren't as enthralling as Boston's Civil War adventure or Colin's Battle of the Bulge heroics. (When my thoughts were my own, it was easier to admit I believed Colin Bisseau—by whatever name---was five hundred years old. I had not even hinted to Janice, Kenny, or anyone, even in joking, about people who call themselves Immortals.)

Janice had prodded me to let her read the rough draft of *In The Mist*, the one Colin, as Cosmo Ballantrie, had sent me, and I reluctantly let her, not thinking quick enough of an excuse to prevent her. I worried that if she later read the published version she might be curious where the additional information came from, so I casually mentioned that Ballantrie had also given me notes of other material he had intended for the book that wasn't in the rough draft.

Call it coincidence or whatever, a few days later a copy of the USA Today appeared on my desk opened to an article that said a well-known European writer and world traveler, Cosmo Ballantrie, and his wife had died in a boating accident in the Aegean Sea. Apparently their boat, the "Mist of the Mediterranean," caught fire. No bodies were recovered but a man by the name of Dion confirmed that he had sailed with the Ballantries from the island of Illikaria to Kos, got off there and watched as the couple left Kos to continue on to their destination, Crete. For a moment my heart shivered until I remembered what Colin had said about the Cosmo Ballantrie persona being dead soon.

"Poor guy's gone," I told Janice and Kenny, on one of those rare days when the three of us managed to arrive at the cafeteria at the same time.

"What poor guy?"

"The one I went to see in Greece; the one who sent me the manuscript. He died."

"My gosh, that's a shame!"

"Yes, even though he gave his work to me, I'm sure he would have wanted to see it published."

I showed her the newspaper story. She read it, shook her head and again said it was a shame.

"How's is that book coming along? Are you still going to publish it?"

"If I can find a publisher," I said, coyly, knowing it wouldn't be a problem. "Not under my name, however."

Later I sent an e-mail to the address Colin had given me. I asked:

"Are you both OK?"

The response I got was: *"Not to worry."*

Another month passed and despite the e-mail response I feared that the story I'd read of the death of the Ballantries was not merely a plant, which I had assumed until now. If it was the last of Colin Bisseau, I would not have the faintest idea who to see about publishing the fantasy tale, *In The Mist*. Worse, I would feel another deep loss, piled on top of the loss of Erin.

So I sent a text to Etta.

"Are you sure you're both OK?"

The replay, almost immediate, was:

"Thanks for your concern, Morg. We are fine, I am in London working with M; C still on I; he will join me in a few weeks. Look forward to seeing you soon. Hugs, E."

Satisfied, I returned to reading and editing Bisseau's journals. If Etta and Colin, and Marcus, assuming he truly exists, showed up soon, I wanted to be finished with the journals. As with most diaries or journals, daily events are mainly mundane and routine, which is why few people keep diaries on a regular, long-term basis. Still, these had an authentic sound to them; they reeked of history and as far as I could tell there was nothing that failed the test of historical accuracy, and I read with a keen eye and ear for anything that smacked of mendacity. There were a couple of events that Colin had referred to, ones he said he was ashamed of, and the historian in me debated with the editor as to how much to include in the book.

An entry dated 1773, no month given, was particularly interesting, explaining the mystery of Catherine, and shivery in its clarity of purpose. What I was reading was the digital reproduction of the original (I assumed) journal, and page one declared that this was:

"The Journal of Corbett Barlowe."

I began to read.

Last night several dozen colonists, disguised, not convincingly, as Indians, boarded three ships in the harbor. The rebels dumped the cargo, East India tea, into Boston Harbor, in response to the Tea Act, a measure that, ironically, was devised to make the British East India tea less expensive than the Dutch tea, which was smuggled.

For some of these revolutionists it was a case of enough, already, King George. The value of the destroyed tea was in the neighborhood of 10,000 pounds.

I joined the glee the next night until the wee hours of the morning at The Whalers' Pub. The patrons and the pub walls themselves shook with laughter from the accounts of the activities of the previous night, the tales likely a tad embellished. None of the storytellers admitted they had been a faction in the adult prank; they had heard of it from others, they claimed.

I laughed too, because less than a week ago I had sold my interest in the tea at a fancy profit, my laughter being one of irony, not joy, though I was glad for my fortune. The buyer was not someone I had searched out, rather the opposite. I strongly resisted at first, as I never imagined the tea was at risk on the ships, but the man was insistent, and raised his offer. Finally I relented, partially to rid me of his rather obnoxious manner, but also deciding that it was a good time to realize my gain and move on to other matters. I was already thinking that the talk of revolution was getting a bit hot.

While wryly grinning to myself, sharing the tale with no one, I could not have ever, in all my 250 some years, imagined that the man who lost at his gamble would take such an extreme reprisal, though to be exact, the horror that resulted was surely not the one he intended. Still, it was the consequence of his careless and lawless action. And I will have my revenge.

As I walked home, a bit unsteady I must admit, I wondered for the hundredth time whether I had done right in marrying Catherine. She was only twenty-two, I told her I was twenty-seven, and in twenty years or so she would be over forty, and look it, while I would still look as I do now. I had not married since I left Nicole, so long ago in a country so far away my life with her was barely a memory, a faded dream of a life that might have been something I read about, not lived. Of course, Nicole would have passed away two centuries ago; still, I at times felt the pang of guilt at having abandoned her.

Not that I hadn't love and lusted; but I played the cad, not always meaning to as a time or two I could say I was truly in love, though I was loath to write of such emotions as I believed it was bad luck to do so.

I crept in quietly so as not to waken Catherine. She wanted children and again, vaguely remembering the children I had with Nicole, I was reluctant, yet, didn't she have a right to live the life she had, albeit one that would surely end long before mine did? Nothing was more of a conundrum for me than my relations with women.

I stepped carefully in the dark so as to not bump into anything, and slid into the bed. I reached for Catherine, to touch her, and my hand found a cool sheet, but no body. I jumped up and called her name. I crashed around until I found a lamp and lit it, again and again calling for Catherine. There was no answer.

I carried the lamp into the main room intending to go outside and search for Catherine, thinking crazy thoughts, such as, I was in the wrong house, or she was visiting her sister and forgot to tell me, or that she had found me out, a freak of nature, 250 years old, and had rushed out in a panic, akin to the panic that was now bubbling up inside of me. Then I saw the paper on the table. A farewell letter?

My heart skipped, my mouth, so recently wet with ale, felt like it was stuffed with cotton. I held the paper up in one hand, the lamp in the other, and read:

"Barlowe: you cheated me! You knew what was going to happen to the tea…you were probably one of them! You owe me 400 pounds and until paid you wont (sic) see your wife. I will meet you at 6 this morning near the Old Well at the end of Harbor Road. Bring the money."

It wasn't signed; didn't need to be. It was from Smyth, the man who had begged me to sell him my interest in the tea that now gurgled in Boston Harbor. I had done no wrong but would gladly pay him the 400 pounds to get back Catherine unharmed. But I did not have such an amount of cash on hand and could not get it to him by 6 this morning.

365

To calm myself while I pondered what to do, I built a fire, then climbed into the clothes I had shed a few moments ago, and put on a pot of water to boil.

You fool, I berated myself again. Catherine's dilemma is my fault. I should not have married her; she should be with a man nearer to her age, one who would grow old with her and share the joys of parenthood and beyond. Even as I vowed to stay true to her I had already contemplated when I would have to leave; in twenty years, twenty-five? But now I must rescue her; then I'll try to convince her it was a mistake for us to marry.

From under a board in the corner of the bedroom I retrieved a bag containing a little over 100 pounds; not nearly enough for Smyth. There was only one person I knew who might get the cash I needed at this time of night. An acquaintance, not a close friend, but one I felt could help or at least point me to someone who could. I won't name names, lest my journal fall into the hands of someone who would not be as circumspect as I with the contents.

It was half past two on that clear, chilly night when I tapped on his door. I wanted to awaken him but not his neighbors.

"Who wakes me?" A voice called from a window two stories above me.

"One Corbett Barlowe, Mr..."

"Is it such urgent business as to ruin my dreams, sir?"

"A thousand and more pardons, sir, but yes it is. I am in frantic need of help and I hoped you might…" Again I couldn't finish my words for being interrupted by him.

"Yes, give me a minute, sir, I will be down."

I waited in the chill, rubbing my hands on my arms and looking all around, wary of anyone seeing me, especially a British soldier.

The door opened and I entered, my host holding a candle in one hand and pistol in the other. He held the lamp up to my face.

"Oh, yes, Barlowe, I wanted to be sure." I heard him set the pistol down on a table. "Come in. Tea or brandy, sir?"

I wanted brandy. "Tea, please, I need my wits."

"Then come in and explain yourself. I don't take lightly to having my precious sleep destroyed; I might have dreamed up a great invention tonight."

"Sorry, sir."

"Well, well, come on, explain yourself," he said, impatient, as he led me to the kitchen. He pointed to a chair and went to the stove where a kettle of water was heating.

"It's like this…" I told my story.

"And the rascals name?" I hesitated. "Come now, you can't expect me to help you if I don't know the name of the rapscallion."

"A common name, one John Smyth, spelled with…"

"Yes, yes, I know of him. A bit mysterious, sneaky looking, a homely sort, but I don't have any first-hand knowledge of him."

"What I told you is the truth."

He nodded. "Yes, yes, I believe you. I know you, Barlowe, know your work. I have friends who have spoken kindly of you, and of your lovely bride. I may be able to help. I don't have all the funds you need at hand, but I have some and I know another who will gladly, once he is calmed from being stirred at this hour, assist you with the needed cash."

"I will write a note."

"Yes, it is best you do, for who knows what may become of any of us in these dangerous days."

To move on with my story, my friend served me tea, excused himself to dress, then led me through the dark streets to a friend of his, one of the more notable citizens of Boston, one I knew only by reputation. He listened to my story without interruption and without any complaints about being called from his warm bed in the middle of the night, relieved, he said, to be disturbed by friendly folk when he feared it might be the British, looking to avenge the "tea party."

Now we had to visit yet another so it was three of us parading down the streets. The sky was already beginning to lighten and I shivered not from cold but from concern I'd be late to meet Smyth.

"Have you considered waiting for the miscreant at the well and shooting him dead on sight?" my friend's friend asked.

I nodded. "Yes, that was my first thought, and truly I could, as I am competent in the use of firearms, but it is my wife at stake here, sir, and I would dread that the slightest mistake result in a worse disaster."

"You are right, of course, I just wondered about your state of mind."

"Shoot him after you retrieve your wife," he suggested.

"My thoughts exactly, sir."

To again skip ahead lest my entry becomes tedious, between my friend and his two friends I acquired the 400 pounds I needed, and wrote out three IOUs, which I felt would be easy to repay as I had no intention of letting Smyth get away with the money, if I had to chase him across the continent.

(My research revealed that 400 pounds in 1773 would be the equivalent of between 60 and 70 thousand dollars today, a fortune indeed in Barlowe's day.)

"You'll have your money back soon," I promised.

"Do you wish us to accompany you?"

"No, thank you, all of you. I fear Smyth would be confused if he saw more than myself. I will report to you later today on how things go."

"Bring your beautiful wife," my friend said, "we will dine tonight."

I thanked them all and hied to the rendezvous, a saddlebag filled with the money draped over one shoulder. Smyth's declared time was near and I was still a quarter-mile from the meeting place. I increased my gait.

As I approached the well, a solitary structure shaded by a copse of oaks centered in a small meadow where horses grazed, a faint hue of orange was tickling the horizon and a slight breeze, crisp and redolent of the sea, drifted across the meadow. The well, indeed, was called the Old Well, one not in use anymore and, I believe, gone completely dry. It was a quiet spot and it was not likely anyone would be around at this early hour of the day, though residential buildings were not far off.

I smelled smoke as fires were stoked in kitchens, and with the smoke the pleasant aromas of crackling bacon and strong coffee. Normally such scents would rouse my appetite but now I was focused on one thing— rescuing Catherine.

I reached the well, still in darkness from the cover of the copse. I saw no one and sensed something had gone wrong and Smyth would not show. Suddenly there was a sound behind me, a rustle followed by a thump, and Smyth stood before me, having leaped from one of the oaks. He held a pistol on me and his pockmarked face, blemished from a childhood disease, sneered at me, his gaping mouth displaying rotting teeth.

For a second I thought he would fire his gun, take my money and leave me for dead, and Catherine, it flashed though my mind, was already dead by the hand of this malefactor.

"Where is she?" I demanded.

"The money!" Smyth scowled.

I tossed him the saddlebag. "Four hundred, you bastard. Now where is she?"

"Down there," he said, pointing at the well.

"Down...what, where?"

"Pull up the rope...she's tied to a chair and she's probably getting cold by now."

I ran to the well and peered in—nothing but a black hole down to infinity. I turned and saw Smyth running off. I could have overtaken him and brought him down but my primary concern was Catherine---was she really in there or was this a ruse by Smyth to give him time to get away?

A rope, frayed from age and dirty from years of use hung down into the well. I tugged on it; it did not seem particularly heavy, so I began to pull it up. The more I pulled the more I knew there was nothing attached. And to my dismay, a sight that sent me to my knees and made me gasp in horror, the end of the rope was shredded. The tired old cord had been unable to maintain its grip on the weight that it had been tied to.

Uselessly I called into the well, but my voice only bounced off the circular walls and sunk in the blackness, eliciting no response. I felt helpless; I wanted to climb in but feared I'd have no way to bring Catherine and myself up without help. I rued now that I hadn't taken the offer of the three gentlemen who had rustled up the money.

I found a small rock and dropped in into the well; I listened carefully for any sound and when it came it was a splat like the sound of a horse's hoof stomping in mud. I decided to risk the rope, praying it had enough fiber, literally, for one last task.

I checked that it was tied securely to the frame of the well and began to ease myself down. In seconds I was enveloped in darkness. I looked up and saw the morning sky, a perfect blue, but no light could reach me, and the people awakening for the day unaware of the frantic man a stone's throw from their kitchen. Maybe I should have called for help, knocked on doors and screamed until I convinced someone of my desperation; yet even as I wished for help I continued down, trying not to pull too hard on the rope, hearing, if not in my ears then in my head, the cricks as the fibers stretched and tore. A minute, two minutes, the time it might have taken to get help, could cost Catherine her life.

Suddenly my feet slopped into mud, and I sunk nearly to my knees. It was absolutely pitch dark and stank of decaying plants and mud and manure. I could see nothing so I groped with my hands in the muck until I felt something. It was a body, my first guess.

In near panic my hands dug into the mud and flung it off the object, the mud splattering against the walls. But the more I dug the more than watery muck slipped back, until I felt hair, the long, once golden hair of my beloved. I yanked her up and still unable to see I cleared mud off her face and out of her mouth, crying, moaning, calling her name, weeping and cursing with every breath.

Smyth had tied Catherine to the rope, and then to a chair, thinking she would sit there in the dark until I came for her. He probably didn't realize that the rope was old and weak, had broken and dropped Catherine, knocking her unconscious until she drowned in the mud, though his ignorance makes the result no less an atrocity.

I sat there in the mud holding her to me, my tears dripping into her hair, until I was exhausted. I might have stayed there until I starved to death had not my friend and his acquaintances come searching for me, having feared for me since I had not returned to report to them.

I heard a holler from above, saw the shadow of someone, and I called back. There is not much else to say about this event other than the men pulled me up with a new rope. There is though, some to be said about Smyth.

A quick funeral was arranged. I may have seemed hasty, but my mind, now freed from worry about Catherine, was engaged in one sole purpose, all else be damned: to find and kill Smyth.

"You are certainly within your rights as a husband, but take care, Barlowe; we do have laws in the land you know. It's not like what we hear of in the frontier."

"The way I feel now I'd kill him in broad daylight in the heart of the city with the entire citizenry as witnesses."

"Yes, and such anger as yours can make a man careless."

"I thank thee," I said, as I mounted a horse I had purchased, ready to give chase.

"I will return with your money, friends, have no fear."

"Return safely, and without a noose around your neck."

I waved to them as I rode off, having already learned of Smyth's route out of the city. He had been seen riding in a westerly direction by the stable hand. He was easy to follow—he was noticeable because of his unpleasant facial appearance and also his overall manner, and was not moving as rapidly as one might thank he would, having committed kidnapping, apparently assured I would be satisfied to have my wife back.

As I pursued Smyth I made no bones to people I met that I was after him for having stolen money from me; I made no mention of Catherine. And because Smyth treated everyone rudely people were prone to tell me what they had heard from Smyth as to his travel plans. It was too easy; I feared Smyth was leading me into a trap. I slowed my pace; from the rate Smyth was moving, and as I gained on him, I estimated I could catch him by the time we reached Lake George, which appeared to be the direction he was headed, with Canada his possible eventual destination.

My fears were uncalled for though the caution it galvanized in me was worth it. I actually had Smyth in sight for three days before we reached the woods around Lake George. I camped outdoors on the penultimate day of my mission a mere hundred yards from the inn at which he bedded that night.

In the morning I followed Smyth cautiously until he stopped to rest on the shore of the lake. He let his horse water and Smyth leaned back against a tree; he appeared to sleep. I dismounted, carrying my rifle until I was within twenty yards of the tree against which Smyth rested.

Across the short end of the lake I could see a cabin. Far in the distance a canoe glided across the glassy water.

There is a French novel by the writer Joseph Marie Eugène Sue, called Mathilde. *In it the author uses the phrase—if I can remember my French—"la vengeance se* mange très bien froide," *best translated as "revenge is very good eaten cold."*

Still, I relished letting Smyth know I had pursued him, though I had no qualms about not giving him a fighting chance, as the phrase goes. I called his name and he stirred, then jumped up, confused at being awakened from a deep nap. I let him see me for less time than it takes to blink before I shot him. The bullet caught him in the center of his chest and he reached for the wound with both hands, as if he could repair the damage if he covered the hole. He looked down at the spot on his shirt and his knees buckled. He looked up at me in astonishment and spat blood. I pulled my pistol from my belt and shot him in the forehead.

I found my the money in the saddlebags on Smyth's horse—actually there was over five hundred pounds, but I only took the four, unsaddled his horse and slapped it to set it running, returned to my horse, mounted and rode away.

I slipped into Boston after sunset three days later. I went to the home of the man I had first awakened that awful night. He began to question me but I hushed him.

"The less you know the better." He nodded.

"Here is the money you and you friends lent me. I will be off." No other words were exchanged, though he shook my hand and smiled, a gesture that said farewell and good luck.

I didn't return to Boston for many years, by which time everyone I had known there had passed away, and Corbett Barlowe was long forgotten.

Cold blooded murder, and yet I couldn't blame him, Barlowe, that is, Colin Bisseau, as I knew him. Would I have done the same thing? Probably not, but I was not alive in those days when men often took the law into their own hands. I would not be much of an historian or an editor if I didn't include the above passage; readers would assume it was fiction, anyway. It gave me pause to wonder what events Colin choose not to record in his journals.

Nicole, Catherine, Clare; yes, Colin knew what it was to lose a loved one. For weeks I'd been imagining that no one understands what it is like—what a foolish notion!

There was so much material it was going to be difficult to determine what to keep and what to exclude, and to do it in a way that the tale of a person who has lived for five centuries sounded interesting and lively, but assuring that it was accepted as clever fiction by a man now deceased, Cosmo Ballantrie, and not the claim of some vacuous crank. The last thing I, and certainly Colin, wanted, was too much publicity.

Four months and ten days after I returned from Greece, while working in my office at Lyman Wilson, the fourth draft of *In The Mist* strewn on my desk, nearly complete, there was a knock on the door.

A split second before the knock I scattered a batch of papers onto the floor. As I bent down to get them I called out, "Come in," without looking up.

The door opened, the door closed, and I heard footsteps as my visitor entered and walked slowly to the chair and sat down, me still face to the floor gathering papers.

"Sorry," I said as I rose up, my hands clutching mixed up pages of the manuscript, my face flushed. I looked at my visitor---then saw there were two; one, a woman in dark slacks and a light green blouse----sitting in the chair facing me, but with her head down and a large hat covering half of her face.

Standing behind her was a tall, nearly bald man, his face adorned with a thin mustache and a goatee, both as black as a raven. He wore dark glasses that completely shut out any glimpse of his eyes and a turtleneck and slacks that matched the deep ebony of his goatee. His lips lay bare a thin smile, almost if he was trying not to smile but something had amused him. If panache was illustrated in the dictionary, this man would be the image.

"Who..."

Then I noticed the cameo locket strung around the woman's neck. A hand reached for the hat and whisked it off, the head shook and ash blonde hair bounced and settled into its proper place; Etta smiled and said, "Hello, Morg."

I broke into a smile broader than any I'd exhibited in many months. I stood up and walked around the desk to greet her and we hugged and grinned like kids seeing reindeer fly over the rooftops.

Then the man removed his glasses. He must have been wearing shoes with thick heels, as he was definitely taller when I'd last seen him.

"Looking good, C.B." I said.

"Are you ready to give away a billion dollars, Morgan?" he said.

END

www.ingramcontent.com/pod-product-compliance
Lightning Source LLC
Chambersburg PA
CBHW022141010726
47493CB00002B/294